WELL, THAT WAS UNEXPECTED

JESSE Q. SUTANTO

DELACORTE PRESS

This is a work of fiction. Names, characters, places, and incidents either are the product of the author's imagination or are used fictitiously. Any resemblance to actual persons, living or dead, events, or locales is entirely coincidental.

Text copyright © 2022 by PT Buku Emas Sejahtera
Jacket art copyright © 2022 by Risa Rodil

All rights reserved. Published in the United States by Delacorte Press, an imprint of Random House Children's Books, a division of Penguin Random House LLC, New York.

Delacorte Press is a registered trademark and the colophon is a trademark of Penguin Random House LLC.

GetUnderlined.com

Educators and librarians, for a variety of teaching tools, visit us at RHTeachersLibrarians.com

Library of Congress Cataloging-in-Publication Data is available upon request.
ISBN 978-0-593-43397-3 (hardcover) — ISBN 978-0-593-43399-7 (ebook)

The text of this book is set in 11-point Maxime Pro.
Interior design by Cathy Bobak

Printed in Canada
10 9 8 7 6 5 4 3 2 1
First Edition

Random House Children's Books supports the First Amendment and celebrates the right to read.

Penguin Random House LLC supports copyright. Copyright fuels creativity, encourages diverse voices, promotes free speech, and creates a vibrant culture. Thank you for buying an authorized edition of this book and for complying with copyright laws by not reproducing, scanning, or distributing any part in any form without permission. You are supporting writers and allowing Penguin Random House to publish books for every reader.

To Indonesia, tanah airku, and Indonesians everywhere

PART ONE

CHAPTER 1

Sharlot

"Bradley, I'm ready. I want to do it." I look in the mirror and try again. "I want to have, uh, to have se—"

"SHAR, YOU WANT JUICE?" Mama's voice, loud enough to be heard all the way in the next city, is like an electric jolt straight to my already-shot nerves.

"No, Mama," I call back down. I give myself a little shake. "Bradley, it's time." Okay, that sounds way too ominous. "Bradley, I—"

"OKAY, I MAKE YOU JUICE."

For crying out loud. "I said I don't want any!" But she can't hear me over the sound of the blender. Argh. Another deep inhale. Okay. "Bradley—"

"COME DRINK YOUR JUICE."

I slam my fists on the dresser and stomp down the stairs. "I told you I didn't want any," I snap.

Mama frowns as she pushes the glass of bright-orange carrot juice toward me. "But I already make. Don't waste food. There are children all over the world who are starving."

"Why did you even ask me if you weren't going to listen anyway?" I should know better than to get angry, but seriously. She's always doing this, and I am not in the mood for juice.

"Shi Jun, you are being so ungrateful right now."

It's the Chinese name that sets me off. You might think naming me something that looks like a cross between "shallot" and "harlot" is the worst thing that a mother could possibly do. But nope. There's worse. Much worse.

Don't get me wrong, naming your only child Sharlot is pretty unforgivable in my book. But whenever I bring it up, Ma just tuts and says, "Mama tuh was wanting 'Charlotte.' Who knows why all these English names are not spelled the way they sound? Not like Indonesian names. Indonesian names sound exactly like they are spelled. Kartika. Hartati. All of them spell exactly like how they sound. Not spelled Car-*tee*-car. Kar-*ti*-ka! Easy, not like crazy English names."

"Why give me an English name if you can't even spell English words?" I'd yell (by the time we reach the part of the conversation where I weaponize my name, we're usually yelling).

"Because I want what is best for my daughter!" she'd yell. "Everything I do is to give you a better life."

And now here she is, using my Chinese name, even though she knows I hate it. And for good reason too, not because I'm ashamed of my heritage or anything. "Don't use my Chinese name," I snap snappishly.

"It's good name," she shoots back. "'Scholar Army'! Good, strong name. All other girls name stupid names like Beautiful

Flower or Beautiful Sky. I want my daughter to have the best name."

"You used the wrong Chinese characters and ended up naming me Correct Bacteria." See what I mean about the name Sharlot not being the worst thing she's done? "How are you this bad at languages?" To be fair to Ma, Mandarin is hellishly difficult, with multiple different characters pronounced the same way. There are a lot of different characters that are pronounced "jun," for example. Army, for one. Monarch, for another. It could also mean smart. But of all the possibilities, Ma had mistakenly picked the character that means bacteria. What are the chances?

"Chinese is a very hard language. You think I so spoiled like you, have private Mandarin teacher? No! I have to learn alone. I do everything myself—"

"Put yourself through school," I mutter as she says, "Put myself through school." I know the rest of this speech by heart, so I tune her out as she babbles on and on about how she raised me all by herself—no help from anyone!—and did I know how hard that was? *REALLY HARD, SHARLOT. Really, really hard. So hard I almost die, you see my wrinkles?—I'm not even forty yet—Asians are not supposed to have wrinkles until they are sixty! You see? YOU SEE?*

Usually I let her carry on for a while, get it out of her system. But not today. I just can't deal with this today, so I fling the only weapon I know will work at her. "I have to go—gonna study before classes start."

It works. Mama's lips immediately clap shut and she rushes

around the kitchen, finishing up the lunch that she always insists on making me.

The familiar feeling of guilt twinges in my chest as I watch Mama close the Tupperware container. Lately, she and I have been having more and more of these fights. They're triggered by all sorts of things—me spending too much time playing computer games, me taking art electives instead of AP classes, me coming home late, and of course, the fact that I told her that when I apply to colleges in the fall, I'm choosing to major in art instead of something Asian-parent-approved like pre-law, pre-med, or business.

Which is why I'm so grateful for Bradley. Sweet, clueless Bradley Morgan, who's so hot he takes my breath away every time I see him.

My phone beeps.

[Bradster 7:15AM]: Here!

I grab my schoolbag and mumble, "Michie is here."

Mama slides the Tupperware container toward me, and I'm about to run for the door when the guilt becomes too much. Gritting my teeth, I grab the glass of juice and force it all down.

Mama smiles. "Good girl."

"Don't make me any more juice EVER." I don't know why I bother; I know she won't listen. I pull on my shoes and run out the door. It's a typical day in Southern California—blue skies, scorching heat, total bikini weather even though it's technically not yet summer. Bradley is parked around the corner so that Ma, peering out the window, won't see me climbing into his convertible instead of Michie's sturdy Volvo. Every morning, my heart rate rises as I round the corner and see his silver car. And when he pops his face out the window and gives me that cheeky, boyish grin, my entire body relaxes.

"Hey, babe," he says. "You look beautiful."

No, you look beautiful, I want to say, but I manage not to. One should try not to appear too eager, even if one is this close to pouncing on another.

"I wish I could pick you up at the house instead of making you walk all the way down here," he says. He always says this, and it always makes me melt a little more, knowing that he wants to do things properly, knowing that I'm being treated like something precious.

"I know, babe. But you know my mom." My mouth tightens at the thought of Mama seeing Bradley on her doorstep. There's one surefire way of scaring off a guy. Another thought brightens my mood. "My mom's going to be working late today."

"Oh?" Bradley drives out onto the main road carefully, looking left-right-left, his hands on the ten-two position. He's like that: everything by the book. If he weren't as chiseled as a Greek god, he probably would've had the shit beaten out of him every day. As it is, he's the star of the basketball team, so he's got everyone eating out of his huge, rugged hands. Even his hands are hot. I can't stop stealing glances at them as he drives, admiring the way they make the steering wheel look tiny.

Okay, so I'm horny. And Bradley is a good-looking guy, I've established that, right? And we've been going out over a month, and like I told Michie, I'm ready. He and I have talked about this—hey, I'm a responsible girl and he's a decent guy—and we've decided we should definitely totally do it before spring semester ends and junior year is over, which is in—ack!—three days. Just three days before summer vacation begins and Bradley's whisked away to the East Coast for two weeks to visit his dad. His dad. I wish I could spend two weeks with my dad. Too bad I know nothing about him, aside from that he's white. Anyway, back to the more urgent topic. Bradley's had sex before, so I feel slightly self-conscious about it being my first time. But I just got to take the plunge, and Bradley's probably the best guy to have my first time with.

"Yeah," I say. "Her accounting firm landed a huge deal with some architecture firm—New Country or whatever. She actually told me last night that I'll have to get used to not having her around as much like it's a bad thing." I snort at that.

"Oh, hey, is the deal with New Land Architecture?" Bradley says, his voice all bouncy and excited.

I frown. This is not how I foresaw this conversation going. "Yeah, I think so. Anyway—"

"Oh man, that's so exciting! They're the ones who built that new opera house in the city! The one I showed you on Instagram?"

Aside from being a beautiful jock, Bradley also happens to be an architecture buff, which is kind of how we got together. We had one of those classic rom-com meet-cutes where we reached for the same book at the library. I still can't bring myself to tell him that I was, in fact, reaching for a book titled *Modern Art* and not *Modern Architecture*. Not when he so gallantly told me I could have it first, but only if I told him how I liked it. I'd slogged through *Modern Architecture* just so we could discuss it, and about thirty minutes in, we'd started making out.

"Yeah, cool, cool. So anyway, the house is going to be all empty, no one but you and me . . ." I trail off suggestively.

"Yeah?" He checks the rearview mirror and glances at me with a cheery smile.

I resist the urge to sigh. The guy's so hot it's practically blinding, but sometimes, Bradley can be a bit slow. Then I hate myself for being so mean, even if it's just in my own head. That's totally something Mama would do—measure everyone against some crazy lofty standards and then judge them when they inevitably fail to meet them. Plus, I guess it's kind of unfair of me to consider him dumb when he's actually brilliant when it comes to all things architecture.

"Um, I was thinking we could—you know." I wiggle my eyebrows and then belatedly wonder if that came off creepy. Doesn't matter, he's got his eyes on the road. If only Mama knew what a safe driver Bradley is.

"Ooh, you wanna have a LAN party? We could invite Michie and Joel."

For fuck's sake. How can I make it any clearer that I'm not talking about gaming? "No, Bradley, I do not want to have a Fortnite party," I snap. "I want to have sex!"

The car swerves. Honks blare, and I grip the door handle as the car swings to the side of the road and screeches to a halt.

Bradley turns to face me, his eyes wide. "Holy shit. Seriously?"

My insides twist, and suddenly, my cheeks are on fire. "Um, unless you don't want to, which is fine—" I'd just kill myself, but it's totally cool.

"No, of course I want to! I just— Whoa." Bradley's mouth forms a perfect circle. "Okay, yeah. Cool!" He grins, leaning over to kiss me on the cheek. He checks the road and eases back into traffic.

Okay, cool. I have to stop myself from grinning like a loon. In just a few hours' time, I, Sharlot Citra, will cease being a kid and become a *~~woman~~*. Or something less gross.

That afternoon, I stand in front of my mirror and practice posing for when I open the door to greet Bradley. Sexily rumpled hair, check. Minty-fresh breath, check. Spinach-less teeth, check. I take a deep breath and am somewhat surprised to find that it's slightly shaky. But I'm going to do this, damn it. And Bradley is the perfect guy to do it with. But my stomach is churning and there are sweat droplets forming on my nose and above my upper lip, which is definitely not sexy. Please stop sweating, dear body. Just to be safe, I grab my tube of deodorant and roll it aggressively over my pits, then under my boobs.

There's a knock at the front door, which makes me jump. I put down the deodorant with some reluctance. Holding it had been fortifying somehow, like holding a magical sword. Which is a totally normal way to feel about a tube of deodorant.

This is it. I go down the stairs with mounting trepidation and open the front door.

Bradley looks amazing, as always, even with his hair still wet from the school showers. Ew, the school shower. I push the image of the mold-infested showers out of my mind.

"Hey, you." He grins that amazingly boyish grin at me and lowers his head to kiss me.

Normally, his kisses are all it takes to make me forget everything, but this time, I find myself stiffening and wanting to pull away. No, self! Why? I squeeze my eyes shut and kiss him back fiercely.

"Okay, whoa," Bradley murmurs, stepping back slightly. He gives me a confused smile. "You okay?"

"Yeah, of course. Come on, let's do it." I pull him up the stairs and into my bedroom. I kick the door shut and practically pounce on him. Our hands are suddenly everywhere on each other, his fingers trailing fire down my waist. I yank off my top and Bradley actually stops breathing for a second. Thank you, Victoria's Secret. This purple lacy bra cost me an entire month's allowance, and it's all worth it for that wide-eyed look on Bradley's face.

When he finally exhales, it's in the reverent sort of way that a curator might do when presented with priceless art. He swallows, his Adam's apple bobbing, and then kisses me again, gently this time. "God, you're perfect."

And again, though there's an aching need to feel the entire length of his body pressing up against mine, a tiny—or maybe not so tiny—part of me quails. He catches the flicker of hesitation on my face and frowns.

"Babe, if you're not ready, it's okay—"

"Oh, I'm ready." He doesn't look convinced, so I prattle on. "It's going to happen, Bradley. Your penis is going to go inside my vagina. Well, actually, your penis is going to go inside a condom, and then go inside—"

"I get it, okay!" He laughs. "If you're sure."

"I am." Probably everybody gets last-minute jitters. Definitely probably. I shake off my doubts and grab his shirt, slightly more roughly than I had intended to. He stumbles a bit—why is this not as sexy and smooth as the movies make it out to be? His shirt comes off at last, and the sight of his abs literally makes me salivate, which is just as gross and creepy as it sounds.

"Can I . . ." His voice trails off as his gaze flicks down at my bra.

"Yeah, of course. Yeah." I bite my lip as his beautiful hands go behind my back and unhook my bra. Or try to, anyway. Should I help him? Is that going to ruin the moment? I should definitely help—no, I think he's got it—nope. I snake my hands up my back and a few excruciating moments later, I feel the release as my bra unhooks. This is it. It's going to happen. Finally. But instead of relief, what floods me is white-hot panic. Right before my bra falls to the floor, I catch it and hug it to my chest. My face is on fire. I don't know what's going on, everything feels right but also really fucking wrong, and my eyes are filling with tears.

"Oh shit, babe." Bradley puts his arms around me and pulls me close. "Hey, it's okay. We don't have to."

"I'm sorry. I'm so sorry."

"Stop apologizing, it's fine," he murmurs, kissing the top of my head.

I sag against him and close my eyes. Despite how mortified and disappointed I feel, I also feel relief. So much relief. "Bradley, I—"

An unearthly shriek pierces the moment. My head jerks up, slamming into Bradley's chin.

"Ow!" he cries.

But I can't pay him any attention right now, because there at the doorway is Mama, wearing the most awful, thunderous expression I have ever seen. She looks at me like she's seeing an entirely different person, like I'm some stranger who's broken into her house.

"WHAT THE HELL IS GOING ON HERE?"

CHAPTER 2

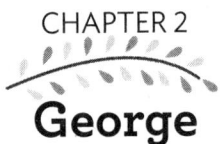

George

Sometimes I like to daydream about what life might be like if Mama hadn't passed away. I don't really remember her; I was only four when she died giving birth to Eleanor. I like to think that life around here would be a lot different with her around. A little less hectic, maybe. I think Mama was a calming force. Her family's certainly a lot quieter than Papa's. I think I take after her, is the problem. No one on Papa's side of the family seems to know what "quiet" or "peace" means, Eleanor included.

Usually, I use this to my advantage. They're just so loud all the time that it's easy to hear them coming and slip into my usual hiding places. Our house in Jakarta, Indonesia, is humongous and provides an obscene number of hiding spots—Papa's unused study, Nainai's unused library, the playroom that Eleanor and I have grown out of. But today, I guess I got carried away. I didn't catch the stomping feet in time.

The only thing I can say in my defense is that I'm a healthy teenage boy, and I'm doing what healthy teenage boys do in their spare time. Also, I even finished my homework before I started doing this super-healthy thing.

There's a knock on the door, which makes me lurch, my heart ramming up my throat. *Ohmygodohmygod—*

I only have time to minimize the porn before Papa barges in. He thinks that knocking a split second before coming in counts as knocking. I bet he's regretting it now, now that we're staring at each other in complete and utter horror, me struggling to do up my jeans. Luckily, he looks away, his cheeks painfully red, and mumbles, "Waduh, sorry, George—"

Unluckily, what he looks away to is the computer screen. I'm not sure why he looks even more horrified—I'd closed the video, and it was pretty vanilla as far as porn goes—but I'm too busy battling with my jeans to notice. I swear my fingers have turned into sausages and forgotten how to work a button.

Then—oh god, no—more loud stomping feet accompanied by a jaunty humming.

"Hi, Papa." Eleanor appears in the doorway next to Papa. "What're you doing—EWW!"

"Eleanor, it's not what it looks like—" Well, it is. It's exactly what it looks like, actually. Finally, *finally,* I manage to button my pants, and I look up to see my dad and my sister staring back and forth between me and my computer with unspeakable horror on their faces. Shit, did I not close the window after all? But seriously, it's completely vanilla, it's— Ah.

When I closed the window in a hurry, the screen went to the next tab I had open, which was a game I'd been playing before nature reminded me I'm a horny teenage boy. *Fields of Dreams* isn't really the type of game I usually go for. It's a farming game with adorable characters and bright primary colors. I'm usually an FPS guy, but I'd just had a particularly rough session of *Warfront Heroes* with the guys and needed a break. Anyway, I have no idea why Papa and Eleanor are staring at *Fields of Dreams* like the cute gnome and even cuter badger have just decided to decapitate each other.

"Um, sorry." Speaking now is amazingly hard, as though my words have to fight through honey to even come out. I should say something else, explain myself, but I'm not sure there's anything to explain. I mean, again: I'm seventeen, I'm healthy, and I wasn't doing anything weird or wrong, right?

With obvious effort Papa and Eleanor tear their gazes from my computer and look back at my face.

"George Clooney," Papa whispers. He always uses my middle name whenever he's angry at me, which just goes to prove that he and Mama gave me that damn name to punish me. "Were you masturbating to—uh—to—"

"To what looks like an elf and a badger gyrating with each other," Eleanor says helpfully. She seems to have recovered from her initial shock, and the familiar smirk has crawled to its usual position on her face.

"What the fu— NO!" I look at the screen again, and I see now that the little bearded gnome is indeed dancing with a large badger. "That's just— No. The gnome's dancing because, um, the badger gave him this special gift, see . . ." I desperately click on the mouse to open my inventory and belatedly realize that what the badger has given my character is . . .

"An extra-large, juicy eggplant," Eleanor reads out in an excruciatingly clear—and of course, loud—voice.

"The animals give you crops if you do quests for them. Don't make it sound like a weird thing!" I'm getting shrill and I know it, but I can't stop myself. "Pa, I swear I was watching normal porn. Like, it was totally vanilla porn, super boring and respectful! Look, I'll show you my browsing history!"

But Papa and the rest of his family aren't known for keeping calm. They're more of the flap-a-lot-and-wail type. It's during these situations that I really wish Mama were still around to calm him down. I stand there helplessly as Papa rushes out of the room and away from me, leaving me alone with Eleanor and her smirk.

"Oh god," I moan, covering my face with both hands. "I swear I wasn't— It's not like that."

Eleanor gives a dramatic sigh. She's definitely got the Tanuwijaya family gene. All drama and flair, go big or go home. "Duh, I knew that."

My head whips up. "You knew?"

She rolls her eyes and sits on the edge of my bed. "Oh, George Clooney. I'm thirteen, I'm not stupid. I've seen the stuff you watch. Like you said, super boring."

"How— What? Wait. What?" I'm so shocked by this revelation I don't remind her to call me gege—Mandarin for "older brother."

"Your computer password is Mama's name," she says with

another aggressive roll of her eyes. "Took me about two minutes to figure out."

"So you were snooping in here?" Jesus, I don't know how to feel. Violated, for one.

"Only when I'm bored. It's all your fault."

"What? How is it at all my fault?"

"Uh, you're supposed to help me persuade Pa to buy me a smartphone, remember? Just think of how much of my time a phone will take up. I won't have to resort to snooping in everyone's rooms to occupy myself." She raises her eyebrows at me like she's pointing out something really obvious. Which, in a way, I guess she is.

I pinch the bridge of my nose. There is so much here to parse through, not least the fact that Pa is still out there, probably wailing through the rest of the house. Lucky that Nainai—my grandmother—is hard of hearing. He'd have to wail extra hard for her to hear, and she probably won't understand what he's saying.

Okay. I need to focus. One thing at a time. Change my computer password. Yeah. I pointedly ignore Eleanor and start typing. New password. Hmmm. Mama's birth—

"I bet you're changing your password to Mama's birthday," Eleanor mutters with derision.

My head snaps up and I try to not look as surprised as I feel.

"So predictable," she mutters again.

Argh. I can't deal with this now. I look around and then type in the first thing I can think of: mousepad. Right. I'll change that later, when I've put out all the flames around me. I straighten up and point an authoritative finger at Eleanor. "Don't ever snoop in my room again, you hear me, Eleanor?"

"Are you forgetting something?"

I grit my teeth and manage to grind out, "Eleanor Roosevelt." So yeah, my parents have a thing about names. It's a Chinese Indonesian thing. They either hopelessly butcher Western names or join two perfectly innocent names together in a Renesmee situation, or they go for famous white people. I, a perfectly normal person, am embarrassed that my full name is George Clooney Tanuwijaya. Eleanor, on the other hand, adores that she's named Eleanor Roosevelt and has spent the whole of last year reminding everyone to please call her by her first and middle name. I speak in the lowest, most threatening tone of voice I can muster: "Do not EVER snoop in my room again."

Eleanor's mouth drops open in an affronted way, and she's no doubt about to give a snarky retort, when we hear voices from downstairs. My heart, previously recovering from its bout of shock, suddenly stutters back to a jumpy canter. Even one floor up and at least three rooms away, there is no mistaking that voice.

We turn to each other and say, *"Eighth Aunt."*

I race out of my room, Eleanor scampering behind me.

Despite being the youngest of eight siblings, Eighth Aunt is the matriarch of the Tanuwijaya clan, and it's not just because she owns the largest share of the family corporation, but because she's charming and wily and the only one of eight siblings who is able to keep her cool in any situation and figure out the best solution. I shudder to think of what solution she'd come up with if Papa were to tell her that he caught me jerking off to a badger. And Papa will definitely tell, because Eighth Aunt will sniff it on him, like some sickly perfume, and start to pry, and when Eighth Aunt pries, she does so with all of the cunning and eloquence of a CIA agent. There is no chance in hell that Papa—the earnest, lumbering big brother of the family—will be able to keep it from her. There are no secrets in our clan, especially from Eighth Aunt. Not even things that normal people would consider private. She knows everything, even information like the exact dates my cousins had their first periods. Nothing is safe from Eighth Aunt. Nothing.

God, run faster, feet! Why is our house so freaking huge? How much space does a family of four really need?

By the time I've rushed down the grand winding staircase, past the foyer, past the formal living room and then the formal dining room and then the casual dining room and into the less formal living room, which is meant for close family, I'm out of breath. I smash my shoulder into the huge double doors, and Eighth Aunt and Papa look up, their mouths falling open. Irah, the head housekeeper, is just taking the last plate of crudités from the silver tray. Oh thank god: if Irah is still here, that means Papa hasn't told Eighth Aunt. They wouldn't say anything that could tarnish the family name with her around.

But my relief is short-lived. Even as I stand there, Eighth Aunt mutters in Mandarin, "Mm, I understand, yes. Very tricky matter."

Mandarin. Nooo! Sometimes I hate that most Chinese Indonesian families speak three languages—Indonesian, Mandarin, and English. This means that Papa and Eighth Aunt would've been able to speak freely without Irah understanding what they're saying. Then Eighth Aunt turns her head and looks at me in a new way, a way that says: "How did generations of good, careful breeding turn out with you? How did genetics fail us so badly?" Usually, she looks at me the same way, but there's also an undercurrent of "Aww, look at little George Clooney. He's not much, but he's the only boy in his generation of the Tanuwijaya clan, so I suppose we should all cherish him and pinch his cheeks and make him eat his vegetables." Now that loving undercurrent is gone. Papa has definitely spilled the beans. Hell, he's spilled the entire casserole. It might seem strange, sharing that you caught your son masturbating, but my family has zero boundaries. I once overheard Fourth Aunt asking Third Aunt if my newlywed cousin Kimberli and her husband were expecting yet, and when Third Aunt said no, Fourth Aunt called the couple and gave the poor guy actual play-by-play advice on the best positions to increase chances of conception. I couldn't meet Fourth Aunt's eye the rest of the day.

"Aduh, George. Sit down here and explain yourself," Eighth Aunt says, her eyebrows scrunching together as she pats the seat next to her. Out of my dad's siblings, she's the only one who's comfortable speaking English, though she does pepper her sentences with bits of Indonesian.

Like a terrified puppy, I approach slowly. Eleanor bounces in, oozing glee.

"Oh, my poor darling Eleanor Roosevelt." Eighth Aunt is also one of the few people who's taken Eleanor's demand to use her full name seriously. "Come here." Eleanor does so with unabashed affection and practically flings herself onto Eighth Aunt's lap, very nearly knocking Eighth Aunt's huge hairdo askew. Eighth Aunt has a professional hairdresser come to her house every other day to wash and style her hair. Eleanor tells me that Eighth Aunt sleeps sitting up so she doesn't squash her hairdo, and I honestly can't tell if she's kidding. The rest of Eighth Aunt looks just as over-the-top as her hair—today, she's wearing full Dior, everything from the full-length tulle skirt to the thick leather belt to the blazer is emblazoned with the CD logo, and I have no doubt that even her flawless makeup is Dior. It's the kind of attention to detail that Eighth Aunt applies to every aspect of her life, which is partly why she's such a successful matriarch. I perch gingerly on the edge of the couch, as far away from them as possible.

"Poor, poor baby," Eighth Aunt says, stroking Eleanor's hair.

"Oh, it was so freaky," Eleanor wails.

Seriously?

I have to resist the urge to glare at Eleanor. I swear my entire head is a ball of flame right now. "I can explain—"

"No need," Eighth Aunt says, waving me off. "I understand. It's what happens when you don't have a mother figure. I have failed you, George." And she looks so completely heartbroken that I squirm uncomfortably, unsure what to do. "I have heard of this trend, you know," she says in a conspiratorial tone.

"What trend?" God, I bet she thinks masturbation is a trend.

She winces and lowers her voice. "This trend of—ah—abusing yourself to cartoon animals."

Papa shudders, letting out a low moan of horror.

"I wasn't!" My voice comes out so high and fast that only dogs can hear it. I clear my throat. "Eighth Aunt, I really wasn't—"

She raises her hand to cut me off. "It's okay, George. I understand that you have strayed a little from the right path. Your papa and I will think of how to resolve this. In the meantime, he and I have agreed that you shouldn't have access to your phone or computer."

My mouth drops open with horror. "No, please—"

Eighth Aunt's expression switches, just like that, from sad to wrathful goddess. "George Clooney, you are going to be the face of our latest product."

The latest product she's talking about is OneLiner, an app we're launching in about a month's time that's aimed at teen boys. It's one of our do-good-for-the-human-race apps—we've got a handful of those under our belts, and they always do wonders for our corporation's image. OneLiner is supposed to be a fun way of teaching teenage boys how to behave appropriately and treat girls with respect. As Eighth Aunt says, it's sad that we have to teach my kind how to treat girls with respect, but since we do, might as well turn it into good publicity for the company. I'm actually kind of proud of the app. It had been my idea, and I didn't think they'd go for it. When the family was informed that it was time for another do-good app, there had been a barrage of suggestions from all my cousins, because traditionally we've always used one of my cousins to be the face of these kinds of apps.

My cousins, their mettles forged in the fires of private schools and/or overseas schooling, make very good mascots. I would've been happy to let any of them be the face of OneLiner, but unfortunately, because it's aimed at boys and the clan was cursed with me as the only boy in my generation, I've become the face that no one wanted to have on the app.

"Listen, I understand that teenagers do—ah, teenage things," Eighth Aunt says with a grimace. "But we live in a conservative country. I know it's, ah, healthy, but the spokesperson of OneLiner cannot be caught doing anything like this."

"It wasn't anything deviant, I swear!" I cry, my voice breaking a little.

She holds her hand up. "It doesn't matter, George. Everything, no matter how innocent, can be taken way out of context here. Remember what happened to Millisent."

Two months ago, while exiting a karaoke lounge, cousin Millisent (as far as misspellings go, hers isn't too awful, I think) threw her arms around her two best friends and planted kisses on their cheeks. A journalist waiting outside had captured the kisses. An innocent gesture, but because their high-fashion outfits revealed a bit more skin than people here are used to seeing, the gossip sites blew up and accused her of having had some wild threesome at the karaoke lounge. The lounge was vandalized by hard-line groups, and Millisent and her friends quickly took off to Singapore to escape the outcry for a while. The family company stocks had taken a dip for two whole days until the media frenzy moved on to another scandal.

"We just need to play it very, very safe, you understand? No risks." She takes a deep breath, then says, "No electronics for you until after OneLiner has been launched properly, titik." Period. Eighth Aunt is used to having the last word.

"And you too, Eleanor," Papa rumbles in Indonesian.

Eleanor's head whips up so fast the back of her skull smashes into Eighth Aunt's chin. "Ouch!" they both yelp. I bite my lip to keep from smiling. I know it's petty as hell, but seriously.

"What, Papa?" Eleanor says, rubbing the back of her head.

"No phone for you."

Eleanor looks affronted. "Why not? We were just about to go to PP to get me an iPhone!"

"I don't feel safe about you having one. Just look at what happened to your brother."

"That's gege! I'm different, Pa, you know I am. Pleaaaase."

But for once, Papa is unmoved by Eleanor's charms. "No. There are too many weirdos out there. We'll wait another year, then we can discuss it again."

The look on my pesky little sister's face is almost worth enduring the whole unfortunate incident. Almost.

CHAPTER 3

Sharlot

The moon is shining silver bright, so clear that I can practically see every crater and hill on its surface. Beneath it is a blanket of clouds, reflecting the moonlight like a silvery sea. As our plane slips through the night sky, I imagine it parting the sea of clouds, breaking the soft cotton apart as it leaves the only home I've ever known. It's a breathtaking sight, but I'm not in the mood to have my breath taken. Instead, I slam the plastic window shade shut and turn to face Mama, who's reading one of the in-flight magazines.

"This is kidnapping," I say for the millionth time.

Mama snorts. "Oh, Sharlot, you so funny."

Usually, I'm not bothered by her broken English—it's so mildly broken it's more like a crack here and there. But now, I'm in the mood to be annoyed by everything Mama does, so I snap, "Sharlot, you *are* so funny. Not 'you so funny.'"

Her lips close and thin, and my chest squeezes guiltily. That was a low blow. Mama had immigrated to the States from Indonesia when she was seventeen and taught herself how to speak like an American by taping and rewatching *Ally McBeal* and *The X Files*. It's a marvel how good her English is. I doubt I could do the same if I were plopped into a foreign country as a teenager. Which is exactly what she's doing to me now, I remind myself. She's completely ruining my life and she deserves all the petty jabs I have to give.

Still, I grit my teeth and grind out a small "Sorry."

Mama doesn't say anything, but her chest falls slightly as she releases the breath she's been holding.

"But, Ma, surely you see how craz—how you're overreacting? I mean, what about your job? Didn't you say you just landed that huge client at the firm?"

"I spoke with the partners. I can do most of the work online, and what I can't do in person will be handled by Gregory."

"Oh god, Gregory? You've been bitching for years about him and how he's always coming after your position."

"Yes, and this should show you how much I'm sacrificing for your sake, Sharlot," she hisses.

"But you don't have to sacrifice anything for me! I swear, nothing was about to happen with Bradley. I was just—" Tears sting my eyes at the memory of my catastrophic foray into sex. How terrible it was and how much worse getting caught by my mother made it. I was so incredibly humiliated that I pre-emptively broke up with Bradley. He was confused, and who can blame him? He asked me what he did wrong, which made it even worse because of course he'd done nothing wrong. It was all me. But when I said those words: "It's not you, it's me," they felt like a stupid cliché.

And now, three days after the most humiliating event of my life, Mama has completely lost her shit and is whisking me off to Indo-freaking-nesia. I pointed out to her that I should take malaria medicine for days before the trip, and she smugly told me I'm up-to-date with my vaccinations. Argh, of course I am. Ever since I was a kid, Mama has been insistent on making sure she and I have every vaccination we need to travel to Indonesia. Malaria, hepatitis A and B, typhoid fever, and rabies. I used to think it was just paranoia on her part, but now I'm wondering if she meant to spring this trip on me all along.

What even is there in *Indonesia*? It's not like Singapore, land of Crazy Rich Asians, all glitz and glamour. I mean, no offense to my own mother's culture, but when I think of Indonesia, I think of, like—well, this is going to sound completely awful, but I think of, um, *National Geographic*-style huts. Which I know is probably not what it's actually like. I hope. I don't know. Everything I hurriedly looked up sounds bad. BBC has a bunch of articles on Indonesia, mostly about how its capital, Jakarta, is sinking. It's also got photos of really sad-looking slums and flood after flood. What a miserable place. And I know how ignorant it makes me sound, but case in point: In all of my seventeen years of living, Mama has never taken me back to Jakarta. And now, she's taking me back as punishment. Even my own mother, who was born and raised in Jakarta, sees the place as purgatory.

"We are not going to discuss anymore," Mama says. "We spend summer in Jakarta, that's it."

"For fuck's sake."

Mama's gaze hits me like a hot laser beam.

"This is exactly why we need to go back," she says. "You become too Americanized. Too loose with everything. Your words. Your body."

The way she says "your body" makes it almost shameful, like I wasn't supposed to have one. "Wow, here we go with the slut-shaming."

"I not slut—" Mama catches herself and takes a sharp inhale. She lowers her voice a notch. "I not saying you cannot ever have sex, Sharlot. You can. But not yet. Not now. You still so young! You're only seventeen!"

Is it my imagination, or did her voice quaver then, just a little?

But when she next speaks, it's turned back to steel. "My job as your mother is keep you safe, show you how to—how to jadi orang."

Jadi orang. Those two words have plagued me ever since I can remember. I think they're supposed to mean "make it," but the direct translation is "become a person," which I hate. As though kids aren't people. As though we need to jump through hoops and cater to the whims of our elders in order to become a legit human being.

"I know you hate to be reminded of it, but I am actually a person in my own right already."

Mama huffs with impatience. "Aduh, Sharlot, why you must be so difficult? Of course I'm not saying you are not a person. I'm saying . . ." She gestures with frustration, trying to pluck the right words out of her head, and I take some pleasure in watching her struggle. "I'm saying you need to learn how to be an adult. Sudah. No more discussion." And she yanks her sleep mask down over her eyes and leans back in her seat, pretending to fall asleep. She's so committed to acting like she's sleeping that she doesn't stir even when an air attendant starts serving us snacks and drinks. The attendant places a cup of iced water on Mama's tray, and I sit there fuming, watching the ice melt, each minute a reminder that I'm being carried far, far away from the only home I've ever known.

Okay, so as it turns out, Jakarta has a really nice, modern airport. Who would've thunk it? In fact, the Jakarta airport is so shiny and modern that it kind of makes LAX look like a dump. I mean, more of a dump than it already is.

Of course, I can't let Mama see how impressed I am with the stupid airport, so I'm careful to keep my expression a curated mix of bored/unimpressed/pissed off. All the way through the long lines at customs and waiting around for our luggage, Mama and I don't say anything. Silent treatment it is. Only thing is, I can't tell which of us is giving the silent treatment and which one is receiving it, and it's not like I can ask. Mama's passive aggression is of legendary level. If I were to come out and ask her point-blank whether she's giving me the silent treatment, she'd give me a surprised, innocent look and be like "What you talking about? I thought we were being quiet because we both meditating." And then somehow, I'd be the petty one of the two of us. Story of my life.

Finally, our bags arrive and Mama and I drag them toward the exit, where huge throngs of people are waiting. Though we're still inside the airport, the constantly open gates allow the humid heat to waft in, and suddenly, I'm sweating like crazy in my light cardigan. I start to take it off, but I'm aware of how revealing my tank top is compared with everyone else's outfits, and how my skin is practically neon white in contrast with that of most people around me. I get the overwhelming sense, again, of being very far from home. I wrap an arm around myself and wheel my luggage silently, keeping my head down and following Mama very, very closely.

As we're about to reach the exit, Mama whips around and says, "Listen, Shar, people here might not be accepting of—" She hesitates, and for a moment, I sense a crack in her usual armor. My mom seems small and young and uncertain. I can practically see her asking herself if bringing me here was the right thing to do. "Just don't . . . just . . . Never mind."

"Pei! Qing Pei!" Someone from the crowd is calling Mama's Chinese name, and from the sea of people, a tall, thin man appears. I'm dying to know what Mama was about to tell me, but when I glance over at her, her walls are back in place. I look back at the man. I recognize him vaguely as one of Mama's many brothers. Despite everything, I find my heart rate rising. This will be the first time I'm meeting a relative in the flesh. I don't know what happened seventeen years ago, but suffice to say, none of Mama's relatives have visited us, though not from lack of trying. I've overheard phone calls from them asking when's a good time to visit, and Mama always says, "Oh, not now, I'm so busy at the office you know, *so* busy. But yes, you must come for a visit when things less hectic, ya?" Problem is, things are never "less hectic," not when Mama's involved.

"Qing Li!" Mama rushes over to him and they give each other a really awkward Asian half-hug, then stand there grinning at each other for a few seconds. "Aiya, you shouldn't have come. I could have taken a Grab."

Uncle Qing Li frowns at her, and as smoothly as anything, Mama switches to Indonesian and says something about . . . something. Why's she speaking so fast? Or has she always spoken Indonesian extra slow for my benefit? I stand there feeling very lost and very alone and with a sudden urge to burst into tears.

Then Uncle Qing Li looks at me and smiles. I smile back at him. My whole body is just one giant heartbeat. This man is related to me! He says something in Indonesian, and when I stare blankly back at him, Mama tells him to speak slower because my Indonesian is terrible.

"Ah, okay! Welcome . . . home . . . Sharlot!"

I have to actually bite my tongue to keep from blurting out "This isn't my home, bruh." Instead, I say, "Thanks, Uncle."

He laughs like I've said something hilarious. "Waduh, you are so bule, ya?" *Wow, you are so white, huh?*

My cheeks must be tomato red by now. I shouldn't be taken aback; I know that Asian aunties and uncles have no filter and they rarely mean any harm when they say things like that. I also know that, being half white, half Asian, I'm always an other. I guess I just didn't expect it to be said so explicitly to my face.

Mama flaps her hand at him and tuts dismissively, then tells me to call him Li Jiujiu, which apparently means "maternal uncle Li" in Mandarin.

With the introductions over, Li Jiujiu grabs both of our bags without asking and wheels them outside, where a huge minivan is waiting for us. A chauffeur climbs out of the car when he spots us and takes our bags from Li Jiujiu.

"Thank you, Roni," Li Jiujiu says.

"Um, yeah, thanks," I say.

The chauffeur gives a small Geralt-of-Rivia grunt in reply and lifts the bags into the car like they weigh nothing.

We duck inside and I exhale, savoring the air-conditioned coolness on my melting skin. This is the fanciest minivan I've ever been in. The seats are a luxurious leather, the interior is ridiculously spacious, and when the chauffeur starts the car, it says something in Japanese. Mama and Li Jiujiu start speaking rapidly in Indonesian, so I tune them out and gaze out the window as we leave the airport.

Jakarta. Mama's hometown. When I was little, I was obsessed with finding out more about the place. I'd ask Mama a million questions about her country, about her family, about her past. But at the time, she'd only tell me little boring details like "It's a tropical country" or "It's very hot." Each nonanswer she gave was a cut, and as I got older, the pain turned into resentment. I decided to get back at her by going in the other direction. Give her a taste of her own medicine. Every time she brings up anything about Indonesia, I shut down the conversation. Spiteful, I know, but after so many years of her shutting me down when I ask, I had to get used to not being curious about Indonesia. Plus, she doesn't get to decide when to reopen the subject, not after rejecting my queries all this time.

The area around the airport is as I expected—rural greenery, not much to look at. I check the time on my phone. Three in the afternoon, local time. My head feels heavy and muzzy. After our twenty-hour flight, I feel utterly defeated, but my mind is too scrambled for me to take a nap. Instead, I glance out the window. The sky is a murky gray-blue, but not because it's cloudy. It's haze from the air pollution. Great. I take out my drawing tablet and start sketching, knowing the act will kill two birds with one stone—it'll soothe my frayed nerves (yay) and irritate Mama (double yay).

Li Jiujiu glances over and laughs indulgently. "Wah, have we got a little artist here? Just like you, Qing Pei!"

What? I turn my head toward Mama sharply. She scowls at Li Jiujiu. "It was just a hobby. A useless one, at that."

I grip my stylus hard and press so heavily on the tablet that my strokes end up a lot thicker than I wanted and I have to undo them. "A useless hobby." That's how she views my dream job. My teeth grind until my jaw hurts, and I force myself to take long, slow breaths. Focus on nothing but the art. Before long, my hand moves in even strokes and I lose myself in the lines of my sketch.

About twenty minutes into the car ride, Li Jiujiu nudges me and says, "There's the city."

Sure enough, there it is. My eyes widen. What in the . . .

I thought Los Angeles is a big city. But there, everything is spaced so widely apart and most buildings are short—not many skyscrapers outside downtown LA. Jakarta is the exact opposite. We're surrounded by skyscraper after skyscraper, and in between them are houses and shops and everything bunched in together in a never-ending metropolitan sprawl. It's both incredible and intimidating, and oh my god, how have I gotten it so wrong this whole time? My insides squirm as I recall all the awful things I've said to Mama. Like when she says Jakarta is a huge, modern city, I roll my eyes or snort and say, "Okay, Ma," in a horrible, condescending way. The dozens of little jabs where I thought I was stating facts but I wasn't. I was just being an asshole. A misinformed, ignorant little asshole.

I turn away from the window and look down at my tablet instead, struggling to calm myself down. I don't care if Jakarta's a modern city after all. It's still not home. I know what it's like to feel out of place. And I have never felt it more than right now.

CHAPTER 4

Sharlot

The car ride takes forever. Literally. Once we get to the heart of the city, we run into traffic that would put LA's to shame. We're stuck for so long that I grow tired of drawing and pack up my tablet, taking out my phone instead. Thank god I've got my spare battery with me. We're fourteen hours ahead of LA, so it's now almost two a.m. there. I aim the camera out the window and take a photo, then post it on Insta Stories with the caption "Loving the big city!" It only makes me feel worse. But it's not like I'm going to post it and say "Stuck in purgatory for the rest of the summer yay #fml." That wouldn't be cool. Instagram is for toxic positivity only. Twitter, on the other hand . . .

Nah. Not in the mood for that hellscape. Instead, I text Michie, telling her I miss her, which is true, at least. Then I open my text thread with Bradley. The last few texts have all been from him.

Bradley [07:34PM]: Hey, I know u broke up with me and stuff, but like . . . r u ok? No one's heard from u

Bradley [07:34PM]: I'm so worried, I hope ur mom hasn't done anything bad

Bradley [08:11PM]: Text me when u get this

And so on and so forth. My thumbs hover over the keys for an eternity, my heart thumping wildly. I should reply to him. The poor guy deserves better. I mean, is there another human as decent as him out there? I literally dumped him, and here he is, concerned about my well-being. I hadn't even told him that I'm being kidnapped to Indonesia.

But every time I think of Bradley, I think of me falling apart in front of him like a complete idiot. I think of him seeing me unmasked, without the layer of acidity I always wear, and the thought is like an ice pick stabbing straight through my brain. I shake my head a little and shove my phone back in my pocket. Texting Bradley is definitely something that needs to be done, but not after a twenty-hour journey with my mother.

Eons later, as I'm nodding off, Li Jiujiu announces, "Here we are!" in the type of voice that makes me think he really needs us to see the entrance to the driveway. I jerk awake and—okay, it actually is worth seeing. Apparently, Li Jiujiu lives in an actual mansion.

"Ah, the old house." Mama sighs happily.

I stare at her. "What do you mean, 'the old house'? This is where you grew up?"

"Yes, this is Ah Gong and Ah Ma's house. Was," Mama adds, her expression turning sad for a moment.

"But we've remodeled it, obviously," Li Jiujiu says.

I have to tell myself not to gape as the ornate front gate swings open and we go into the driveway. Dang, Mama's family is loaded. How come I never knew? I mean, in LA we've always been comfortable in a very firmly middle class way. "Are we Crazy Rich Asians?" I blurt out.

They both throw back their heads and laugh. "No," Ma cries between peals of laughter.

"Of course not!" Li Jiujiu says. "We are just average Chinese family. Qing Pei, you not teach her about Chinese Indonesian history?"

Mama sniffs, and I grind my teeth, biting back yet another acidic retort.

"Ooh, okay, Li Jiujiu tell you later. Come, now we go inside and you have shower, everything, then later dinner."

As soon as I get out of the car, I go to the back to get my luggage, but Li Jiujiu tells me not to bother and ushers me inside the mansion. The interior of the house can only be described as a rococo explosion. Everything is exceptionally ornamental and theatrical—the pillars drip with bouquets of flowers and birds carved painstakingly out of stone, the walls have layers and layers of curved molding, and the furniture is all curved with dainty legs and bursts of intricate engraving. There are huge, elaborate chandeliers in every room—the foyer, the living room, the dining room. I feel as though I've just stepped into an opera house. It all feels a bit ornamental, though, like a stage set.

"Ah, Qing Pei!" a woman calls out from the other end of the house. She hurries over with a big smile and outstretched hands.

Mama's smile is a bit less open. "Sao sao, you look very healthy," she says. I estimate that *sao sao* means something along the lines of "older brother's wife." Chinese family titles are painfully specific, and I have no idea what I should call my maternal uncle's wife. Maybe I can just call her Auntie.

"Aduh, no need to call me that, just call me by my name." The woman air-kisses Mama and then turns to look at me. When she speaks to me, she does so in English. "You must be Sharlot. How lovely to finally meet you. I'm your auntie Janice." Whoa. Her English is flawless, with a vague British accent. I mean, it's better than Mama's, and Mama has spent half her life in America. I sneak a glance at Ma, and sure enough, she's noticed how much better Auntie Janice's English is. I can tell by that tiny pinch in one corner of her mouth. I try to feel smug about it—hey, it was Mama's idea to come all the way here—but I can't. Instead, I'm almost overcome by an urge to pat Mama's shoulder. We're not really the hugging type. With some effort, I squash the urge and give Auntie Janice a smile big enough to rival hers.

"Hi, Auntie Janice. It's nice to meet you."

"Gosh, aren't you pretty?" she says, pinching my cheek like I'm all of five years old. "Oh, there's Kiki. Kiki, come. KIKI. KIKI."

I turn, expecting a Pomeranian, the way Auntie Janice is calling, but it's a girl around my age.

"This is my youngest, Kristabella," Auntie Janice says, pulling Kristabella and positioning her in front of me like some mannequin. "Kiki, this is your American cousin, Sharlot."

Kiki gives me a once-over and I have to stop myself from

quailing under the scrutiny. It's weird: in America, Asians from Asia are called FOB—Fresh Off the Boat. It's a disparaging term, but everyone in school uses it, especially the Asian Americans. And right now I feel like the out-of-place FOB. Which I guess, technically, since I literally just got off a plane, I am? I really did not see this plot twist coming.

Kiki isn't gorgeous, but she's the kind of cool that would make people stop mid-sentence and stare as she walks by. I don't know what it is. Maybe it's her clothes—she's just wearing a button-down and slacks, but somehow they fit her so well they look tailored, clinging to her silhouette without being tight. Maybe it's her asymmetric bob that falls elegantly over one side of her face. Maybe it's her flawless skin. Whatever it is, she oozes effortless perfection, and I am seriously regretting my choice of fashion. The ripped jeans I thought would symbolize defiance and coolness now make me feel totally dumb. And my shirt, after my long-ass journey, is not faring well at all. Rumpled, stained, probably has an intense stink too.

"Hi," I manage to finally say. It comes out as a squeak. "I'm Shar."

"Kiki. Come, I'll show you to your room." Like her mother's, Kiki's English is perfect, with a slight British accent.

I look back at Mama, for once seeking a bit of comfort from my mother, and find her thin-lipped. She gives me a little nod. *Go.* I'm not sure what comes over me, but I reach out and give her arm a squeeze before I follow Kiki.

We go up the richly carpeted stairs, and Kiki points at the first door. "This is you. I'm next door, and my parents' room is at the end of the hallway. Your mum's room is that one." She points at the door across from mine. Mum. I've never heard anyone call their mom "mum" outside of a Netflix show.

The inside of the guest room is just as lavish as the outside. There's even a four-poster bed. And, of course, another chandelier. Do they sell these things at every street corner or something? I mean, there was one above the landing of the stairs and there's another out in the hallway.

Kiki catches me gaping up at the chandelier and scoffs. "They're Chinese-made, so they're dirt cheap. The wiring isn't great. We need to change the bulbs, like, once a month. Everything in here's like that. Looks great but is actually a cheap copy."

"Oh, okay." I'm not really sure what to say to that. I look around and see with a start that my luggage has been placed here. I wonder if Kiki's going to go so I can unpack and then go shower the smell of airplane travel off me and—I don't know—probably have a good cry or something. Instead, she crosses the room and plops onto a sofa right next to the picture window.

"So, what's your story, Shar? Is that short for Charmaine? Charlene?"

"Sharlot."

Kiki nods. "Did she spell it correctly?"

I bite my lower lip.

"Because there's a Michael in my class," Kiki says with a grin.

"Michael? That sounds fine."

"It's spelled M-a-i-k-e-l."

"Ah." I sigh. "She didn't spell mine correctly, no." I walk over to my luggage and unzip it pointedly. This should be a hint for

Kiki to leave. It's not that she's being unpleasant, exactly, but I'm so tired, and I am desperate for a few minutes to myself. What time is it in LA? Maybe Michie— Oh. It's around four a.m.

"Mum says you got knocked up." She says this so casually, with her pert little chin in her pert little hand like she's asking me about the weather.

I straighten up so fast I get dizzy. "Excuse me?"

Kiki shrugs. "My mum. She says you were sleeping with some American boy and got pregnant, that's why you're here."

"Jesus."

"Not true?" Kiki gives me that calculating glance I'm fast becoming very familiar with. "You don't look pregnant."

"I'm not—god. Fuck your mom."

We both gasp. I didn't mean to say that. Oh my god. What is wrong with me? Why do I do this? Why am I all fight and no flight all the time?

But then Kiki's mouth quirks into a grin, and before I know what's happening, she's laughing uproariously. It feels like the first true thing I've seen ever since I got here, and the relief is so immense it floods through my entire body and I start laughing too.

"Oh my god, I can't believe you said that!" she cries between cackles.

"I know, I'm so sorry."

She shakes her head, still laughing. "It's fine." She takes a deep breath and composes herself. "If it makes you feel better, I don't think Mum believes it herself. Well, actually, I don't know.

I never can tell which lies Mum believes and which ones she pretends to believe just so she can tell everyone about it. She's a bit of a c-u-next-Tuesday, you know?"

Whoa. Okay. And here I thought I had a difficult relationship with my mom. But I have never called my own mom—or any other woman—the c-word and I have to say, it's pretty shocking hearing it from someone who looks like Kiki. I plop down on the sofa next to her.

"So. Not pregnant. Why're you here?"

I shrug. "Am I not allowed to visit my mother's homeland? Don't tons of our cousins visit here?"

"Yeah, the ones in the US and UK come back once a year, usually. Ones in Aussie come back twice a year. But you," she says, pointing a finger at me, "have not set foot in this country in the entire seventeen years you've been alive. So everyone is just a tad curious about why you're suddenly here."

This sends a shot of dread crawling down my spine. "Everyone?"

"The family. You know."

"I don't know, actually. Um. How big is it again?" I mean, I know Mama has six siblings, and each of those siblings had more than two kids, and some of those kids—my cousins—are grown-up and have gotten married and produced their own kids . . .

"Big. Last I checked, there are sixteen of us in our generation and—I don't know—maybe seven in the next gen? I'll have to check if Ci Genevieve's given birth yet."

Sixteen of us. Fifteen first cousins. Good lord.

"And they're all wondering and, like, making up stories about why I'm back here?"

"Not all." Kiki rolls her eyes. "I mean, some just don't care. Like Ci Genevieve, she's all about her firm. And her babies. Ah, good ol' Ci Genevieve, always making the rest of us cousins look bad. This will be her third child, you know, and she still hasn't taken a single day off work."

"What does she do?" I vaguely know of a family business in . . . real estate? Plastics? Pipes?

"Private equity. She didn't go into the family business. She's making it all on her own and setting the bar way too high for the rest of us."

"Ah." Great, so the only person who doesn't care is some ancient overachieving cousin. "So, Genevieve doesn't care—"

"Cici Genevieve. You can't just call her by her name, that's so rude. She's older than us by like, fifteen years."

I resist the urge to roll my eyes. It's like this all over Asia—age matters a lot, so if you're older, the younger person needs to call you by a title and definitely not just by your name. "So Ci Genevieve doesn't care, but everyone else does?"

"Yeah." Kiki looks closely at me. Way too closely.

"You're really different from how I thought you'd be."

I shift uneasily, unable to tell whether she means it as a good thing or a bad one, but before I can ask, she springs off the sofa and tells me to get some rest before dinner, then leaves the room. And just like that, I'm alone, feeling emptier than I have ever felt in my life. It's not just the long journey, it's that I've returned to my mother's homeland to find that I'm a complete stranger, an outcast even, and there's something so painfully lonely in that realization.

Tears prick my eyes. Before I can stop myself, I reach for my phone and send a WhatsApp message to Bradley. Just two words: *Save me.*

CHAPTER 5

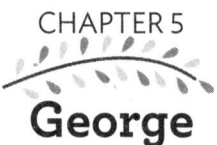

George

As it turns out, confiscating my electronics isn't a logical punishment, given I need them for school, so for now, the new rule around the house is that the Wi-Fi password is off-limits to Eleanor and me unless we need it for school assignments. To circumvent our computers saving the Wi-Fi password, Papa changes it after every use. It sounds terrible, and it sort of is, but Papa and Eighth Aunt seem to think that if they don't, I'll be spending all my time rocking back and forth in a dark corner, pining for the internet.

In hindsight, I should've done that once or twice at least, just to appease them. Instead, I foolishly took it as a long-needed break from the everything-ness of the internet and spent the whole of last week coming up with new features for OneLiner. I have so many ideas for the app—how to streamline it so it loads faster, how to make it more user-friendly, and how to make it stand out in the app store. My favorite idea is to have a share-your-story section where our users can post about how toxic masculinity has affected them. I think it would help for boys to hear how their actions affect others. There are a gazillion apps aimed at teen boys, and admittedly, apps that take more of an educational slant are less popular than the flashy ones. Even Eighth Aunt doesn't think it'll actually get many users; she just thinks it'll look good for the company's profile.

When I get tired of thinking of all the things I can do with OneLiner, I take a break and start going through my TBR pile. My poor books, they've been so neglected, especially since Simon and I started playing *Warfront Heroes*. It's been nice getting through the pile of hardbacks—

There's a single knock. The next second, the door crashes open and Eleanor comes bounding in, her face shining with excitement, her pigtails bouncing wildly. She's learned the art of the non-knock from Papa.

"Oh good, you're not doing your gross-teenage-boy thing again," she says by way of greeting, bouncing onto the sofa at the foot of my bed.

I don't bother looking up from my book. "Go 'way."

"You're going to want to listen, big bro."

When I don't respond, Eleanor jumps off the sofa, scampers to my reading nook, and puts her face up against the book cover. "Hellooo, gege."

This is hopeless. "What?" I sigh, putting the book down and giving Eleanor a pointed I-am-not-interested-in-whatever-you're-going-to-say look.

With a grin, Eleanor straightens up. "Okay, so. Despite the fact that you've completely ruined my social life—"

"How did I ruin your social life?" The moment I say it, I realize I've walked into her trap. I should've just stayed quiet.

"Did you forget that Papa was about to take me to—"

"Pacific Place to get you your first-ever phone, yeah, yeah."

"Sooo! I've thought of a way that you can prove to Papa that you're not this"—she gestures vaguely at me—"this sad, pathetic weird guy."

"Thanks."

"And that's to find you a proper, age-appropriate, family-approved girlfriend. A human one."

"What?" I shake my head and snort. "You're being ridiculous. As usual. Are you done? Because I'd really like to get back to my book."

"Harry Potter can wait, George."

"Okay, first of all, it's not Harry Potter, it's a Hugo-winning fantasy by a Black writer named N. K. Jemisin—"

"I hope you realize you sound like a thirty-year-old nerd. This is exactly why you need my help to get you a real, human girlfriend."

I groan into my hands. "Okay, I've listened to your pitch. Now please go away."

"But you agree to it, right?"

"What?" I think of my annoying little sister finding me a "human girlfriend" and sigh. Where's she even going to start? She's like this, always starting little projects and then getting tired of them half a minute later and moving on to the next thing. "Sure, whatever. Go crazy."

The effect is immediate. She practically lunges at me, gives me a huge hug, and then springs away before I can hug her back.

"Papa! Pa! PA! Gege said okay!"

"Wait, what?" Papa's involved? Oh no. I have a really bad feeling about this. "Hang on, Eleanor—"

But it's too late. Like some terrible, vengeful god rising from the depths of the sea, Papa appears in the doorway. I gape at him. "Have you just been standing outside my room the entire time?"

"Yes. I wanted to come inside from the beginning, but Eleanor said not to." He pats Eleanor on the head with obvious pride, and she gives him one of her I'm-such-an-adorable-precocious-sweetheart grins. He's no match for her. Then again, I guess I'm not either, because, wow, she got me good.

Papa holds out his hand. "Give Papa your phone."

I snort. "Uh, not a chance."

"George Clooney." He uses that voice, the one that probably every Asian kid knows, the one that reaches deep into our central nervous system and makes all our senses prick up. There's so much weight behind it—disappointment, quiet anger, and an ocean's worth of expectation that threatens to crush me.

"No!" I say again, but I already know it's useless. Whenever I watch US or British TV shows, it always strikes me how free the kids are, how rebellious and how daring, especially toward their parents. I wish I could be more like them. But nope. I've been raised all my life to *never* go against my elders. All Papa does is glare at me, and my hand moves, as though of its own accord, to take my phone out of my pocket. I watch helplessly as he takes it from me and gives it to—

"You're kidding me," I hiss. "You can't give my phone to Eleanor!"

Papa frowns. "She's just helping me navigate this app you kids use." But as a compromise, he says to her, "Don't snoop into any of gege's apps, okay?"

She nods obediently. "Promise, Papa." Then she types in the unlock code—how the hell did she even know my unlock code?

"How did you—"

"It's your birthdate," she says with a roll of her eyes. "It's, like, literally the first thing I tried."

I sit back, defeated.

"Don't worry, gege, I swear I won't snoop into your emails or anything. I am doing this from a purely professional standpoint."

"You're thirteen years old. That's, like, the very definition of nonprofessional!"

She levels a stern gaze at me. "Stop being such an ageist." Then she turns to Papa with a grin and says, "Okay, here we go. Opening ShareIt. It's what's called a social media app . . ."

I stare in mild horror and disbelief as my little sister gets our dad up to speed on ShareIt, an Indonesian app that's pretty much a knock-off Instagram. She scrolls through my feed and points out my various friends. Papa listens to her with the gravity of a serious business merger.

"So if I 'Like' this photo, it means I like the person?"

"No, just the photo. Technically. But obviously, Papa, if it's someone you've had some tension with, then they'd probably notice you liking their post."

Oh my god. Someone kill me now.

"And now, let's open up the search settings. This way, we can look for someone appropriate for gege."

Papa nods and the two of them tinker with my ShareIt settings for a while, muttering stuff like, "Location . . . age . . ."

I have no idea what to do now. "I don't think you can do this," I say, but my voice comes out weak and they both ignore it easily. "Seriously," I add.

Papa looks up from the phone, his face lined with disappointment. "Son," he says. Uh-oh. He's switched to English. Now I know he's being serious, because his English is terrible and he only ever uses it when he really needs to get through to me. "You are what you call it, hmmm."

Eleanor and I wait for it. He's going to say something like "privileged" and then go into a whole lecture about don't I know how fortunate I am to be his son, etc.

"Loser," Papa says.

"Excuse me?"

Next to Papa, Eleanor is raising her brows and obviously trying not to laugh.

"Yes, you are what you call this 'loser.' Every day just in your room, playing games. Not out doing sport."

"Doing sport?" Sports aren't a huge part of the Chinese Indonesian upbringing. They're there as extracurricular activities, definitely not something to be taken too seriously, and this is what's been drilled into my head from the start of kindergarten. "Have you forgotten that you've brought us up to *not* do any sports? I mean, you give me such a hard time every time I swim laps or hit the gym!"

Papa fidgets in his seat. "Yes, you are right, sport is waste of time when you should be studying. But you know what I mean, George!"

"I really don't."

"And now I realize, I fail you. Is all my fault."

Oh no. Here we go. This is why Chinese Indo kids are so obedient. Because our parents raise us with a healthy dose of emotional blackmail.

"You didn't fail me, Pa."

Pa's face scrunches into a half sob. "I fail. I fail your mama. If she see us now, she would cry in her grave. I should have spend more time with you, not worry so much about business. Business fail is still okay. Lose the house, lose everything, is fine. You two are my priority."

"Aww, Papa." Eleanor puts her arms around his shoulders and hugs him while glaring at me.

It's a ruse, I remind myself. Papa and his siblings are masters of guilting their kids into doing what they want. Stay strong.

Despite that, the sight of Papa's heartbroken, defeated face is too much. I can only take a few moments of it before I relent. "Fine," I say, and sigh loudly. Damn it.

"Papa is so proud, son." He pats my shoulder.

"Just. Argh. Never mind. Stop speaking English. I'm gonna take a shower." I leave the bedroom, unable to withstand the sight of the two of them poring over my phone, and head to my bathroom. Inside, I take an extra-long shower, hoping against hope that by the time I go back out there, both my dad and my sister would have got bored and gone out of my room. Unlikely to happen, but one can hope. When I'm done, I towel myself dry and look at my reflection. The face of the company's new app. Sigh.

A squeal of excitement comes from the bedroom. Guess I should get out there and face the music. Unfortunately, the music is the theme to *Jaws*.

With no small amount of trepidation, I walk out of the bathroom.

"We did it. We found the perfect girl for you. *And* she's already replied to your message!"

"WHAT?" Just how long was I in the shower? I grab the phone from Eleanor's hand and look at it.

And wow. Okay. I'm not sure what I was expecting, but SharSpy10 is definitely not it. Just like Instagram, ShareIt is focused on images. SharSpy10 only has three posts, all of them of her, and she is very, very pretty. Like, forget-what-you're-about-to-say kind of pretty. She's also my age, apparently, and newly transplanted to Jakarta.

"Look, she even grew up in California, so that's, like, major cool points," Eleanor says.

"Normally I wouldn't approve of these ABCs," Papa says, using the abbreviation for American-born Chinese, "but we have to take drastic measures. Maybe an ABC is just what you need."

I ignore them both and look at the messages my dad and sister have sent to this poor unsuspecting girl.

CuriousGeorge [10:13AM]: Salutations!

Oh my god. "Nobody says 'Salutations,'" I bite out. "What the hell? I expected more from you, Eleanor."

"I'm being classy. Setting you apart from all the other randos who probably message her every day. Plus, look at her replies."

SharSpy10 [10:14AM]: Salutations back to you!

CuriousGeorge [10:15AM]: Org Indo, ya?
Are you Indonesian?

SharSpy10 [10:16AM]: Iya. Wah, senangnya ketemu org Indo
Yes. Wow, I'm so happy to meet a fellow Indonesian.

CuriousGeorge [10:17AM]: Sudah "for good" ya di Indo?
Are you back in Indo for good?

SharSpy10 [10:17AM]: Just for the summer, ha-ha. But I love it already!

Despite myself, I'm actually impressed by Eleanor, because somehow, against all odds, she's managed to start up a conversation with SharSpy10. And Eleanor's right that given how SharSpy10 looks, she's probably inundated by messages from randos all the time.

"You liiike her," Eleanor says in a singsong voice.

"No, I don't. She's a complete stranger that you and Pa

are catfishing. Do you two realize how insanely inappropriate this is?"

"What's catfishing?" Eleanor says.

I pinch the bridge of my nose. "We watch *The Circle* together, El, you know exactly what catfishing is. It's when somebody pretends to be someone else, especially online," I add for Papa's benefit.

They both look at me blankly.

Why do I even bother?

CHAPTER 6

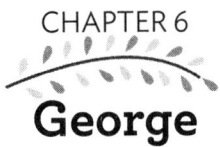

George

CuriousGeorge [4:17PM]: What do you do as a hobby?

SharSpy10 [4:18PM]: I cook! I looove cooking.

CuriousGeorge [4:18PM]: Wonderful! What kinds of food do you cook? Western?

SharSpy10 [4:19PM]: Oh no. Western food too easy—you just fry everything. No, I like to take good care of my family, make sure everyone well-nourished, so I cook Chinese food. A lot of bone broth soup, ginseng, etc.

"SON," Papa cries, looking up from my phone in wonderment, "we have find perfect wife material for you!" Great, he's speaking English again. The past few years, it's become more in vogue for people to speak English instead of Indonesian—many here see it as a sign that they're well-educated. So despite his broken English, Papa often insists on speaking it just to show that he can.

Next to him, Eleanor grins and nods so hard that her pigtails bounce wildly. "He's right, you know, gege. SharSpy really does sound like the kind of girl you marry."

I snatch the phone from their hands and scan the messages. Oh god. How many freaking messages are there? When they'd found SharSpy a week ago, I'd thought (and prayed to the universe) that they'd realize the ridiculousness of this whole endeavor and stop after an hour or two. But oh my god, I was so wrong. There's like a novel's worth of chat messages in here.

The messages have switched from Indonesian to English. And worse still, to Papa's broken English. I glare at Eleanor. "Why didn't you at least correct his grammar?"

She looks at me innocently and shrugs. "Her grammar is awful, too, so I thought I'd make her feel better by hiding my eloquence. It's called empathy, gege."

I close my eyes and pinch the bridge of my nose, but Eleanor is right. For an ABC, SharSpy's grasp of the English language is . . . somewhat wobbly. But I shouldn't judge her for that, though I *can* judge her for everything else, like her cooking, for example.

SharSpy loves cooking traditional Chinese food. With ginseng. Eurgghh. Nothing against ginseng, but this is old-people food. Literally! It's actually what Nainai eats every day—chicken, pork, or beef ribs stewed for hours and hours with Chinese herbs until the soup is milky and rich with nutrients and collagen from the bones. To be fair, it's actually delicious, but again, it's old-people food. Also, she sounds kind of judgy about it, like it's something she believes a woman is supposed to do, which eurgghh.

"Can I just remind you both of how wildly inappropriate this is?" I say. "Also, really freaking creepy. Pa, you're leading a teenage girl on. This is—it's gaslighting!"

"What this gaslighting?" Papa says. "Lighting a fire?"

Eleanor rolls her eyes. "Gaslighting basically means lying. And we're not doing that, because it's your real account, and here you are, CuriousGeorge, a real-life teenage boy."

"Yeah, but it's not me sending those messages to her! It's you, a thirteen-year-old kid, and you, a forty-year-old man, which makes this incredibly creepy and wrong."

Eleanor waves me off. "Chill, gege. God, you're acting like we're asking her for her bank account or something."

"Enough of this. Give the phone back to us," Papa says. He's switched to Indonesian, which means he's trying to exert authority, which means he's back to serious mode.

I take a step away from him, unsure what to do, but I don't see Eleanor slithering up from the other side. She plucks the phone out of my hand smoothly and scampers to Papa's side. They settle back down on the sofa, both wearing the same eager expression.

"Okay, now ask her if she's ever had a boyfriend," Papa says.

Eleanor nods and starts typing.

"Don't ask her that! That's just—no!" I'm getting shrill and I know it, but seriously. I start walking toward them and Papa looks up and shoots me a look. It's a look that probably most kids know well. A look where he's somehow transformed from loving, gentle dad to Old Testament patriarch. And I hate that it stops me in my tracks. Papa has never hit us, but we've been raised with enough Asian guilt that I still can't find it in me to go against him when his mind is set.

"She says 'Of course not, I'm not a hussy,'" Eleanor announces.

Okay, first of all, that was really fast. Second of all, ugh, now she's slut-shaming. Honestly, the more I know of SharSpy, the less appealing she is. Of course, I am still the less appealing of the two of us, given I'm standing here watching helplessly as my little sister and my dad deceive the poor, innocent girl.

Papa is nodding with much parental approval. Kind of like the way he often looks at Eleanor, I guess. "Ah, she is a very good kid, very good."

Then Eleanor says, "Uh-oh."

I rush over and look over their shoulders.

SharSpy10 [4:23PM]: What about you, what do you do as a hobby?

"What do we say, gege?" Eleanor asks in faux panic. "You have no hobbies outside of gaming!"

I roll my eyes at her. "Thanks. Um, tell her I like working out with the guys?" The mention of my school friends makes me a bit sad. I'm not close to any of them because my family considers most close friendships to be a bit of a liability. We never know when someone might betray us for attention or money, so I don't really have close friends. But I do miss my gym buddies.

Papa shakes his head again. "No girl wants to hear that. Tell her he likes to do homework. Mathematics."

"Wait—"

Eleanor types at lightning speed. For a girl who's never owned a phone, she is suspiciously adept at typing on one.

CuriousGeorge [4:24PM]: Calculus.

Great. Just great. If SharSpy didn't suspect anything before, she sure as hell will now. Or at the very least, she'll think I'm the world's biggest nerd. Actually, that's not a bad thing. Maybe it'll turn her off so much, she'll ghost me. Huh. I should've just let them run with it. No girl in her right mind would fall for the version of me they're creating online. I almost laugh out loud at how quickly this whole inane ploy has been shut down.

Three dots appear next to SharSpy's name. Here it comes. She's going to tell "me" that I'm a loser. My chest squeezes with anticipation.

SharSpy10 [4:25PM]: Wow. You are perfect.

Like I said, no girl *in her right mind* would fall for the version of me they've created online.

CHAPTER 7

June 8

SharSpy10 [2:18PM]: I just think WHY? Why is it that so many girls my age they don't like to cook? And not only they don't like it, but they think it's like something to be proud of, you know?

CuriousGeorge [2:19PM]: Yes, exactly! Same like boys my age, they think not knowing what they want to do in life is something to be proud of!

SharSpy10 [2:20PM]: This is a very strange generation, very strange.

CuriousGeorge [2:21PM]: Oh yes, so strange. You know, back in my parents' times, things make a lot more sense. The boys know they have to work hard so they can provide for their family.

SharSpy10 [2:22PM]: Yes! And the girls know they have to learn to cook well so they can feed their children when they get marry.

CuriousGeorge [2:24PM]: It's like you are reading my mind!

June 10

CuriousGeorge [2:36PM]: Yes, so this app I design is name OneLiner.

SharSpy10 [2:37PM]: Ugh, don't tell me, is it like to pick up girls?

CuriousGeorge [2:38PM]: Oh no! Actually it is the opposite! It is to teach boys how to treat girls right.

SharSpy10 [2:39PM]: Oh, you mean like how to be gentleman?

CuriousGeorge [2:40PM]: Yes, exactly! Because nowadays boys are so hopeless, you know. They not know how to treat girls right, make them feel like special treasure, you know.

SharSpy10 [2:42PM]: Yes, I feel the same way.

CuriousGeorge [2:42PM]: I think is so important for boys to make girls know they are precious, need to be treated very carefully.

SharSpy10 [2:43PM]: Yes, definitely. Wah, I am so surprise, George. You are like modern-day gentleman. It's so rare nowadays. You are such a good boy. This is so rad!

CuriousGeorge [2:44PM]: Ha-ha-ha, aduh, no, no. You flatter me.

June 11

SharSpy10 [7:38PM]: Look what I cook for my family! [Sends a picture]

CuriousGeorge [7:42PM]: WUAH. So much good food! Your family so lucky to have you.

SharSpy10 [7:47PM]: Braised sea cucumber with pork belly and shiitake mushrooms, chicken collagen soup with sliced abalone, fried bamboo shoots with pork trotters, and fried pork and shrimp balls. This one recipe from my grandma, she is from Hakka region of China. You ever try Hakka pork balls?

CuriousGeorge [7:48PM]: Those are favorite! My ah gong was from Hakka also. One day I shall like to try your recipe.

SharSpy10 [7:49PM]: I'll save some for you! But better eat them fresh. Maybe we can meet up tomorrow?

CuriousGeorge [7:50PM]: Yes! Great idea.

SharSpy10 [7:51PM]: I can't wait!

CuriousGeorge [7:51PM]: Me neither!

CHAPTER 8

Sharlot

"Why the hell would you do this?" I yell at Mama. I shouldn't yell, I know, the walls aren't thin, but they're not shout-proof and people will hear. Well, I say people but I am mostly referring to Auntie Janice, who at this very moment is probably pressing her ear against the damask-patterned wallpaper to try and catch every word. I can picture her so vividly I can even see the expression on her face as she does so, but still I can't rein in my temper, because—

"Out of all the fucked-up things you've done, this tops it, Ma!"

"Enough!" Ma thunders back. We both know I got my temper from her. "Is been a week since we arrive here, have you gone out? NO. You just staying in your room, moping, 'Oh, I'm so sad, oh no, poor me!' The whole family is worried about you."

The mention of family makes my stomach curdle like spoiled milk. If only Mama had taken me here as a child, back when I wanted to know everything there was to know about the place and my family. But now, all I feel when I think about them is the sharp tang of fear and resentment. All that stuff Kiki told me about them the day I arrived . . . about how they'd been gossiping about me and the only reason I'm here is that I got pregnant.

"I didn't think you could do even worse than confiscating my phone the day we arrived," I hiss.

I was sure it wouldn't be long before Ma realized the error of her ways and gave me back my phone. Instead, this morning, she came rushing into my room all breathless and happy, saying she's found me "the perfect boyfriend."

"I don't understand you, Sharlot," Ma says, and suddenly all the fight leaves her. Her shoulders sag, and her face is lined with a mixture of sadness, worry, and disappointment—the look she gets when she sees me lately, that is. "I thought you'd be happy."

"I don't even—I—what? Why would I be happy about my mom trying to match-make me to some boy I don't even know?"

"Because it shows that I care! It shows that you are loved. And you haven't even seen this boy I find for you. He is perfect. Please, Sharlot, I just trying to help."

Wow, Ma said "please." To me. That's kind of a momentous occasion. I know it's kind of a stereotype, but none of the Chinese parents I know believe in saying things like "please" or "sorry" to their kids. Or maybe it's just a Ma thing. Either way, I'm pretty sure this is the first time I've ever heard her say please to me. Her voice is so sincere, her expression so earnest, I find I can't easily fire back a retort. Oh, FFS. I can't believe I'm about to say this. I am definitely going to regret it. "Fine, let's take a look."

Ma squeals. An actual squeal like she's some excited little kid. My heart twinges, and I wish I could overcome this gaping barrier between us and give her a hug, but I'm still too mad. Anyway, I have no idea how she'd react to that. She's never been one for physical affection. With some trepidation, I take my phone back. The familiar weight and feel of it back in my hand brings out a sigh of relief. *Welcome home, sweet, sweet phone.*

Then I look at this supposed "perfect boyfriend" she's found me. Huh. He's actually really cute. Good skin, strong jaw, broad shoulders—wow, I do not hate it.

Doesn't matter, though, a small voice in my head pipes up. *Check your messages! Has Bradley replied? What about Michie? They must think you're dead!*

But with Ma hovering next to me, I can't quit the ShareIt app.

"This boy, out of the blue, he message you," Mama says. "Is fate! Meant to be!"

I ignore her. I get messages all the time, mostly from creepy older men, but I choose not to tell her that. She'd freak out and then who knows what she'd do? Instead I open up the chat history with CuriousGeorge—god, what a dorky screen name. The first few messages are in Indonesian. My Indo is bad enough that I have to read them while pointing at the words with my index finger and mouthing them as I go, but fortunately, after that, they both switch to English. Unfortunately, CuriousGeorge's English is just as broken as Mama's.

CuriousGeorge [4:31PM]: When I grow up? I'm definitely joining my family business.

SharSpy10 [4:32PM]: What does your family do?

CuriousGeorge [4:33PM]: This and that. A bit of land development, a bit of tech, a bit of raw material production. Everything, really. I want to be their finance manager. I'm good at saving money.

SharSpy10 [4:34PM]: Wow. You are amazing, so intelligent.

Good-fucking-lord. *Amazing* and *intelligent* are definitely NOT the words I'd use to describe CuriousGeorge. *Nerdy* comes to mind with *overly privileged asshole* a close second. What the hell kind of seventeen-year-old boy wants to be a finance manager? What even is a finance manager? No seventeen-year-old boy in the world is good at *saving* money. But of course, that's not even the worst of it. No, the worst bit comes right after that.

CuriousGeorge [4:35PM]: Thanks. I believe that men should provide for their families.

SharSpy10 [4:35PM]: Oh WOW. Your future wife is so lucky!

Kill me now.

Of course, Ma isn't satisfied with me just seeing the chat messages she's exchanged with this poor, weird asshat. Poor, weird asshat. Hah. I keep swinging back and forth between feeling horribly guilty about CuriousGeorge (seriously, that screen name, c'mon) and judging him really harshly, because:

1. He sounds like exactly the kind of son Chinese parents would die to have: hardworking (boring), conscientious (yawn), and a total narc. I mean, I don't actually know that the last one is true, but I'd bet money that if George saw a classmate doing something that isn't completely kosher, he'd totally squeal on them.

2. He seems to think my mother's version of me is really great, which should tell you everything you need to know about his taste in girls.

3. He sounds really gross and sexist. All that stuff he said about his app, OneLiner? Eww. Treating girls like "something precious"? So. Much. Nope. He's way too ready to praise Mama every time she talks about cooking. Clearly, he thinks a woman's place is in the kitchen. He's just so wrong in every way that it is possible to be wrong.

But is Mama willing to listen to reason? Of course not. Just minutes after she hands me back my phone, she tells me that I'm going to meet up with George for a coffee.

"Like hell I am." The words slip out of me so effortlessly. I don't even bother waiting for a reply. I continue scrolling through the messages, hating this boy more and more with each text I read. Then I come to the end of the string, and . . . Oh god. "You asked him out?!" I half scream. "You offered to bring him homemade pork balls? What the fuck, Mama?"

"Sharlot." There's that warning tone in her voice, the one that sets the little hairs at the back of my neck on end. Then she stops herself and sighs. When she speaks again, her voice is conciliatory, though I still sense the tension lurking. Won't take much to make it break through and snatch us straight into a shouting match. "You don't have to cook the pork balls yourself. I already made some and put in Tupperware for tomorrow. Please, have coffee with him. Not date. Just a coffee."

"To be fair, you are on an island that's literally called Java," Kiki says, popping her head through the door.

We both whirl around, mouths agape. "Kiki!" Ma cries. "How long have you been there?"

She shrugs as she walks in. "From the very beginning, I reckon. You guys should lock your door if you don't want anyone listening in. And, you know, speak in softer voices. Mami's on the other side listening, by the way. She's got a stethoscope pressed up against the wall and everything. She ordered one online when she found out you were coming."

"What?"

Mama's lips thin, like she's sort of surprised but not really.

Kiki turns to Mama. "Can't believe you catfished some teenaged boy, Auntie. Can I see his photos?" She leans over and whispers to me in a very non-whispery way, "I bet he looks like a total nerd. Amirite?"

All I can manage is "I— Wha— A stethoscope?"

With a sigh, Mama says, "You talk some sense into her," and passes the phone to Kiki. Kiki looks down, and her impish grin freezes.

"Um." She glances up at Mama. "This is the guy you fooled into talking to you? CuriousGeorge?" She shows Mama the screen to double check. Mama nods. "Wow."

Curiosity overcomes my shock. "What? What is it?"

"This is George Clooney Tanuwijaya."

I don't even bother holding back my laughter. "George Clooney?"

"Yeah, yeah okay, move on, the middle name isn't the interesting bit."

"He's actually named George Clooney?" I'm still cackling away. Suddenly, Sharlot isn't the most unfortunate name I've come across.

"Yeah, he is. Stop laughing and listen. Have you two never heard of the Tanuwijayas?"

I swallow the rest of my laughter and try to look like I'm paying attention.

"I knew a Tanuwijaya when I was young," Mama muses.

"Probably a different Tanuwijaya," Kiki says dismissively. "You'd know if you were friends with the Tanuwijayas. They're Indonesia's second-wealthiest family? I think they were number seven last year in *Forbes Asia*."

"Ah yes, definitely different Tanuwijayas," Mama says. "My friend Shu Ling so secretive about her family background. My parents told me it must be because she was so poor, so she was embarrassed of her family."

"Well, these Tanuwijayas are the opposite of poor. We're talking the real Crazy Rich Asians. Old money, not like those Singaporean tech and finance guys. Money from the Dutch days."

"Dutch days?" I echo uselessly. Kiki stares so hard at me I cringe. "What?" I hate how defensive I sound.

She turns the stare on Mama, who flinches too. Geez, Kiki can be scary when she wants to be. "Auntie, you never told her the history of Indonesia?"

"She never wanted to learn," Mama sniffs.

"Uh, not true," I pipe up. "I used to want to learn, but you were always shooting me down, so I got tired of it."

Kiki holds up her hands. "Doesn't matter. Okay, quick lesson: Late fifteen hundreds, the Dutch came and colonized Indonesia. A ton of Chinese immigrants were already here, and they were hired by the Dutch as skilled artisans. Those are our ancestors, in case you haven't figured."

"I have," I bite out, sounding a lot like a surly toddler.

"They didn't just stay skilled artisans, though. The Chinese were entrepreneurs and were, like, obsessed with improving their guanxi."

I must have looked confused by this, because Kiki rolls her eyes and says, "Is your Chinese as bad as your Indonesian? *Guanxi* just means 'relationships.' We're obsessed with building good relationships with others. Specifically, business relationships. Our ancestors strengthened guanxi with a ton of other Chinese immigrants in Southeast Asia, trading and building and working their asses off, and by the time the Dutch left, almost all businesses in Indonesia were owned by Chinese."

"Oh. Wow."

Kiki nods. "That's also why even though the Chinese make up only two percent of Indonesia's population, we now own seventy percent of its wealth. There have been laws put into place to curb the wealth of Chinese Indos, but it's kind of hard to curb such a huge head start. Obviously it's unfair for the native Indonesians. I hope that we can find a way to fix the inequality somehow. The Tanuwijayas are one of these old Chinese Indonesian families. They own everything—coal mines, palm tree and coffee plantations, real estate. And they manufacture everything—plastics, pipelines, houses. Lately they're branching out into tech. They literally do everything."

"You fooled some billionaire's kid?" I say to Ma, who's staring with mouth agape at Kiki.

"I didn't know—I—"

"Not just some billionaire's kid," Kiki adds, her grin widening. "George Clooney is the only Tanuwijaya boy in his generation."

"The only boy?" Mama says, her eyebrows disappearing into her hairline.

"What's wrong with that?" I say.

Kiki sighs. "Gosh, Auntie, you really haven't told her anything, have you?" She turns to face me. "The Chinese Indo community is super traditional. Some families more than others. The patriarchy is definitely far from being smashed here. You know, when George was born, they threw a banquet so stupidly lavish and over the top it was on the news. So, Auntie, you didn't just trick some billionaire's kid, you tricked some billionaire's only male heir."

Mama and I stare at each other in horror.

"Are we in danger?" I manage to choke out after a while.

"Of course not. Don't be so melodramatic, my dear," Auntie Janice says, striding in.

Mama and I gape at her. Sure enough, there is a literal stethoscope hanging from her neck.

For someone who's just scolded us for being melodramatic, Auntie Janice gives a *very* dramatic sigh before flopping onto the chaise longue. My bedroom is suddenly very full of people.

"Really now, Kiki, why do you always have to paint everything in the most dire way possible?" Auntie Janice shakes her head. "You just made it all sound so threatening, as though your auntie Qing Pei has done something awful, instead of commending her for landing such a catch."

"I—I didn't mean to," Ma stammers. I've never seen her this unnerved, and it's unnerving to see. "I didn't—I wasn't seeing him as a catch like that. I just thought he was a nice boy."

"Well, he is," Kiki says. "I hear things about him. He's not like one of those gross jocks or anything. He doesn't drive flashy cars or whatever."

She has Auntie Janice's full attention. "You know him and you never told Mami?"

"Aduh, Mami, of course I don't know him. We don't even go to the same school."

"Papi's fault," Auntie Janice says immediately. "I told him, 'Send her to Xingfa School, that's the biggest, most famous school in Jakarta. Traditional Chinese schools are the best!' But did he listen? No, he wanted you to go to a smaller, new school, so now here you are in Mingyang. Is there anyone famous there? No, of course not." She turns to face me. "Anyway, Sharlot dear, you must meet this boy."

"Not if it's dangerous," Mama snaps.

Auntie Janice and Kiki stare at her. "Why would it be dangerous?" Auntie Janice asks.

Mama shrugs, her face turning red. Auntie Janice has a way of speaking that isn't, like, overtly rude or anything, but makes it clear that she thinks you're not on par with her brilliance and she's having to accommodate your lack of intelligence. I feel protective of Mama, which is a really weird feeling to have. "You hear many thing about these super-wealthy families," Mama says in a small voice. "They hiring military police, escort them everywhere . . ."

Military police? What the hell?

"Oh, military police," Auntie Janice says with a laugh, waving Mama off.

I relax a little. Okay, so I wasn't overreacting. Mama's just exaggerating. As usual.

But then Auntie Janice says, "We employ them too. Just a handful. Roni, our driver, is a retired colonel!"

My mouth drops open. "What?" I think of the tight-lipped, broad-shouldered chauffeur who drove us from the airport and my mind goes: Does not compute.

"We had Roni and his old platoon mates escort us to the hotel for cousin Lyonel's wedding," Kiki pipes up. "They helped us clear the traffic and stuff. It's pretty common here. I think most Chinese families here have at least one or two of them employed full-time."

"Holy what?"

"Kiki's right," Auntie Janice says. "You've been away from Indo too long, Qing Pei. Things are different now, not like they were in the nineties. Jakarta is very safe now."

Mama nods slowly, though she doesn't look fully convinced.

"Right, so we're all agreed that Sharlot will have a coffee with George Tanuwijaya," Aunt Janice says. Kiki nods eagerly.

Mama chews on her bottom lip. "If you say it's safe . . ."

My cheeks heat up and all my frustration blurts out: "Hells no!" Mama looks at me with wide eyes, and Auntie Janice looks slightly miffed but mostly bored. "Sorry, but you guys don't just get to peddle me out like I'm a piece of meat to some rich asshole! Maybe that's the done thing over here, but it sure as hell isn't acceptable where I come from. I'm a person. Don't I get a say in this whole thing?"

"She doesn't mean that—" Ma says. She's scrambling to smooth things over because I've just done a huge no-no: talked back to an elder.

Auntie Janice's gaze crawls over my face and I resist the urge to run away and hide. She just has this effect on people, like she's always calculating their worth and finding them lacking. Worthless. Her gaze says, Hello, little cockroach, let's see you run around, then. Mild interest combined with mild revulsion, like she can't believe we're somehow related.

Then her gaze moves to Mama. I've always thought Mama a

formidable woman, but under that horrible, dehumanizing gaze, she quails. A silent conversation happens between the two of them. I can practically hear the unspoken words flying back and forth.

Auntie Janice: Are you really going to allow your daughter to speak to her elder and better like that? What a failure of a mother you are.

Mama: NOOOOOO. (*Sob.*) I am not a failure.

Auntie Janice: Shame on you, Qing Pei. Shame. SHAME.

Mama: Oh god, I must prove to everyone that I haven't failed as a mother.

By the time Mama turns back to look at me, I know my fate is sealed. She's got this look of determination written all over her face. I prepare for the fight.

When she speaks, her voice is quiet but deadly. "Sharlot, if you do not meet up with George, you are never go back to California."

CHAPTER 9

Sharlot

I can't believe this. Or I guess I can, since the fact that I'm being chauffeured to some dumb mall to meet up with a stranger my mother's fooled isn't even the craziest thing to have happened this summer. It doesn't help that Mama, Kiki, Auntie Janice, and Li Jiujiu are all in the car with me. Each one has made up some inane reason for "needing" to go to the mall—Mama wants frozen yogurt; Auntie Janice wants a dress; Kiki needs a haircut; and Li Jiujiu had stared blankly at me for a bit before saying, "I need a... shoe?" Not "a pair of shoes," just "a shoe."

So here we are, packed into Li Jiujiu's humongous minivan, driving into what Li Jiujiu proudly calls the Sudirman Central Business District area, or SCBD for short. It's actually really well-built, with shiny glass-and-steel skyscrapers among well-manicured greenery. A lot more impressive than the gray buildings in downtown LA, that's for sure. But I would rather die before admitting to Mama that Jakarta's a lot different from what I'd envisioned.

We arrive at the mall and—okay—like the whole of the

SCBD, the Sudirman Plaza Mall is exceeding all expectations. Starting with the lobby, where employees wearing uniforms complete with white gloves and hats open the doors for us and say, "Selamat datang di Sudirman Plaza Mall." Everything is shiny and glittery. I am very much regretting my choice of outfit: a ratty-jeans-and-T-shirt combo that I thought would seem cool in a very I-don't-give-a-crap way but instead feels dowdy now. I should've listened to Mama when she tried to persuade me to wear something nicer before we left. Of course, I would rather eat a live snake than admit that now.

As soon as we get out of the minivan, the sweltering tropical heat slams into us and we all hurry up the steps and into the cool refuge of the mall.

And wow. I look up and up and up. Floor after floor of shops soar above me, and in the center of the huge mall is a display of hot-air balloons, hanging at different heights from the ceiling. At the ground floor is a huge hot-air balloon, and kids are clambering all over the basket while their parents take photos. A few steps away, a pianist plays a tune on a grand piano. The entire scene screams decadence, an over-the-top show of wealth. The shops on the ground floor are all brands I will never be able to afford—Prada, Louis Vuitton, Hermès—each one boasting elaborately decorated display windows.

Giving myself a little shake, I check my phone and say, "Okay, I have like two minutes to get to the café, so . . ."

Auntie Janice pats my arm. "No, my dear. You can't be on time."

"Seriously?"

"Auntie Janice is right," Li Jiujiu says. "Better you not be on time."

Kiki shrugs. "I mean, they have a point. It's called Indo time. People are always at least ten minutes late. If you get there on time, you'll just seem way too eager."

Argh. "I'm not eager, I'm just eager to get it done and over with!"

"I know," Kiki says easily. "But patience, young Padawan." With that, she twines her hand through the crook of my arm and leads me up the escalator. "Come, we'll go check out a few local designers, eh? See you later, Mami, Papi, Auntie Qing Pei!"

The three grown-ups nod at us and wander off, Li Jiujiu telling Mama that she must try the food at this restaurant and that café. Kiki takes me to level one, where to my relief there are more affordable brands like H&M. We go inside a shop called (X)SML, and she tells me this is a local brand. The clothes in here have the kind of look that I've been admiring on Kiki—understated outfits that look well-tailored and fit on the body in such a way that's both modest and yet alluring. She gets me to try a peach-colored top with a navy-blue sash that ties into a bow at the waist, and when I look in the mirror, I feel ridiculously different. Put together. Like I've got everything under control. Like I'm a good Chinese-Indo girl. I'm about to take it off and leave it rumpled on the rack when Kiki pops her head into the changing room.

She gasps with delight. "Look at you! I knew these clothes would fit you better than those ratty shirts you've been wearing. No offense."

"Not sure how I can take that without offense, but okay," I mutter.

Before I can stop her, she plucks the price tag from the nape and snaps it off. Then she grabs my "ratty" shirt from the side and walks out of the changing room.

"What the—" I scramble to put my shoes on—why did I even take them off?

Outside, Kiki's already at the counter, paying for my top and a green dress she'd found for herself. She smiles when she sees me.

"Kiki, what are you doing? Give me back my shirt!"

She ignores me and taps her PIN onto the payment thingy. "Trust me, Shar, you can't meet up with George Tanuwijaya wearing this—ugh—stained T-shirt, okay?"

"It's not stained, it's the design—ah, okay, yes that particular blob is a coffee stain, but Kiki! Give it back now."

She turns to the cashier and hands her the shirt. "Please throw this away, thank you," she says in Indonesian, before sauntering out of the store.

I rush after her, ready to tell her off, but she glances at her phone and says, "Okay, now you are suitably late, you should go to the café."

That takes me aback. I was so ready to tell her how annoying she is, but being told I'm late for my coffee non-date is disarming. Argh!

"Third floor," Kiki says helpfully.

I point a finger in her face. "We are not done here. We'll discuss healthy boundaries with you when I'm done with the boy my mother has catfished." With that, I stalk off and spend the time walking toward the café doing deep breathing exercises. By the time I find it, I'm somewhat calm-ish. Well, as calm as I can get about meeting a billionaire stranger my mom has tricked into meeting me, anyway. Huh, I've never met a billionaire in real life before. Come to think of it, I don't think I've ever met anyone I got to know online, never mind someone my mom got to know online on my behalf. Okay, my calm is dissipating. This is fine, this is a totally normal coffee non-date. I'll sit there for half an hour, to be polite, and then make up some family emergency. A quick look at my phone tells me that I'm now thirteen minutes late. That's an omen if I've ever seen one.

Like everything else in the mall, Kopi-Kopi is a super fancy café—it definitely puts all the places I go to in LA to shame. But I'm unable to admire the lovely décor, because as soon as I walk in, I spot him. George Clooney Tanuwijaya, sitting casually in a booth and scrolling through his phone.

He glances up, sees me, and there's a moment of something. Something that makes my breath catch. Something real, like for a split second, both of us are unmasked and I'm seeing the boy behind the big name and finding that he's just as vulnerable and lost as I am.

I blink, and the moment's gone. I remind myself to breathe. Here we go.

"Hi, George?"

He stands up and holds out his hand for me to shake. Kind of formal. Maybe that's how people do things around here. His hand's warm and firm. Mine's probably clammy. This is off to a great start. I sit down opposite him.

It's hard for me to ignore how good-looking the guy is. I mean, he's the kind of hot that would make me take surreptitious glances at him throughout classes if we'd gone to the same school. I can totally see myself eyeing him in AP Lit, admiring the nape of his neck and the strong, hard lines of his jaw, and those dark eyes that—

"Hey, SharSpy, how're you doing?" he says, sliding back into his seat with the easy grace of an athlete and jarring me out of my thoughts. His voice is a bit of a shock—it's deeper than I thought it would be and has an accent I can't quite place. Not American, not British, but sounds familiar all the same.

"Uh, yeah, good. You? Oh, and it's Sharlot, by the way." He nods and smiles at that. God, I'm so flustered, and it's not just because George in real life is so pretty. I remind myself that Bradley is just as hot as George, and look how that turned out. Doesn't matter if they're pretty if we can't connect on a deeper level, and after reading those chat messages between Ma and George, I already know there's no way in hell he and I would ever connect on a deeper level.

"Good, good." He slides a menu toward me and I stare hard at it. It's kind of really difficult to focus on the words when I'm so fully aware of the stranger sitting in front of me who thinks he's been chatting with me the past few days but really has been chatting with my mom. I mean, there's no precedent for this kind of thing! How the hell am I supposed to behave?

I must be taking way too long with the menu, because after a while, George says, "If you're new to Jakarta, I suggest the Kopi Susu Batavia. It's basically an iced latte with palm sugar."

"Um, okay, that sounds good." I wait as George calls for a waiter and asks for two Kopi Susu Batavias. The menu is whisked away, and now there's nothing between us but a whole lot of lies. Our gazes meet and quickly dart away, both of us breaking eye contact as though it burned us.

I try to think of what I know about him. "So, you go to SIS—"

At the same time, he says, "You grew up in the States?"

We stare at each other for a second, then George says, "Sorry, you go ahead."

"Uh." It takes me a couple of seconds to remember what I was going to say. "You go to Xingfa?"

"Yeah."

"What's it like?" I have no idea what private schools are like, never mind international ones.

George shrugs. "It's okay. Like a normal school, I guess. Really strict. But I think that's par for the course in Asia—you'd be hard-pressed to find a school here that isn't strict."

"How strict are we talking? 'Cause you know, I would describe my school in Los Angeles as strict, but somehow I think you're talking on a whole different level."

He gives a little laugh, and I feel my cheeks warm at the sight of the corners of his eyes crinkling. Ugh, he's even cuter when he laughs. Dimples. Argh, dimple alert. Why does he have to be cute? "How strict . . . hmm." He considers it for a second, then says, "Okay, for example, in addition to our school uniforms, the girls are only allowed to wear black or navy-blue hair bands. No other hair accessories allowed. And the boys have to have hair of a certain length and style. Like, we can't have a buzz cut or anything like that."

"Wow." I'm about to give some smart-ass retort as usual, tease him a bit for being in a school that is so stereotypically Asian, but at the last second, I recall that George isn't like the people I usually hang out with. Based on the chat messages I've read, George *loves* rules. With some effort, I say, "That's, uh . . . nice."

The dimples disappear completely. Something in his expression closes up a little. "Yeah. It's nice. Orderly."

Ugh, gross. I was right. He does like rules. In fact, he probably thinks it's great that the girls in his school aren't even allowed to wear cute hair accessories because otherwise it might distract the boys. Asshole. I have to actively remind myself not let my upper lip curl up into a sneer.

"What about your school? What's it like?"

"Well, we don't have uniforms, for one. So we can wear whatever we like." Actually, that's not quite true. Even without a uniform, there are still a ton of rules that dictate what we can and cannot wear, especially for the girls. But I am not in the mood to get into those details with someone like George. He'd be, like, "Oh yeah, girls should definitely not be allowed to wear tank tops. How would the boys focus on their studies if girls are walking around dressed so provocatively?"

Luckily, we're interrupted by our drinks arriving. When the

waiter leaves, I take a sip, and holy crap, it's the best coffee I have ever tasted. It's creamy and rich and the palm sugar tastes like buttery caramel. "Holy fuck, this is amazing."

His eyes widen a little and I realize he's probably taken aback by me swearing. Gah. I bet he's judging me for being crass or whatever. For being different from his idea of how girls should behave.

"I'm glad you like it," he says finally. I nod. My head is a mess. The thing is, before I arrived, I'd daydreamed about being so awful to George that he'll run off screaming and then I'll cackle about it in Mama's face. Okay, so that's a bit of a reach, but I had every intention of being surly and unpleasant toward him. But now that I'm seeing him in person, I'm finding it impossible even though I find his opinions repulsive. It's a lot harder to be horrible in person. He's just so . . . there. A whole other human being. I don't know how to behave.

An eternity passes before I decide: I'll be polite, but boring. By the time this non-date ends, he's going to be so glad it's over.

CHAPTER 10

George

I know the stereotype about teenaged boys: we're awkward, gangly idiots who are led everywhere by our dicks. It's not wrong, I guess. I am an awkward, gangly idiot, but I like to think I'm led by my actual brain most of the time. Take this poor girl Papa and Eleanor have tricked into meeting me, for example.

Sharlot's beautiful, no doubt about it. She's got these huge, expressive eyes and dark brown hair that ends right below her shoulders in thick waves, and her lips are soft and very much the kind of lips I'd like to kiss.

But.

But she's also really, really boring. See? I can look past the gorgeous exterior and judge her by her personality. Which is sorely lacking. I mean, I even told her about the crazy rules that Xingfa has, and instead of laughing and agreeing that whoever wrote the rules must've been on a power trip, she freaking said it was "nice" to have all those rules. Also, it doesn't help that she even dresses like the kind of girl that Papa has always wanted me to date. She's wearing the kind of top I see on my cousins and schoolmates all the time—well-tailored, soft pastel shade, pleasant to look at and completely devoid of any character.

Wow, I'm being really mean. I guess I'm in a bad mood. Hard not to be when I'm sitting across from Sharlot in the flesh and knowing that everything that's led up to us meeting was a lie. It's so wrong, me sitting here and pretending to be someone I'm not. Whenever I feel the urge to just blurt out the truth, I force myself to take a sip of my drink.

It's ironic, being the one who's deceptive for once. A couple years back, I started dating this girl from school, Alisha. Whenever I worked out at the school gym, she was always there. She'd start chatting with me, and before long, I was smitten. Of course, once Eighth Aunt found out (don't ask me how she found out, she's basically like Varys from *Game of Thrones*—she knows everything there's to know about everyone), she told me she didn't like Alisha. I'd dismissed her concerns. I mean, how the heck did Eighth Aunt know enough about Alisha to know that she disliked her, anyway? Then I noticed the paparazzi were always showing up whenever Alisha and I went out, as though they knew exactly where we were going to be. Then I found out that they did know, because Alisha would tell them beforehand. After that, I never really dated anyone else. Kind of hard to trust people after that whole thing. Which is why this is so, so awful. I'm being such a slime bag, tricking Sharlot like this.

It's okay, I tell myself for the hundredth time. Just sit here another twenty minutes or so, and then make up some excuse and leave. I don't have to actually befriend Sharlot; it's way too weird and I feel too guilty about everything.

"So, is this your first time in Jakarta?"

She glances down at her drink, and I wonder if I've accidentally asked something hard, something too personal. Then she says, "Yeah." And that's it. No follow-up or anything. God help me, this must be the worst conversation I've ever had. I swear I've had better conversations with my own reflection.

Still, I try my best. "How do you like it here so far?"

"Um, it's nice. Kind of humid. LA's hotter, but it's a dry heat, so it's not as bad."

The weather. We're literally talking about the weather. Which is good, because it's boring, and therefore safe. I lean into it. "Well, during the rainy season, it gets really rainy." Wow. Great job, George. Really smooth. At some point in my life, I should probably learn how to talk to pretty girls. But this is fine, because I don't want to impress Sharlot. Right? Right.

The corners of Sharlot's mouth tremble like she's fighting back a smile. "Never would've guessed that the rainy season would be rainy," she deadpans.

We look at each other and I could've sworn that like me, she's trying not to laugh. I almost burst out laughing stupidly, but then I remind myself that this is creepy because catfishing etc. The mirth dissipates and the moment is over. Phew. I mentally rifle through the messages she and Papa/Eleanor have been exchanging and pounce on another safe-ish subject.

"So, you like to cook?"

She looks taken aback by this, as though I just asked her what color bra she's wearing. But then she recovers and says, "Yeah."

Okay. I was kind of expecting her to give more than a one-word answer, but maybe it's on me to try and find out more.

"Um, what kind of food do you like to cook?"

Her upper lip twitches and I swear she sneered at me for just a split second. That's definitely a look of contempt. But then as fast as it appeared, it's gone, and I wonder if I imagined it.

"All sorts," she mumbles.

Oh my god, this is painful. "You mentioned you really like making bone broth stews?" What are these words coming out of my mouth? Who cares about bone broth stew? What a fucking weird thing to say: BONE BROTH STEW, like I'm some weird serial killer who collects the bones of his victims to throw into the slow cooker with Chinese herbs.

That contemptuous look crosses her face again, and I can't blame her. "Yeah, bone broth stews . . . love making them. With, like, ginseng and shi—stuff. Very nutritious."

I nod, wondering what to say that wouldn't come off weird. There's very little I know about cooking and if I have to say the words *bone broth stew* one more time I'm pretty sure I'll spontaneously combust.

"And you," she says, "you said you like to do . . . finance? It has to do with your family company?" She gives me a polite smile, her eyebrows rising.

My stomach drops. Here we go again. This is the reason why I don't have many close friends or any serious relationships. Because the Tanuwijaya name precedes me. My dad and aunts and uncles have always instilled in me and my cousins a "healthy" dose of paranoia. "You be careful, George," Eighth Aunt started telling me when I was three years old, bending over slightly so she was towering over me, "you are the only male heir of the Tanuwijaya clan. There will be many, many people throwing themselves at you, pretending to be your friend, many pretty girls wanting to be your girlfriend. Do not trust them." I had nodded and then promptly wet my pants.

The worst part is, technically it doesn't even matter that I'm the sole male offspring in my generation; my family is progressive enough to not let gender stand in the way of meritocratic nepotism. Second Uncle's firstborn, Luna, is primed to take over as the company's CEO because she's very clearly the most capable out of all of us. But the patriarchy is entrenched enough into Asian society that as the only boy, I get a lot of attention from the media, our competitors, and our business partners alike. If any of the other cousins aside from Luna make a mistake, they're largely ignored. If I make a mistake, I get to see it splashed across every news outlet and every social media app—SOLE MALE HEIR OF TANU CORP CRASHES LAMBORGHINI. That had been me and my classmate, Ramtaro of Halim Group Corp., and I wasn't the one driving nor was it my Lambo we were in. But it had been enough to teach me a lesson—better stick to online gaming where I can be completely anonymous.

It's not Sharlot's fault that Papa thought that telling her I want to join the family business—something completely untrue, by the way—would be a good thing. Benign. Right. That's what we're aiming for.

"Sure. Sort of. I guess I just like math." I mean, math is okay, but nobody *likes* it, okay? Nobody aside from this persona my dad and little sister have taken on for me that's supposedly going to nab me a girlfriend.

She nods. "Wow." It's the least-impressed wow in the history of wows. "So what is it that your family company does?"

Immediately, my walls clap back into place. "This and that."

She stares at me, probably waiting for me to expand. I'm not trying to be an ass, so I add, "Mostly land development." I fail to tell her that the mall we're currently sitting in is one of the many buildings we own.

"That's interesting."

Is it? No, it really isn't. She's not even really looking at me, she's stirring her drink for the millionth time, and so am I, because this "date" is dying a long, slow death and, god, why can't it end already?

"What else do you like to do aside from cooking?" I say after a constipated second.

Sharlot looks up like she's thinking real hard. Oh my god, I am on a date with a girl who has no hobbies aside from making stews. Don't judge her, I scold myself. Of the two of us, she's not the one who's lying to the other person. So what if she has the personality of a stale water cracker? At least she's not a creepy-assed liar.

"I, um . . . I . . . like to read," she says after a while.

"Cool. What do you read?"

"Mostly books," she says, nodding, her expression completely serious. I can't tell if she's kidding or not at all.

"What sort of books?"

"Like . . . novels. You know."

I don't, actually, but I do know that I'm done trying. Not that I was really trying in the first place, but I'm done with straining my brain to make small talk. I glance up at the clock and am relieved to find that it's been almost twenty minutes since we sat down. It wouldn't be completely awful of me to end this date now. It's clear we have nothing in common, no chemistry whatsoever, and the date is taking its last sips of air and needs to be put out of its misery.

I take out my phone like it's just vibrated in my pocket and pretend to read a text. "Uh-oh." Okay, that came out hella fake, but maybe she won't notice.

"What's up?"

"Uh, there's been a—a family situation. I need to go." Oh my god, could the words sound any more made-up? I stand and Sharlot does too.

"Oh no." She grabs her bag and walks out with me.

Outside of the café, we stop and turn to look at each other. I hold out my hand again. "It's been really nice meeting you, Sharlot."

"Yeah, I'm glad we did this. I hope everything works out okay with your family." She smiles at me, and I think it's the first real thing I've seen today. The realness in it is so disarming that I forget, just for a moment, what we're doing. Then she reaches out and instead of shaking my hand, hugs me. Her scent fills my senses—summer fruit and fresh laundry. And there's something behind the hug, some sort of raw emotion that catches at my throat and leaves me feeling breathless.

"Sharlot—"

"George!" someone calls out.

The hairs at the nape of my neck prickle to attention even as my stomach drops. It's an instinctive reaction to that voice, the voice of the matriarch who has our entire clan eating out of her hands. I turn to see that Eighth Aunt and Nainai are here.

CHAPTER 11

Sharlot

I once saw a tweet that said something along the lines of "When will writers learn that negative emotions don't make people paler?" I had laughed and clicked Like because the sheer number of times I've come across a description of a character going pale due to shock/horror/sadness is ridiculous. But now, here I am, witnessing this exact phenomenon happening before me. I mean, just a moment ago George's skin was a very typical shade of salmon-beige. And then this group of people appear, and *boom*, his complexion can only be described as ashen, or maybe taupe if I were feeling fancy.

"Oh, George, what a nice surprise," the auntie—she's not my aunt but she's the very definition of a Chinese-Indo auntie: huge hair, shoulder pads for days, a Birkin bag, and of course, the requisite Chanel tweed jacket. I'm half Indo, which means, thanks to Mama, I recognize all the high-fashion brands not only by their logos, but by their trademark looks. I don't know what it is about the Chanel tweed jacket. Sure, it's pretty, but it's also hellishly hot. I get wearing it in mild LA winters, but in the sweltering humidity of Jakarta, that's just a death wish. She's holding the arm of a white-haired old lady who's also in full-body Chanel, though the old lady is also wearing a fat string of flawless pearls around her neck.

Next to the auntie is a young, attractive Chinese-Indonesian woman and two cameramen. I watch them with barely concealed interest. A TV crew? Or magazine? Their gear looks very big and official and very in-your-face. The one carrying the massive video cam swings round and aims it at me and George, and now I wonder if I've gone taupe as well. It's one thing to be an outside observer, quite another to be the subject of that disconcerting lens. I have no idea what to do with, like, my hands and my legs and for that matter my face.

"Eighth Aunt, Nainai!" George stammers. "Hi! Um, it's so great to see you here." It's an obvious lie, but both Eighth Aunt and Nainai smile with obvious affection as George gives them each a careful hug. The photographer clicks away at them hugging. "What brings you here? Nainai, let's find you a seat."

"We're having an interview, of course." Eighth Aunt—good god, just how many aunts does George have?—says this like being interviewed is something that happens every Tuesday and Thursday afternoon. "This is Rina from *Asian Wealth*. We thought it would be fun to do the interview at one of these cafés that you kids like to go to so much, rather than the usual high-end places."

"I don't know about this," Nainai grouses. "I'd have much rather go to my usual place at the Ritz."

"Aiya, Ma. I've told you, the Ritz is so yesterday."

The reporter smiles and nods. "Yes, we've done a lot of coverage at the Ritz. This will make you look a lot more approachable. More relatable."

Eighth Aunt nods, obviously pleased at being described as approachable. I wonder if she's forgotten that her entire outfit costs over fifty grand. Nainai sniffs, looking around her like she's not at all impressed by the beautiful mall we're in. She's a tiny old lady with equally impeccable makeup, and though she's so petite, she manages to look intimidating as hell.

"Hi, George," Rina says, holding out her hand to George. "We've spoken on the phone? I called to ask for an interview about OneLiner."

"Oh, right. Yeah, I remember." Wow, George is a really bad liar. But Rina smiles and shakes his hand anyway. Then—horror of horrors—she turns and holds out her hand to me, and I have her full attention and it's just as disarming as the camera lenses.

She smiles, reminding me of a shark that senses blood in the water. "And you must be George's girlfriend, based on that hug we saw!"

What? It takes a second to realize what she's referring to. The goodbye hug? The one I gave out of pity because George is some poor idiot my mom had deceived for no good reason? Belatedly, it hits me that in a place as conservative as Jakarta, hugs must carry a lot more meaning. People don't just go around hugging each other. So Rina assumes that since George and I hugged, we must be close. Ah, shit.

"Uh." I swear I'm usually better with words than this, but the cameras are seriously in my face, and having Rina's, Nainai's, and Eighth Aunt's gazes on me is too disconcerting. For a second, I actually forget my own name.

"This is Sharlot," George says after a painful silence.

"Oh, Sharlot!" Eighth Aunt cries. "How nice to finally meet you!"

Before I know it, she's giving me that same Asian hug, complete with air-kisses. I manage to recover enough of my senses to return the non-hug, fully aware of the camera that's recording everything and the shutter clicks of the other one. I almost ask her how the hell she knows who I am, but stop myself in time. Obviously she's putting up a show for Rina and her crew. I don't know what's going on, but poor George looks about ready to faint, so I say, "It's so nice to finally meet you too, Eighth Aunt."

"Oh, aren't you sweet? Isn't she lovely, Ma?" Eighth Aunt says to Nainai.

Nainai glances at me before looking away again, obviously uninterested.

"Very lovely," Rina says, her shark grin widening. "And she is . . ."

George stares at me in a panic. I stare back, probably also with that deer-about-to-turn-into-venison expression. In hindsight, I could've said I'm a school friend or a cousin twice removed or literally anything else. But in that moment, the only thing my mind spits out is CATFISH! FAKE! FRAUD!

Eighth Aunt grabs my shoulders and turns me to face the cameras. Then she says, "His girlfriend, of course!"

Nainai gasps, her head whipping back to face me. My mouth drops open. The camera shutter clicks.

The last thing I need is another superstrong Indonesian coffee laced with enough palm sugar to give an elephant a sugar rush, but I seem to have completely lost my voice. So here I am, back at Kopi-Kopi, this time with George, his grandmother, his aunt (the eighth one, apparently), and a TV/magazine/newspaper crew. I have yet to figure out what *Asian Wealth* actually is, and it seems rude to ask.

"So George, OneLiner is the first app your family is releasing with you as the face of it. Are you excited?" Rina says.

George to his credit seems to have recovered a little from his initial shock, and now I'm seeing a whole new side of him that I never would've thought could exist. He gives her a smile so easily charming and confident that I wonder how many times he's practiced it in the mirror. It works, anyway. Rina returns it with a slight blush. Not bad, George. Not bad. "Yeah, I'm very excited. And it's such a necessary app, you know? I hate to say it, but a lot of us have grown up with the whole boys-will-be-boys mindset, which is really harmful."

Rina nods. "Yes, toxic masculinity is a subject we've tackled here at *Asian Wealth*."

Really? Color me shocked. No offense to Rina, but I wouldn't have expected a publication called *Asian Wealth* to touch on anything outside of finance.

Eighth Aunt nods and says, "With OneLiner, we hope to educate boys on how to be proper gentlemen. We've spoken with the education minister about including it in the schools' curriculum, and everyone who's used it has been impressed. I daresay there are many grown men who could use a bit of time with OneLiner." She throws her head back and laughs. Rina laughs along with her, so I titter politely as well.

Titter. I literally titter. It sounds like something between a squeak and a laugh and makes me want to punch myself in the face. Instead, I poke viciously at the ice in my coffee with my battered straw.

"You must be so proud of your boyfriend, Sharlot," Rina says. "Not many boys are so passionate about this subject." She smiles at George. "I'm so happy for you, George. I'm proud to have you representing the Chinese youth community here. You're an amazing role model. He's a favorite amongst our younger audience, male and female alike."

George smiles, but is it just me or do his eyes look somewhat panicky?

"Mm-hmm." I take a long sip of my coffee to avoid having to say anything, but Rina is unrelenting.

"So, tell me, Sharlot, how long have you and George been seeing each other? Do you go to Xingfa as well?"

I shake my head, my mouth still stubbornly around the straw.

"Oh? How do you two know each other?"

The worst sound in the world fills my ears. The sound of a straw desperately sucking at an empty cup. NOOO. I have run out of coffee with which to cover up my silence! Jesus wept. Oh god. Now what?

As the millionth thought fires through my head in less than

a second, it strikes me that I should've asked for decaf. But too late now.

"We, uh—this is kind of dorky—but we actually met online."

"It was on this program for, um, really hardworking teens, it's called, um—" George practically shouts. "It's called Hardworking Teens?"

"Yeah, that's right," I babble. "You wouldn't be able to find it online, it was a long time ago." What are these words falling out of my mouth? Somebody stop me.

"Oh, wow, so you two have known each other for a while, then?"

I nod with such vigor I almost break my neck. Is it the crazy amount of caffeine? The sugar? The adrenaline? The cameras? Psych, it's ALL OF THE ABOVE! Okay, please calm down, self. "Oh yeah, totally. George and I have known each other forever!" What? No, we haven't. We literally met half an hour ago. Oh my god, what is wrong with me? I reach under the table and pinch my thigh so hard that tears spring into my eyes. The pain is bad, but also good because it forces my thoughts to slow down a bit.

"Is George your first-ever boyfriend?"

Fuck no, I almost blurt out. I'm seventeen, lady, not seven. But again, I realize that I'm in a very different culture and the way that everyone is watching me now makes me bite my tongue before I can tell them that I've been in plenty of other relationships. Plus, Mama had told George over chat that I've never had a boyfriend before. "Uh. Yeah . . . ? He is?"

Eighth Aunt nods with a satisfied smile. "That's because she's a good girl, you can tell, can't you? You can just tell that Sharlot is a proper, good girl."

I try not to squirm under their approving smiles.

"Is this true?" Nainai says. "You have known this girl forever?" Her voice is gentle, but there's something about Nainai that arrests everyone's attention.

"Um. Uh. Yeah."

Nainai looks at me then. Really looks, not the careless glance she did outside the café. Despite her obvious old age, her gaze is as sharp as anyone else's, and I feel as though she's carving me open and looking straight into my blackened soul.

After a century has passed, she nods and smiles her first real smile at me. It transforms her entire face, her wrinkles shifting and curving dramatically. "You have good face," she says in English. "Look, she got lucky nose, ya? Mancung sekali. And her forehead so high. Is mean good luck, you know." Then she leans forward. Before I can react, Nainai grabs my left earlobe. I jump up like a shocked rabbit, and she laughs, still gripping hold of it. For an old woman, her grip is surprisingly strong. "Look at her ears!"

"Er, Nainai, could you maybe let go of Sharlot's ear?" George says.

"Tch, don't interrupt your grandmother!" Eighth Aunt snaps, and George and I shrink back automatically. Well, I try to shrink back, but it's impossible with my ear still caught in Nainai's unforgiving grip.

"This," Nainai announces to everyone, "is what we call Buddha ears. You see how the lobe so fat and so long?"

Okay, I have never had my ears be fat-shamed, but I guess there's a first for everything.

"Very good-luck ears. Means you will have very great fortune," Nainai says. Finally, *finally*, she releases my ear and I sag back in my seat, my heart racing and my pits sweaty. I really did not foresee having my ear accosted by an old woman today. Nainai smiles and reaches out for me once more and I can't help but flinch. But this time, she just pats my cheek gently. "Oh, Nainai is so happy you are Ming Fa's girlfriend."

Who the hell is Ming Fa?

"Ming Fa is my Chinese name," George mumbles, as though reading my mind.

"Ah, right."

"And what is your Chinese name?" Nainai says. "I don't like all these modern English name, they have no meaning. How can you tell what kind of person if the name has no meaning? You see, *Ming Fa* means 'Intelligence and Fortune,' and my grandson exactly like that, ya kan?"

George gives a forced smile and shrugs. "Sure, Nainai."

Oh my god. Welp. She's about to learn that the kind of person I am is all wrong, just like my Chinese name. With some trepidation, I mutter, "Um. My Chinese name is Shi Jun."

"Shi Jun," Nainai says. "Oh my." She nods at Eighth Aunt, who nods back with a smile. "Very good name. Warrior Scholar."

Ah, she's got the wrong characters, but who the hell is going to correct her and say, *Well actually, it's not Warrior Scholar, it's Correct Bacteria*. I nod. "Yep, Warrior Scholar, that's what my Chinese name means."

"Oh, so good. So, SO good!" Nainai cries happily. "Aiya, not like all these other girl, their names always so silly—Pretty Flower lah, Beautiful Moon lah. Who care about pretty flower? The girl who date my Ming Fa must be strong! Intelligent! Aduh, Ming Fa, Nainai is so happy you meet Shi Jun. Such fortuitous meeting, ya? So auspicious!"

"Ha . . . Uh-huh, so auspicious." I laugh weakly, wishing I could disintegrate into an atomic level and dissipate into thin air.

"Am I detecting an American accent?" Rina says.

"Yeah, I'm American. Just visiting for the summer. Temporarily. You know, just for the summer," I say again, making sure they all understand that I'm not hanging around.

Rina's eyes widen. "Wow, a long-distance relationship. At your age, that must be really hard. I mean, it's hard at any age, really."

"Aduh, must be so hard for my poor Ming Fa!" Nainai says. "But you not worry, okay? You two can fly, visit each other often, ya?"

George and I smile at each other with wide, horrified eyes. "Yeah, totally . . . ," I hear myself say.

Eighth Aunt says something and the cameras swivel back to capture her. I take the chance to catch my breath and try to regroup my thoughts, which are shattered. Just completely and utterly destroyed. My whole mind is a mess. It's such a mess, in fact, that it takes a moment to realize that Rina's speaking to me again. "I'm sorry?"

"Will you be attending the launch as well?"

"What?" What launch?

"Yes, oh, what an excellent idea, Rina," Eighth Aunt cries. "Just brilliant! Yes, who better to make an appearance at the launch of OneLiner than Sharlot? She of all people would know what a gentleman George is and what a great role model he makes for teenage boys. Oh, I love this idea. Maybe we can even arrange for a speaking slot during the event."

WHAT EVENT?

Rina nods, obviously pleased at Eighth Aunt's approval. "Wow, okay. I'm very much looking forward to that. The launch event for OneLiner is going to be amazing!"

I'm going to faint. Or vomit. Or maybe both.

An appearance? What the hell? Can't they see that I can barely string together two sentences under pressure? What in god's name would make anyone think that I would be a good candidate for anything at an actual *event* with actual real-life humans?

But then I look over at George and his face is a picture of pure panic. He's staring at me wide-eyed and grimacing and it's like watching a really, really sad puppy slowly drown. I can't *not* save the puppy. I don't want to get him in trouble in front of these people, and definitely not in front of these cameras. Plus, Nainai is smiling and nodding at me, and nobody can possibly say no to that tiny wrinkled face. So I say, "Yeah . . . sure. I would love to attend an event here."

"Here?" Rina says, frowning. "Has there been a change in the itinerary?"

"Huh?" I say.

"No," George says quickly. "There hasn't. The launch will go on as planned, and I guess, uh, you'll be appearing then . . . in, uh, in Bali."

Bali. The island that's a two-hour plane ride from Jakarta. Bali. Yep. Of course. I smile at him with wild, panicky eyes. "On second thought, I don't know that my mom would let me fly—"

"Sharlot! What's going on?"

I look up to see Mama, Kiki, and Kiki's parents, and honestly, this is the first time ever that I've felt so relieved to see Mama. So much relief, in fact, that tears rush to my eyes. For the first time in my life, I need Mama to be her overbearing self and tell me that I need to go the hell home right now. I stand up and say, "Sorry, everyone, this is my family."

George is already on his feet, holding out his hand toward Mama. "Hi, Tante." *Tante* means "Auntie" in Indonesian. Mama can't possibly resist the charm of being called Tante so politely, but before she can reply, Kiki leans forward and holds out her hand to George.

"Kiki. I'm Shar's cousin." She glances at the camera and winks.

"Er, yep, so great that we were all able to meet," I say. "Anyway, we'll go and let you have some private time with, uh . . . with the cameras and stuff."

I grab Kiki's hand to yank her away—she's already posing for the cameras. Thank you, universe, for my family being so meddlesome that they couldn't stay away from my non-date. Thank you, thank—

"Qing Pei, is that you?"

All thought screeches out of my head. I freeze as Eighth

Aunt gets to her feet. Her eyes aren't on me, though. They're on Mama, and Mama's looking equally shell-shocked to see Eighth Aunt. The camera is clicking away like no tomorrow, and the video guy is having a hard time deciding whose face to focus on. Rina is watching all of this with unconcealed interest.

When Mama finally talks, her voice comes out small and unsure and very much unlike the strident Mama I know. "Shu Ling?"

"Yes!" Eighth Aunt cries. "Oh my goodness. Qing Pei!" She rushes forward and closes the gap between them, hugging Mama tightly. It's not an Asian hug this time, but a real oh-boy-it's-a-pot-of-honey-and-I'm-a-bear-type hug. A split second later, Mama gingerly hugs her back. Eighth Aunt laughs and releases her before turning to the cameras. "This is my best friend from school. Aduh, I haven't seen you since—wah, since we were seventeen."

Mama stiffens a little but recovers her smile valiantly. Seventeen. Huh. She had me when she was eighteen. Something inside me clicks into place, and for a moment everything else fades away. She must've gotten pregnant here at seventeen and then left for the States because it would've been a huge scandal at the time. When I look at Mama again, I see her in a slightly different light. She'd left her homeland, her family, and her best friend who she was obviously close to. It must have been heartbreaking. I'm only here for the summer and already I miss everyone back home in LA with a fierce ache I can't get over.

Mama seems to have gotten over the slight hiccup, and she and Eighth Aunt are now getting equally flappy and excited about how amazing it is to be reunited after all these years. Li Jiujiu laughs and tells Nainai that Mama and Eighth Aunt used to be mistaken for sisters because they wore their hair exactly the same way as each other and insisted on wearing identical outfits.

"That is so sweet!" Rina says. "And now your daughter is seeing her nephew. What are the chances?"

All eyes and lenses are suddenly on me and George. "Uh . . ." I'm not quite sure which of us is uh-ing. Both. Both of us are.

George, who's probably had a ton more practice in the spotlight, manages to recover first and go, "Ha-ha, yeah, what are the chances?"

"This feels like fate," Kiki says with a grin. I shoot her a glare, which she deflects with an innocent smile.

"This really does feel like fate!" Eighth Aunt cries. She's linked her arm through Mama's and can't stop grinning at her. "You know, we were just talking about having Sharlot give a speech at our event in Bali—oh yes, we're having an event in Bali next week—please come, Qing Pei. Now that I finally have you back in Indonesia, we must catch up. We must!"

Mama's eyes are wide. My insides roil. *Say no, Mama. You've said no my entire life. It's been a series of nos. And now is the time I really need you to say no.*

She opens her mouth.

"Of course, we'd be delighted to."

Aw, fuck.

PART TWO

CHAPTER 12

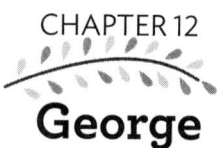

George

The night after my disastrous meeting with Sharlot, I confide privately to Eighth Aunt about what a bad idea it is to have Sharlot join us in Bali because catfishing, fake girlfriend, etc. In my defense, I'd foolishly hoped that Eighth Aunt would be empathetic and tell me she'd handle it the same way she handles every other crisis the family manages to come up with every week.

But now here she is, gaping at me with such a look of horror and disappointment that my balls are shriveling up and trying to climb back into my body.

"Because catfishing?" she says softly.

"Um. It's kind of a long story, but, uh—oh, okay, you're gone." I stand there, unmoving, as Eighth Aunt marches out of the formal living room.

"Shu Peng! Eleanor! You come here RIGHT NOW. SHU PENG. ELEANOR ROOSEVELT."

I wince at her authoritative shouts, flinching at the sound of her footsteps stomping upstairs and into Papa's and Eleanor's rooms. Before long, Eighth Aunt is back, practically dragging them by their ears like they were naughty pups.

Papa and Eleanor give me looks of utter betrayal as Eighth Aunt releases them and barks at us to sit down on the sofa. We all hunker down and she begins her tirade.

"I *cannot* believe how incredibly STUPID and AWFUL and RIDICULOUS you have been!"

"Look, Shu Ling," Papa says, "I just wanted what's best for George!"

"You chatted with a teenage girl!" Eighth Aunt cries at him. "What is wrong with you? That is so highly inappropriate! Do you know what the media would say if they ever found out?"

"To be fair, Eighth Aunt, it was mostly me," Eleanor says. "You know how hopeless both Papa and gege are when it comes to talking to girls."

Eighth Aunt shoots Eleanor a look so sharp that it makes us all cower. "I am even more disappointed to hear that, Eleanor Roosevelt!" she snaps. "I expect this sort of shenanigans from your brother and your dad—"

"Okay, for the record?" I interrupt, "I was—and am—very much against the entire thing from the very beginning."

"—but I expected more from you, my prodigy," Eighth Aunt continues as though I hadn't said anything.

Eleanor deflates visibly, her lower lip trembling. Eighth Aunt sighs. "Never mind. No use crying over spilt milk. We need to run damage control." She paces again, tapping an index finger on her chin as she walks. "All right. It's not entirely terrible, I suppose. As far as fake girlfriends go, you could've chosen worse.

Sharlot is very photogenic and well-spoken. Teens will like her American accent, especially those we're targeting for OneLiner. It's not entirely a disaster."

Papa and Eleanor puff up as though this were a huge compliment. I suppose coming from Eighth Aunt, it sort of is.

"Since we've already publicly invited her to join us for the launch in Bali, we can't possibly uninvite her. So, George, you are going to have to continue fake-dating Sharlot, you hear me? We're going to do a lot of prepping before the event. I'll have Fauzi coach you kids on what to say—you know what? No, I can't let anyone else find out about this. I'll coach you kids myself."

"But, Eighth Aunt—"

"No *buts*! We can't afford a whiff of bad press, not until after the app launches. It's your first-ever official product; if it goes badly, it will follow you for the rest of your life. You need to make sure that the launch goes perfectly. This means you better be nice to this poor girl."

"I wasn't going to be horrible to her, sheesh," I mumble.

"Yes, well, let's aim for something higher than 'not horrible,' okay? Be a perfect boyfriend. She needs to rave to everyone about what an incredible gentleman you are and how well-suited you are as the face of OneLiner."

My insides squirm sickeningly. "But I'd be lying to her—"

Eighth Aunt throws up her hands in frustration. "Just for another week or so, George! Don't be so dramatic."

Dramatic?! Argh! I'm the least dramatic person in the room, why can't they see that? Of course, I have enough sense of self-preservation not to say it out loud.

Eighth Aunt storms out then, leaving me, Papa, and Eleanor staring at one another guiltily. For about two seconds. Then Papa says, "Please, listen to Eighth Aunt and be nice to Sharlot, okay? She is a nice girl. Sharlot is a special kid. Be good to her."

"Does that mean I should treat her as my girlfriend, or my platonic friend, or the truth, which is that she's practically a stranger?" I ask drily.

Papa blinks and looks lost for a while. Then he smiles. "I'm sure you'll figure it out."

"Are these Hermès seats?" Sharlot's cousin Kiki asks as we file into the jet.

I shift self-consciously. "Um, I guess. I don't know."

"Oh yes dear," Eighth Aunt says, looking up from her phone. "We had them custom-made for all our jets."

"Wow, I didn't know Hermès made furniture," Kiki mutters.

"They make the best furniture. Their leather is premium quality, isn't that right, Eighth Aunt?" Eleanor pipes up.

"That's right, sayang," Eighth Aunt says. Eleanor gives one of her trademark I'm-such-a-sweetheart smiles, and Eighth Aunt pinches her cheek with obvious endearment before going back to tapping on her phone.

Eleanor leans close to Kiki, and whispers, "Not that we can tell what's premium quality leather. I once swapped Eighth Aunt's handbag with a fake. She still hasn't noticed."

Kiki laughs. "Eleanor Roosevelt, you are such a treat. I wish you were my little sister."

"I wish you were my big sister! Can you even imagine?"

I roll my eyes and look away from Eleanor's smug grin. Of course Eleanor and Kiki would get along wonderfully. Unlike me and my supposed girlfriend, Sharlot, who's chosen the farthest seat in the back and is staring out the window with an unreadable expression. I hover around Eighth Aunt's seat, wondering if maybe this is the right time to have a quick chat with her about a few of my latest ideas for OneLiner, especially the share-your-stories function. But just as I think that, Eighth Aunt glances up at me and gives me this look that says, WTH are you doing, George Clooney? Be a good boy and sit with your fake girlfriend.

With a deep breath, I pass Eighth Aunt's seat and go down the aisle until I'm in front of Sharlot's seat.

"Hey, is this seat taken?" I say.

She looks around, her eyebrows rising when she sees that Kiki has chosen to sit up front, and shrugs. "I guess not."

Oh-kay. That's not a no, so I slide in next to her. "How're you doing?" Did that come out weird? I still have no idea how to act around Sharlot, probably because that's exactly what I'm doing—acting. Acting like I know and like her as my girlfriend. There is so much deception going on here that I can barely keep up with it.

"I'm okay," she says. Then she snorts. "Well, not really. I'm kind of in shock. I'm on your private jet. That's pretty crazy, right? I've never known anyone who has a private jet."

"If it makes you feel better, it's not my private jet, it's my family's private jet?"

That makes her laugh. The fist clutching my chest eases up a little.

"Also, your aunt said 'for all our jets.' How many private airplanes do you guys have?" Sharlot looks at me with wide eyes.

"Um. A few?" I hate talking about our wealth. It makes me feel slimy. Probably because I've done nothing to deserve it, and yet here I am, enjoying this privilege anyway.

Sharlot gives a mirthless laugh and then looks up the aisle, where everyone else has settled down in pairs—her mother with Eighth Aunt, Papa with Nainai, and Kiki with Eleanor. Everyone is chatting away merrily. Then there's us.

"So—" we both say at the same time.

"You first," she says.

"Okay. Um, I'm really sorry about what happened at the café."

"Oh? What about it?" She looks genuinely confused.

"Um, like, I lie about us being in a long-distance relationship? And then my aunt and my grandmother appear like wraiths and Nainai tells you that you have fat ears?"

She laughs. "Okay, yeah, that was . . . something else. But I like your grandmother. And to be fair, I also lied to the reporter about us dating. I'm not sure why I did that aside from that I was on a real caffeine high."

"I'm sorry about that too. I should've warned you about the coffee. Indonesian coffee is stupidly strong. I think it has to do with us being on an island that's literally called Java."

She laughs again, though it sounds a bit like a half sob. "Oh god. It was like an out-of-body experience. I swear I was just standing to one side watching myself blab all about us, and I was going, '*What the hell are you saying?* Stop talking!' to myself. I was a mess. I'm sorry too. And now you're saddled with me in Bali, which is probably the last thing you want. But don't worry, okay? Your aunt has prepped us well, I think."

I smile weakly at the memory of Eighth Aunt's "prep," a hellishly long day at the house, which consisted of her telling us that if we say one thing wrong, the reputation of the family company will be dragged through the mud. Afterward, Sharlot had barely said two words to me before going straight home looking utterly exhausted.

"And aside from the interviews and the launch, I'll stay out of your hair," Sharlot continues.

"Um." My insides are twisting like snakes. Like . . . like *Snakes on a Plane* snakes. But inside my stomach. I feel like a total asshole, basically. Because last week, after the insane coffee date with Sharlot, Rina immediately ran the story on *Asian Wealth*, and it's blown up on all the socials.

And the family—I should start referring to my family as The Family, *Godfather*-style, since they're practically a mob, except their weapon of choice is guilt instead of guns—called for a meeting about my love life. There are those—Third and Fifth Uncle and Second Aunt—who think that this is a terrible development because it's distracting from the launch of OneLiner. But luckily, or unluckily, everyone else thinks it's a great publicity move. Anything that gets people talking about me means they're talking about OneLiner. Thankfully for me, Eighth Aunt has decided to keep the fact that Sharlot is my fake girlfriend from the rest of the family. If they all found out . . .

I shudder. Okay, don't think about any of that now.

So here I am, sitting next to Sharlot on the plane, making small talk and trying to be nice to her, except I don't quite know what that entails, exactly.

"I don't want you to stay out of my hair," I finally say. "I mean, if you want to, that's okay and I understand. But, um . . . you don't need to." God, I feel terrible saying that, even though it's true—I really don't want her to feel like I don't want her around. I mean, I don't, but I do. Okay, so I might be losing my mind.

Her mouth trembles into a small smile. "You're a really nice guy, you know that, George?"

There's a bitter taste at the back of my mouth. A nice guy. Hah, she'd think otherwise if she ever finds out that the truth is, I'm a huge liar who's been letting my dad and my sister fool her into this mess. Time for a change of subject. I search through my memory for things I know about her. She likes to . . . cook. No, I've touched on that already. I take out my phone and scroll through our messages as subtly as I can and come across a couple of messages where she talked about—of all things—cleaning. Which is a very weird hobby to have, but hey, I'm not judging.

"So, um, one of your hobbies is cleaning?"

She frowns, that vulnerable look fleeing her features, and suddenly looks really annoyed. What did I say? God, I really have no idea how to talk to her.

"Sorry, did I say something wrong?"

"No." She gives me the world's fakest smile. "You're right, I love tidying up. It's something all girls love to do."

The way she says it makes my skin crawl, but I have no idea how to react to that, so I just nod and say, "It's a great pastime to have."

"Of course," she mutters.

"Sorry?"

"Nothing. What do you want to know about cleaning anyway?"

Geez. Her tone could not be more acidic. I find myself subconsciously shrinking back from her. Feeling a little like I'm stepping into a trap, I say, "Um, what do you like about cleaning?" I don't even really know what I just asked; Sharlot's sudden anger is making me flustered.

She looks me in the eye and says, "Sorry, George, I'm really tired. I'm going to take a nap, okay?" Then she turns her entire body away from me and closes her eyes pointedly.

Okay, I can take a hint. Especially one as painfully obvious as this. I look at the cabin. At least everyone else seems to be having a great time. Sharlot's mother and Eighth Aunt are both laughing at something on Eighth Aunt's phone, their heads tilted close to each other's. Eleanor is giggling at something Kiki's saying, and Papa is fussing about with Nainai's (Hermès) blanket. Everyone's paired off.

I glance at Sharlot, wondering what she's like behind those walls, taking in the curve of her jawline and lips.

"It's creepy to stare," she mutters.

I look away, my cheeks burning.

Sharlot "naps" the entire two-hour plane ride to Bali. At some point, she actually does fall asleep, her mouth going slack and a little snore coming out of her. She jerks awake when we hit the tarmac.

"We're here," I tell her, pointing to my chin to indicate that there's a line of drool on hers.

She wipes it, her cheeks reddening.

"Did you sleep okay?" I don't know why I bother asking. It's obvious she slept great, and anyway I'm not really interested in knowing how she slept.

"Yeah." She grabs her bag and looks out the window. Her eyes widen and she says, "How come we're not docking at a gangway?"

"Oh, we don't need to go through the airport. They'll send a customs guy to go through our documents." I lean forward to look out the window as well. "Our luggage will be loaded directly into the car. . . . There. That's our ride to the hotel."

Her eyebrows disappear into her hairline. "Wow, straight from the plane and into a limo. No waiting in never-ending lines at the airport." Her mouth crooks into a wry smile. "I could get used to traveling like this."

I realize that my face is really close to hers—close enough to see the smattering of freckles across her cheeks and catch how the late-morning sunlight makes her dark brown eyes turn a rich chocolate. Cheeks flushing, I lean back quickly. So what if she's really cute? She's still mean and I'm still the asshole who's lying to her.

We don't talk as the customs officer comes to go through

our papers. We don't talk as we climb out of our seats. And we definitely don't talk after that, because Sharlot sidles up to Kiki and links one arm through her cousin's and the other through Eleanor's arm. Great. Even my own fake girlfriend would rather spend time with my little sister than me. Eleanor glances back at me, and I look away, pretending to study the interior of the plane. Damn it, I don't even have my phone to pretend to be busy with. This is ridiculous. Oh! I did bring my e-reader. I take it out of my backpack and stare hard at it, like I'm reading. Maybe I should actually try to read.

When we finally get off the plane, Papa's assistant, Fauzi, greets us and ushers us into the limo. Inside, he sends us all a pdf of our individual itineraries and then starts filling in Papa and Eighth Aunt about how everything is coming along. I look at the pdf on my tablet with growing dread. As expected, the timetable is packed. We'll be here for three nights, and every single day has been planned meticulously, activities arranged in half-hour increments. Today's is the lightest, and even then, I have three interviews lined up. *Plot Twist, Tech World,* and *Young Entrepreneurs.*

"Hang on, this says that I have interviews. Is that right?" Sharlot says. She doesn't look at all amused.

I look at her phone. *Plot Twist, Tech World, Young Entrepreneurs.* She has the same interviews I do. At the same time. Well, shit. Eighth Aunt had mentioned that part of her running damage control was to limit the amount of exposure we have with journalists as a couple to minimize the chances of error. So what the hell is this?

"Fauzi, um—sorry, can I interrupt you for a sec?"

Fauzi, Papa, and Eighth Aunt stop talking and turn to look at me expectantly, making it very obvious that I'm interrupting an important conversation. It's always like this with them. Everything is important; every conversation has the weight of millions of dollars at stake. In contrast, everything I say seems laughably trivial.

"Yep, what's hanging, my man?" Fauzi is twenty-seven or something equally ancient. He makes up for it by switching to what he thinks is trendy-speak whenever he talks to me and Eleanor.

"Um, just—I think you might've sent Sharlot the wrong itinerary? Hers looks the same as mine."

"Ah yes. The lovely Sharlot." Fauzi nods and smiles at her. "Yeah, I thought it would be prudent to pair you kids up for all the interviews. You're welcome."

Papa is staring so hard at me I can feel his eyeballs straining inside his head. Fauzi doesn't know that Sharlot is my fake girlfriend. Of course he doesn't. And because of it, he thinks he's done us a favor by making sure we've got as much time together as possible. Ha. Kill me now. I don't even want to tell Eighth Aunt because she might have him fired, and it's not his fault.

"I just feel bad that Sharlot's first visit to Bali is going to be filled with all these interviews. Maybe I can do them on my own so she can, like, enjoy Bali?"

Sharlot looks surprised by that, which is both nice and annoying, 'cause, man, how low is her opinion of me?

"No worries, my homie," Fauzi says. "Day two of your itineraries is all about exploring Bali. You kids are going to explore the shit out of this island." He laughs like he's just said something hilarious.

My stomach turns and I glance down at my tablet again. Day two. Oh my god. White water rafting. Monkey temple. Island temple in the middle of the sea. Beachside dinner. Okay, that last one doesn't sound so bad. But the rest . . .

I mean, they sound pretty cool too, but not with Sharlot, who's looking equally horrified at the idea of traversing Bali with me.

"The journos are really looking forward to these interviews," Fauzi says. "They can't wait to meet the girl who stole our little prince's heart." With that, he turns back to Papa, who for his part gives me one last meaningful stare. I get it, Pa. Don't let the world think I'm into gnomes and badgers, yeah.

I turn to Sharlot, who's just cracked open the minibar and taken out an icy bottle of sparkling water.

She smiles. Or is it . . . a frown? "I guess I won't be staying out of your hair after all," she says.

CHAPTER 13

Sharlot

Bali is an island of the gods. Even alongside the highway, there are stone statues of creatures with bulging eyes and lolling tongues with fresh flowers on their ears and around their necks and a black-and-white-checked cloth around their waists. Their facial features are grotesque, and yet the effect is somehow beautiful and soothing.

I take photo after photo and send them to Michie. The one good thing about meeting George is that Mama has returned me my phone and I've filled Michie in on the mess that is now my life. I even managed to grit my teeth through all the messages from Bradley, who was understandably concerned after my cryptic "save me" message. I'd replied, "Never mind, ha-ha," and then closed that message thread, unable to bear the humiliation of talking to Bradley. God, I feel so awful about how I've left things with him. Honestly, is there a more decent guy on the face of this planet than Bradley? Who else could remain so nice and caring toward somebody who dumped them out of the blue and then ghosted them without any explanation? I should give him one, I owe him that much at least, but the thought of it is enough to make everything inside me shrivel up into a squeaking mess.

Of course, Michie finds everything hilarious instead of frustrating.

Sharlot [1:03PM]: Look at these cool statues

Michie [1:04PM]: Giiiirl. I am SO jealous right now!

Sharlot [1:04PM]: Ugh, don't be. I'm stuck in a limo minivan with my fake boyfriend and his family. It is tres awkward

Michie [1:05PM]: You mean your billionaire boyfriend? (Money emoji) (Dancing emoji) Sugar daddyyy!

Sharlot [1:05PM]: Thank you for being a sympathetic friend and also setting the feminist movement back twenty years

Michie [1:06PM]: Lol! Any time

Sharlot [1:07PM]: I wonder if the driver of the limovan is retired military too.

Michie [1:07PM]: I bet he is. Is he carrying an uzi? I bet he is.

Sharlot [1:08PM]: Very funny.

But I crane my neck to see if there are indeed any weapons on the driver. There aren't. This is what I get for humoring Michie and her ridiculous ideas.

The Alphard minivan turns off the main road onto side streets that become increasingly narrow, to the point where the driver has to maneuver the limo this way and that to fit around some of the turns. This can't be right. We've gone back in time and have found ourselves in a sleepy village. There can't be a hotel big enough to hold an event with thousands of guests here.

We turn down one last side alley, a narrow passageway flanked by sweeping thin bamboos that curve into a tunnel. I've never seen anything more magical. It feels like we're on our way to fairyland. And then the green tunnel ends, and we're out in bright sunlight and the hotel appears before us in all its majestic glory. My mouth drops open.

I don't know how to describe the Grand Hotel Uluwatu. It's exactly as its name describes, for one. We're dropped off at the vast lobby, and I hop out and stare and stare and stare at the beauty around me. There are cascading waterfalls everywhere, and a never-ending mirror pond with vibrant orange and gold koi gliding underneath bowls of jasmine and candles. The lobby is a giant dome overlooking an impressive cliff, along which the resort has been built, with grand sweeping steps leading to a pristine beach below. The walls are decorated with huge carvings—tropical flowers and animals in a gorgeous tableau, and here and there are the same guardian statues carved out of stone and decorated with fresh, colorful flowers. Despite everything that's happened, despite the very reason we're here, I feel at peace. I exhale, my muscles relaxing. It's impossible to feel anything but happy and soothed in this place.

"Wow, this place is something else, huh?" Mama says.

For a moment, I'm tempted to do my usual surly thing and shrug, but I nod instead. Like I said, it's impossible to feel anything but soothed here. Kiki looks as amazed as I am, which makes me feel better; here's something that even my annoyingly worldly cousin is impressed by. As soon as she hops out of the car, Eleanor takes Kiki's hand and pulls her deeper into the lobby, pointing out various features to her. I can't help but smile. It's kind of sweet how the two of them have glommed on to each other. Unlike me and my supposed boyfriend.

I turn to look for George and find him helping his elderly grandmother out of the car. Oh crap. I take a hesitant step forward, unsure of what to do to help but feeling like I definitely should be offering some help. Once out of the car, she looks up and gives George a smile full of unabashed love, and he leans down and kisses her temple. I look away, feeling embarrassed, as though I'd intruded on a private moment.

"Wah, you all finally arrived!" an auntie with hair even bigger than Eighth Aunt's rushes toward us. Like Eighth Aunt, this auntie is decked out in full-body Chanel and also carrying a Birkin bag, although hers looks like it's made out of crocodile skin. Next to her is an uncle who is in a full-body Gucci tracksuit. He waves at us, nearly blinding me with the huge watch on his wrist and chunky gold and jade rings on his fingers. Behind them are two kids who look around my age, both too busy tapping on their phones to pay us much attention.

"Hi, Third Uncle, Third Aunt," George says. "Did you have a good flight?"

Third Uncle makes a tch-noise. "We fired the air attendant. Look what she did to my limited-edition Gucci!" He tugs at his tracksuit to show us a coin-size stain.

"Limited edition!" Third Aunt says, just in case we all missed that part somehow.

Eighth Aunt, alighting from the car, glances at Third Uncle and rolls her eyes. "Aiya, I told you, gege, please stop wearing Gucci. It's just so . . . mainstream. It's embarrassing, really. Remember the mantra: Hermès, Dior, and Chanel are swell. Gucci, Louis, and Prada are outta."

Kiki glances at Eleanor, who bursts out laughing. "You really need to work on that last rhyme, Eighth Aunt."

Third Uncle looks down and mumbles something about brand loyalty. Third Aunt looks at me and does a double take. "Is this . . . ? Waduh! George! Your girlfriend, ya? Wah, so pretty!"

Luckily, before Third Aunt can say anything more, Eighth Aunt says, "You can properly meet Sharlot at the welcome dinner." I have the sense that I've just narrowly escaped the jaws of a dangerous beast. For now. I gulp, feeling strangely small and helpless. I wonder if the rest of George's family is just as intimidating.

"Come here, Shi Jun," Nainai says, beckoning toward me. "Come walk with Nainai."

I hurry forward and hold out my arm to her so she can hold on to me for support as we walk. It feels kind of awkward and yet also kind of lovely to be walking with this old lady who calls herself "Nainai" around me, as though I were her granddaughter and not just some random girl who's pretending to be her grandson's girlfriend. I never had a relationship with any of my grandparents, and seeing her wrinkled hand on my arm is making me all sorts of emotional.

"Wah, this place is so nice, ya, Shi Jun?" Nainai says, looking around us and nodding her approval.

"Yeah, it really is. Thank you again for having me here."

"Of course. Oh, you are so lovely. I can see why my Ming Fa likes you."

Guilt churns in my belly, turning it sour.

"How are you doing, my girl? You seem tired. Are you a bit stressed?"

I gnaw on my lower lip, wondering how much to reveal to Nainai. The thing is, the last week has been an overwhelming mess. I hadn't foreseen just how much things were going to blow up online once Rina ran the story about George being attached to me. My ShareIt account, which was only opened a couple weeks back, went from seven followers to over twenty thousand overnight, and I swear most of these people are only hate-following me because their comments aren't very nice at all. They're mostly stuff about how I'm not as pretty as this girl or that girl and George could do a lot better and so on. And then there had been the prep that Eighth Aunt had put us through. She made us get our back stories straight and memorize random bits of preapproved information about each other. For example, George's hobbies (reading SFF, gym, app design), his favorite food (rendang), and his dream job (working in the family company, of course. And astronaut). It's all such a farce, and happening so fast that I'm still reeling at the magnitude of everything.

Somehow, I manage to make myself smile at Nainai and say, "I'm fine. Just a bit tired from the journey."

A woman wearing a simple but elegant black dress approaches us and says, "Om Suastiastu." She clasps her palms together and gives a slight bow.

I don't recognize the words, so they must be Balinese instead of Bahasa Indonesia.

"I'm Sri," she says, "the hotel manager. Welcome to the Grand Hotel Uluwatu. May I escort you to your private villas?"

"Don't we need to check in?" I blurt out loud. They all look at me with a mixture of amusement and maybe a tiny bit of pity. Okay, so maybe I'm imagining the pity. Probably.

"It's all been taken care of," Fauzi says, patting my arm reassuringly.

Of course it's all "been taken care of." God, I feel so out of place. Years ago, Mama had saved up enough to splurge on a trip to Disney World in Florida. I had felt so incredibly privileged, especially when we stepped inside the resort, and everything, even the elevator buttons, had some sort of Mickey emblem on them. I had felt like a princess. Most of the people there, I assumed, were much wealthier than Mama and I. But they too had to line up at the reception desk and check in like me and Mama.

This is another whole level of wealth. From the time we left our house to go to the airport, every step of the way has "been taken care of." I never knew that this kind of traveling existed, and I have never felt a larger divide between my world and theirs.

I'm quiet as we walk through the amazing lobby and down the grand stone steps. Nainai clings to my arm and George holds her other arm to steady her as we walk down. She refuses to take the elevator, insisting she's still spry enough to maneuver the steps. The resort stretches out on both sides of the steps, a cascade of rooms built into the cliff side, each one with its own private pool overlooking the beach. At the bottom of the steps on the beach level, we are led down a side path flanked with lush tropical plants. There's a hotel employee waiting with a golf cart for Nainai, who sits down with obvious relief. Without her between me and George, I'm suddenly very aware of his presence once more. Ugh. We start walking in silence.

"Hey," George says.

I look up.

"You okay?"

"Yeah, you?" I want to ask him if I don't seem okay, but maybe that's a bit too defensive. But I am feeling prickly and defensive. This place—it's too nice. I don't belong here. I'm a sore thumb. A squeaky wheel. The wheat stalk that's grown too high and is about to be chopped off. I don't know what other sayings there are, but the bottom line is, I don't belong here, and I hate that he does, that he's so obviously at home in places as lavish as this.

"Yeah. I'm fine."

"Good."

"Great." He must've sensed my mood, because he doesn't say anything else.

The private villas are tucked into one side of the resort, away from the noise and vibrancy of the main building. Here, it's more tranquil, each villa hidden behind a wall.

"This is yours," Fauzi says, handing Mama three key cards. "A two-bedroom villa."

Mama, Kiki, and I wave to the rest of the group and go through the carved wooden gate. We're greeted by a beautiful courtyard complete with a fountain wreathed with more fresh flowers, and our "villa" is larger than our house back in LA. Mama waves a key card at the door and the lock snicks open. We step inside and . . . holy crap.

Kiki squeals and runs in. Without the weight of George and his stupidly rich family, I do the same, rushing through the incredibly beautiful living room to the other side, where there are massive glass doors that open out into a private infinity pool. There's even a cabana on one side of the pool with a day bed that's just begging to be slept in. The bedrooms are equally breathtaking. The master bedroom is obviously designed for honeymooners—there is an astonishingly large tub near the floor-to-ceiling window that overlooks the private pool.

"How romantic," Mama says with a sigh.

"Ew. You can have this room. I'll share the other one with Kiki." I cross the living room into the other bedroom, where Kiki has already claimed the bed closest to the window. I can't resist jumping into the bed. Heaven. The sheets are creamy smooth and the pillows are made of fluffy clouds. The entire villa is set at a comfortable temperature that makes me want to take a warm bath and then burrow into this unbelievably light duvet and read a book until I fall asleep. Oh, please, universe, let me just do that this entire trip instead of—

"Shouldn't you be getting ready for your first interview?" Kiki says.

I groan out loud. "Don't start."

"No, but really. You don't want to look gross on camera. That stuff's forever on the internet, you know. And no offense, but you look like you've been traveling all day."

I glare at her. I guess she's right. I feel like I'm covered in travel grime, despite having traveled in the most stylish way possible. Kiki, on the other hand, looks as fresh as a newly picked rose. "How come you look all perky and nice?"

She smiles and bats her eyelashes at me. "I take my toiletries with me on flights. Before we landed, I went and washed my face and brushed my teeth and redid my makeup. I'm a pro at flying. Off you go. Once you've showered I'll help you get ready. I've got all this makeup from South Korea. Top-of-the-line stuff."

Grumbling, I do as Kiki orders and take a shower. The bathroom has a side that's all glass, which makes me feel a bit exposed at first, but upon further inspection, thanks to the brilliant design of the villa, I realize that no one can look into the bathroom. Cunning. I enjoy the shower a lot more than I thought I would; there's something super calming about showering while gazing out at flowers and plants and our private pool. When I'm done, I shrug on a peach-colored summer dress that has a cute front chest tie. Very tropical beach. Then I go into the adjoining walk-in closet, where Kiki has laid out her makeup bag on the vanity table. She's got a whole arsenal of makeup. Makeup for the barrage of interviews I'm about to face. My stomach knots, but I make myself sit down in front of the vanity.

I hate to admit it, but Kiki obviously knows what she's doing. She slathers primer on my face, followed by BB cream and concealer, and by the time she's done, my skin looks dewy and fresh and spotless. She moves on to my eyes next, lining them with a deep-brown pencil before smudging it so it looks natural. Mama walks in as Kiki's just finishing up with a berry-colored lip tint. "Ah," Mama says with a smile. "Prepping for the interviews?"

I can't help but notice that Mama has had a shower herself and put on a beautiful yellow wrap dress and more makeup than usual. The sight of her looking so much more vibrant than I've ever seen her lights a fire in my gut. How dare she have so much fun while I'm stuck in a nightmare?

"Don't glower like that, you're making it hard for me to put this stuff on," Kiki scolds.

"I can't help it!" I say, and I feel tears rushing into my eyes. Ugh, gross. Stop that, self! I turn away and blink them away before Mama can see, and then I snap, "This is all your fault, Mama. I didn't want to come here to Bali. This is so weird!" My words come out poisonous, dripping with venom. I can't help myself. The thought of Nainai's kind smile spurs me on. Does Nainai know that I'm a fake? Regardless, I'm lying to everyone and it feels so shitty. I want to make Mama feel as crappy as I feel.

Kiki mumbles something about needing her eyebrow pencil and scurries out of the closet.

For a few painful moments, neither Mama nor I speak.

Ever since the non-date at Kopi-Kopi, I've been so furious at Mama that I've taken extra care to avoid her. Now I can't quite bring myself to look at her, so I focus on my hands. I pick at my thumbnail, worrying at it until a sliver tears off and I can rip it out and focus on the sharp burst of pain. Didn't take long at all for the peace that had come with this magical place to dissipate. As usual, all it takes is a few minutes with Mama, then all of the bad stuff comes crawling back out of the ground. I mentally prepare myself for the usual barrage of "Why you so ungrateful" and "I do everything for you."

Instead, when Mama opens her mouth, what she says is "I'm sorry."

It comes out so quiet and so raw that for a second, I wonder if I've misheard. Maybe I've wanted to hear these words for so long that my imagination went ahead and made it up. But no, she really did just apologize.

"When George message you, I didn't think it would come to this . . . this whole entire thing." She gestures around us and gives a mirthless laugh. "I didn't know that his auntie is my childhood best friend. She was always so secretive when we were young. I never thought—she was always so modestly dressed, didn't have branded bags or anything. How should I know it turns out she is a billionaire? I didn't think we would be here in Bali. I didn't think—I didn't think I'd care this much."

"About me?" I hate how needy I sound.

"No!" Ma cries. "Of course not talking about you. I always care about you, you know that."

Yeah, I guess I do know that.

"I mean about all this . . . coming back here, all my old friends, my family. I didn't think I would care so much about them, but—" She stops abruptly and stares up at the ceiling, blinking.

With a twist in my gut, I realize she's trying not to cry. There's something bigger here. Something she's always kept hidden from me, something I've always wanted to know. Something to do with our past.

So I ask the question I've always asked but never received an answer to.

"Why did you never come back to Jakarta? When you had time off work. When I had time off school. You never came back. You never wanted to."

Mama turns away and meets my eye in the mirror instead, as though it's too much to look at me straight on. "When I leave Jakarta all those years ago, it was not a happy leaving."

I kind of suspected that before, but hearing her say it is still a bit of a surprise. "Why? What happened?"

She shakes her head. "Doesn't matter. I don't mean to make you go through all this. I just wanted you to stop moping, you know? You lock yourself up in your room, not want to come out and explore the city . . . I thought maybe if I reply to this boy, then you might want to come out. And now we are all in Bali. I'm sorry, Shar. Mama is sorry."

The only times that my mother has ever apologized were times when she had been absolutely cornered and was proven one hundred percent wrong. And then she'd snap, "I'm sorry, okay? You happy now? I'm *sorry*." Before stomping off and cleaning the house very aggressively.

I've never heard her apologize like this. Like she means it, like her heart is heavy with guilt. And I hate it. This is not my fiery mom. This mom is soft and vulnerable and I don't know how to deal with how exposed this makes me feel. How dangerously close it makes me to bursting into tears and clinging to her like a toddler. So I do the only thing I know how to.

I piss her off.

"Yeah, well. Maybe if you hadn't ruined my life by kidnapping me all the way to this shithole, we wouldn't be in this mess."

"Sharlot—"

"My life was good before you decided to destroy it," I say, getting even angrier because now I'm seriously hating myself and I hate that I'm like this toward her, but that feeling only makes me want to lash out even more. "And you know what? I can't wait to go back to California and get the hell out of the house, because I can't wait to leave you."

I might as well have hit her. She straightens up, her mouth thinning into that familiar tight line, anger and hurt etched painfully into her features. Without another word, she walks away. I can't bear to look at my own reflection, so I look down at the vanity table, where I see that I'm white-knuckling one of Kiki's makeup brushes. Deep inhale. And exhale.

God, I was beastly to her. I didn't mean to be. I don't know why I felt a need to lash out like that, to hurt her. Why am I like this?

I can't stand being inside the villa, its air thick with tension and sharp edges. I can practically feel Kiki listening in from the other room, and I don't want to have to talk about how horrible I am to her. Grabbing my phone and my purse, I duck out of the bedroom and barely glance at Kiki before rushing out.

CHAPTER 14

George

Twenty minutes before the first interview is due to begin, I walk over to Sharlot's villa. I'm about to ring the doorbell when the door swings open and Sharlot rushes out so fast that she crashes into my arms.

"Whoa, you okay?" I grip her arms tight out of instinct and she jerks away like my touch burned her.

"George!" She blinks at me, and I realize that her eyes are shining with tears.

I feel a protective urge come over me. "What's going on?"

She walks briskly away from the villa and I have to hurry to catch up with her. "Wait up." When I fall into step beside her, I say, "Do you wanna talk about it?"

She lets out a long, frustrated breath. We turn a corner and find a bench under a plumeria tree. Sharlot sits down and buries her face in her hands, and I sit down next to her, wondering what the hell to say. After a while, she says, "It's nothing. Just my mom."

"Ah." Okay, now I really don't know what to say, so I just look down at my hands.

Sharlot lets out a little gasp and says, "Shit, I'm so sorry, George. I forgot that your mom is—um. Yeah. Damn it, I'm such an asshole. I'm sorry."

"No, it's okay. She passed away a long time ago, so." I don't know why I said that. It's so stupid. It doesn't matter how long ago my mom passed away, I still miss her every day. "Um, anyway, my dad's kind of a lot, so I get it." Then it's my turn to grimace. Her dad's out of the picture, idiot. Argh. "Sorry. I didn't mean—"

Shalor laughs, the tension going out of her shoulders. "Oh my god, how are the two of us so bad at this?"

"I swear I'm not normally this terrible at talking to other people," I say. "Okay, can we please have a do-over?"

"Deal." She shakes her head and takes a deep breath. "So. I just got into a huge fight with my mom, and honestly? I was such a huge dick toward her. But I've just been so mad at her. Like, she whisked me away from Cali to spend my entire summer here without any warning."

"That sucks."

"Yeah! And all my friends probably think it's the saddest thing, spending the summer in a Third World country." She pauses. "Sorry, that was so offensive. Argh. I'm sorry, I'm just—my head's a mess."

I shrug. "It's fine. I'm used to foreigners thinking we live in huts or something."

Sharlot gives a guilty grimace and is quiet for a while. "It's . . .

been really different from what I expected. Indonesia is a lot nicer than I thought it would be. Hell, parts of it are more well-developed than LA. Not that I'll ever admit that to my mom. I still can't believe she dragged me all the way here."

"Why not? She obviously loves Indonesia. I saw the way her face lit up when she was served gado-gado on the flight here." Sharlot's eyes widen, and for a moment, I forget what I was about to say. At the risk of sounding like an idiot, Sharlot is really pretty. Her eyes are very symmetrical, her nose turns up at a pleasing angle, and her mouth is very proportionate to the rest of her face. Okay, so maybe I'm not the best at describing facial features. I make myself continue. "Your mom kind of squeaked and was like, 'Oh my god, gado-gado!' I've never seen anyone get so excited over a bowl of what's essentially salad."

A little laugh escapes Sharlot's mouth. "Yeah, I guess she does get excited over Indonesian food. Or anything Indonesian, for that matter." She frowns. "Ugh, you're right. She's obviously having the time of her life here. I should probably pull my head out of my ass and be nice to her or whatever."

"If you ever need help pulling heads out of asses, I'm your guy." Oh my god, what are these words falling out of my mouth? "Sorry, that sounded a lot better in my head."

"I got the gist," she says, laughing.

My phone buzzes with a reminder that the interviews are starting soon. My stomach clenches at the thought of the interviews. "We should get going. The longer we make the reporters wait, the sharper their questions get."

Sharlot pales slightly, but she stands up and starts walking next to me. "I won't lie, I'm really nervous about these interviews."

"Tell me about it. I'm not looking forward to them."

"I still feel so out of place here, like I'm totally going to make a mess of everything. Which I already have, which is the very reason I'm here. It's all so complicated. I'm having a hard time trying to keep all the lies straight in my head."

"All the lies?" My heart starts thudding against my rib cage like it's trying to make a break for it. She's only got the one lie to worry about—the one about us supposedly being in a long-term, long-distance relationship. She can't possibly know about the other lie—the one where I wasn't the one she'd been messaging so frequently for over a week.

"Oh. Yeah. I meant the one about us dating."

"Right." I'm too scared to ask what other lies there are that she might be referring to, so I quickly say, "That's okay, I think it's a totally believable lie. Especially with all the different video call apps we've got now. Distance isn't a problem like it used to be."

"But how long will we have to pretend to be a couple?"

There's a tinge of desperation in her voice that kind of smarts a little. Hard not to take it personally, especially when I consider that she'd been so sweet and warm over ShareIt. Come to think of it, Sharlot was all eager on ShareIt and then became cold and reserved after we met. Which can only mean one thing: She finds the real-life me repulsive.

Ouch.

Like I said, hard not to take it personally.

I give a small shake of the head, trying to clear my thoughts. So she doesn't like me that way, so what? I don't even like her on a deeper level aside from her looks.

"Things will die down once the event's over and the app's launched. For now, let's go over the Eighth-Aunt-approved answers again. So let's see, how did we meet? I know we told them we met on Hardworking Teens, but we'll probably need more details than that. Like, what got us to start talking, when was the first time we actually met in person, that sort of thing."

She groans. "We've been over this a million times with your aunt, and honestly? All the stuff she came up with sounded really cliché and dumb. Can't we just say the truth? That you messaged me online and we started chatting?"

I wince. I'm dying, literally *dying* to tell her that I did no such thing, that Papa and Eleanor were behind it. It's just such a creepy thing to do, messaging pretty girls randomly on some app. "Um, talk about cliché . . ."

She shrugs. "Okay . . . so, how else would we meet, given you're based in Jakarta and I'm based in LA?"

"How about we met when I was in LA last year?"

"You were in LA last year?"

I try to think of where I was last year, and with each passing moment as I go through the numerous places I spent last year, Sharlot's eyebrows rise until they practically disappear into her hair.

"Why are you taking so long to answer?"

"I'm trying to remember if I went to LA last year or not."

"Just how many places did you go to last year?" she cries.

"I don't know. Seven? Maybe nine? Do you know how many places you travel to each year?"

"Yeah, the normal number: zero!"

"Oh. Right. Um." The memory hits me: Eighth Aunt rushing us down Melrose Avenue because she had an appointment at Dior to look at some special-edition handbag they'd reserved just for her. "Yes!" I say quickly, eager to get this conversation over with. "I did go to LA last year."

She quirks the corner of her mouth up at me. "Took you long enough to remember. Must be hard to travel so much that you can't even remember where you went a year ago."

I sigh. I'm noticing that I do that a lot when I'm with Sharlot. "So anyway, we met while I was in LA—"

"I saved your ass from kids who were beating the shit out of you for being so clueless."

The laugh escapes me before I realize it. "No. No way."

"Okay. I saved your ass from a barista because you went into a hipster café and ordered a venti caramel macchiato."

"How about we steer clear of you saving my ass from anything?"

"What's the fun in that?"

And somehow, despite everything, Sharlot and I are smiling at each other. Our first real smile in a while, maybe the first one I've seen on her today. God, is it still today? This day has stretched on a hell of a lot longer than it has any right to.

We chat more easily the rest of the way until we arrive at the main building and one of the receptionists escorts us to the meeting rooms. Outside of the door, I steel myself and glance at Sharlot.

"You ready?"

"Nope."

"Great."

Whoever comes up with these interview questions needs to be introduced to the twenty-first century. Seriously, what is up with these super-outdated, sexist questions?

Our first interviewer, whose name I have already forgotten, is from *Plot Twist,* a news website aimed at young people. When it was first launched five years ago, it had been more of a fun news site filled with silly quizzes and memes, but it has since grown into a billion-dollar enterprise that releases surprisingly in-depth and well-researched articles. In fact, it won a prestigious journalism award just last year for covering the devastating effects of climate change on the Indonesian rain forests.

This article that they're doing of us, however, is not that.

As soon as the reporter is done asking me questions about OneLiner, he immediately says, "So, tell me, George, what caught your eye about Sharlot?"

I glance at Sharlot and feel my cheeks warming up. "Uh." God, I am unprepared for this. How the hell did that happen? I grew up doing these interviews. The first rule of the Tanuwijaya clan, hammered into us from when we were young enough to form sentences, is "Never be caught unprepared." And I've always been so good at them. Okay, well, not good. But definitely not terrible. Unlike my cousin Melodi, for example, Eighth Aunt didn't have to put in extra effort to have me sent off to a boarding school in Scotland just to escape the public eye. I have a whole list of vetted and prepared answers for all the interview questions that have been lobbed my way. But now, I belatedly realize that those answers were dependent on my not seeing anyone. They're about deflecting personal questions and redirecting to whatever new venture the company is currently invested in.

A million answers crowd into my head and I reject them all. *She's pretty*—too shallow. *She's smart*—too generic. *She's kind*—yawn.

"She's, um, she's nice." Wow. Way to go, George. I cringe inwardly to think of Eighth Aunt's and Eleanor's reactions when this interview is released. She's *nice*? They're going to be like, "Are you trying to kill all excitement about the app? Because that's what you're doing, George Clooney."

Apparently, the interviewer thinks so too, because he presses a bit harder. "Nice?" he asks with a laugh. "You must be inundated with nice girls all the time! You've been famous for refusing to be involved with anyone, and now that we've received news about the shy, reclusive Prince George finally having a girlfriend, everyone is dying to know more about her."

"Um . . . er . . ." Oh god. I have never choked like this, and especially not in the presence of a reporter. But as soon as I think, I'm choking, it gets even worse. My entire family flashes before my eyes, their faces frowning with disappointment. Come on, George, just think of something to say. Anything!

Sharlot glances at me, frowning at my failure to come up with a coherent sentence, and I'm so embarrassed I could just burst into flames now. I'm supposed to be the seasoned pro at interviews, and here I am, crashing and burning in the most idiotic fashion. Her forehead clears when she sees my panicked expression. She knows. She knows I'm choking.

She turns back to the reporter and says, "Excuse me, Asep, but since you're dying to know about me, shouldn't you be asking me these questions?"

I can practically feel my jaw landing on the floor. Sharlot—soft-spoken, straight-laced Sharlot whose favorite hobby is stewing bones into broths—is kind of . . . badass? And she remembered the reporter's name!

Asep looks at Sharlot with some surprise and then laughs. "Oh, I'm sorry. Sure." He doesn't even bother turning his body toward her or moving his phone, which is recording the interview, closer to her. It's clear he's not at all interested in what she has to say. She's merely the object of my affection, emphasis on "object." I never ever abuse my position of privilege, but fleetingly I indulge in the thought of getting this jackass fired.

"Okay, well." Sharlot straightens up and flips her hair over her shoulder. "I'm pretty amazing, so I'm not surprised that George here went for me."

I bite down on my bottom lip to keep from laughing.

"I won the sixth-grade statewide spelling bee contest. That's the state of California, by the way. It's huge. The word was *derailleur*. Do you know how to spell *derailleur*?"

Asep cocks his head. *"D-e-r-a-i-l-u-r-e."*

Sharlot nods with a smirk. "Yeah, that was the answer Cecilia MacKenzie gave too. The wrong one."

Asep doesn't frown, exactly, but he definitely looks less smug than he did moments ago. He turns to me and says, "So, you were attracted to Sharlot because she's a good speller?"

I don't hesitate. "Yep, that's exactly why." I glance at Sharlot and the knot in my chest releases. I can breathe again.

The rest of the interview, as well as the following interviews we have, go smoothly. Well, maybe *smoothly* isn't quite the right word for them, but I no longer choke for answers. In fact, Sharlot and I have a lot of fun with all the ridiculous questions we're asked. She tells one reporter that it was the way I blew my nose that drew her to me, and I tell them it was the way she ate a burger that attracted me to her.

By the time they end, I'm exhausted, but in a good way. We leave the meeting room just like we entered—holding hands, but as soon as we're safely out of sight from the reporters and the cameras, we immediately let go. Not sure who let go of whose hand first, we're both so eager to not be touching each other. We walk through the grand lobby and stand at the top of the stairs, looking down at the rest of the resort. It's late afternoon, the endless blue sky starting to get a violet hue to it. It won't be long before the lights come on all over the resort, turning it into something magical.

"Thanks for saving me in there," I say to Sharlot.

She shrugs and looks at me from the corner of her eye. "No probs. But what happened in there? I thought you grew up with these kinds of things."

"I did. I don't know, I guess it just hit me that it's the first time I've been interviewed about my personal life."

"Seriously? I find that hard to believe."

"No, I mean like—" I struggle to find the right words. "There have been tons of profiles done on me before, but they're all pretty tame, you know? Oh, George Tanuwijaya's on the swim team. Hobbies include gaming. You know, nothing that would land me on the first page of anything. But now I realize that this is . . . the kind of thing that can really blow up, and I wasn't, um, I guess I wasn't mentally prepared for it. I'm really sorry. I didn't realize how weird it must be for you too. But you were amazing."

"That's because I've perfected the art of not giving a shit."

I'm so taken aback by this that I laugh. "You're so different from what I expected," I blurt out. What I really meant was that she's so much more interesting than I had thought she would be based on our chat messages. Online, she's uptight and prissy and all about maintaining a good-Asian-kid persona. In real life, she's none of those things.

She loses her smile. "Sorry if I disappoint."

"That wasn't what I meant—"

But it's too late. I've killed the moment. Sharlot puts her arms around herself. "Anyway, I should go back to my room. My mom and cousin are probably wondering where I am."

"Okay. Um." I have no idea what to say. "See you at dinner."

"Yep, see you," she says, without bothering to even look at me as she walks away.

CHAPTER 15

Sharlot

Later that evening, we gather at the hotel lobby to find a line of Alphards waiting to take us to the restaurant for dinner. This is definitely a different life from what I'm used to. I feel even more self-conscious than before, despite the pretty dress I've borrowed from Kiki and the flawless makeup she's once again applied to my face. Mama walks ahead of us, her head held high and her ankle-length dress fluttering in the evening breeze. I'm not used to this version of her. I'm used to seeing her in her pantsuits, hair tied back into a supertight bun, exuding an aura of no-nonsense. Here, she's laid-back and cheerful and like . . . a woman instead of a mother, which is utterly weird.

Oh god, it just strikes me that maybe she's got a crush on someone. Maybe it's George's dad. Eww. Can people in their late thirties even have crushes? That's, like, way ancient to have a crush. Still, I can't deny that Mama in Indonesia is so different from Mama in California, and it makes my chest tighten to see how alive she is. I hadn't realized that the mama I knew back home was only a watered-down version of herself. I gaze at her for the longest time, wanting to apologize to her but unable to swallow my pride. With no small amount of difficulty, I tear my thoughts away from the very disturbing possibility of Mama liking George's dad in that way.

Nainai is already there and her entire face brightens when she sees me. I greet her and everyone else, avoiding George's eye, before trying to jump into one of the Alphards with Mama and Kiki. But Nainai stops me and says, "Oh, you lovebirds must sit with each other!" Argh.

George gives me an apologetic grimace. Without any choice, I climb into the back of the Alphard with him. I sit as far off to one side as possible, hoping George would sit at the other side. Instead, he sits in the middle seat. I'm about to ask him to move over when Eleanor clambers in and squeezes in next to George. Even though she's tiny, she somehow takes up a ton of space, pushing George until he's pressed right up against my side. I am painfully aware of the warmth of his body against mine. At least he looks as uncomfortable about it as I feel.

We don't talk to each other the entire ride. Eleanor, Nainai, and Papa chat easily and I answer any questions thrown my way as politely as I can. I swear this is the longest car journey I have ever been on. When we finally get there, George and I scramble out with obvious relief.

Then George turns to face me and says, "Ready?" He holds out a hand.

I stare at it like it's an alien tentacle until he raises his eyebrows. Oh, right, we're supposed to be a couple. Argh. I take his outstretched hand before immediately yanking my hand back and wiping my palm on my dress. Both our palms are equally sticky. Then I take his hand again and follow his dad and Eleanor into the restaurant.

The restaurant we're at is called Café Menega, but it's less café and more beachside seafood restaurant with a huge crowd of people spilling out of it. Most of them are, terrifyingly, George's family members. How are Chinese-Indo families this humongous?

"Um, just so you know," George murmurs as we walk inside, "we have a Tanuwijaya family group chat and uh, everyone has heard about us and they're all dying to meet you."

I only have time to say, "Wait, a family group what?" before the first of the Tanuwijaya clan descends upon us. The aunties lead the charge, of course. A murder of aunties with huge, permed hair and faces painted with thick makeup despite the sweltering heat.

"George!" one auntie cries. "Finally, you arrive!"

"Hi, Third Aunt," George says, "apa kabar?"

I know enough about Indonesian custom to slightly bow my head to the aunties and say, "Hi, Tante, apa kabar?" Their gazes immediately shift from George to me. I feel a little like a zoo animal being scrutinized by visitors.

Third Aunt gives me a once-over, her eyes glittering with interest. "Oh, hello! Is this . . . your girlfriend that I've been hearing so much about?"

I look up at George with panicky eyes, probably looking like a rabbit that's gotten caught in a trap. I should tell her that I am, but now that I'm actually standing here before them, I feel so self-conscious about our lie, so certain that they'll be able to smell the bullshit and call us out. There's only a flicker of hesitation on George's face before he says, smoothly, "Yes, this is Sharlot, my girlfriend."

The auntie's grin widens like a cartoon shark when it senses blood in the water. She grabs a nearby uncle and says in rapid Indonesian, "Eh! Ah Leong, look, it's George's girlfriend!"

I mean, sheesh, I am literally standing right here.

It's not long before there's an even larger mob gathered around us.

One of the aunties takes my hand and pats it. "Wah, cantik, ya?" *So pretty.* I smile just as she says, "Mancung sekali." One of the remaining effects of Western colonization in Asia is that we still hold everyone up to a Westernized beauty standard. Indonesians are so obsessed with Western features that they even have a whole word that means "sharp or pointy nose, or nose that isn't flat"—*mancung*. It's meant as a compliment, but I feel like burying myself in a hole as more and more aunties surround us and make unfettered comments about my looks as though I'm not even here. One of them touches my hair, another one pinches my cheek and tells me how *putih bersih*—"white and pure"—my skin is. Which is . . . cringe-worthy.

"Ow, ow, okay, enough of this," I say, batting away the aunties.

Their eyes widen like I've just slapped them in the face. I have a feeling I've just committed an actual crime. At once, their demeanor turns cold, their gazes switching from interest to condescension. It's clear what they're thinking: How dare she talk back to her elders? My insides shrivel up.

"I'm sorry," I quickly say. "I—uh—"

George waves at someone in the crowd and says, "Sorry, aunties, we should go say hi to Eighth Aunt."

The tension breaks and the murder of aunties say, "Of course, yes. Of course!"

I breathe out with relief and let George lead me away from the aunts, who aren't even bothering to keep their voices down as they chatter about how awful my behavior is. God, I do not feel ready to face Eighth Aunt right now.

As though he's heard my thoughts, George leans in and says, "I was just lying about saying hi to Eighth Aunt. I only said that to get us out of there."

My head jerks up and I stare at him.

"Sorry, I know my aunts can be a bit much."

That gets a smile out of me. I didn't know if he'd noticed how uncomfortable I'd been with his aunts, and the realization that he's made up a story to save me from them is kind of touching. But before I can thank him, a burly guy who looks only a handful of years older than us appears and smacks George's shoulder.

"Georgie!" he shouts. "Hey, everyone, it's George and his girlfriend!"

George winces. His palm becomes more slick, especially as more people approach us. At least these ones are young—some in their twenties, a few who look about our age. "My cousins," he whispers to me.

"That's me!" the first guy says.

"I thought you didn't have any male cousins?" I ask George.

"That's right!" the first guy says. "We're technically George's cousins-in-law, but we're as good as family, aren't we, Georgie?" He turns to me and holds out his hand. "Nice to meet you, kid, I'm Dicky."

I have never met anyone who goes by Dicky, but if ever there was a Dicky, this guy is it. I shake his hand. "I'm Sharlot."

"Hey, Sharlot, I'm Rosiella," a beautiful woman in her early twenties says, "and this is my sister Nicoletta."

I try hard to remember all of their names, but after Nicoletta, they all kind of blur into one large, overwhelming group. Apparently, all these sophisticated, elegant people are somehow George's first cousins. Well, with the exception of the men, who are his cousins-in-law.

"All right, Georgie finally got himself a girlfriend!" Dicky shouts. I think he thinks he's at a frat party or something.

"Ignore my husband," Rosiella says with a roll of her eyes. She hands me a bright purple drink with a jasmine flower floating at the top. I take a small sip and cough. Okay, this drink is strong. Rosiella and Nicoletta are watching me closely. When I sputter after my first sip, they both laugh. "Oh, you are so innocent. I thought you ABCs would know how to party."

My cheeks burst into flame. Honestly, I never thought I'd come to Asia and be the nerdy kid here. What the hell is going on? I feel so out of place. I just want to go back to my villa and hide under the duvet and never come out.

"Have you had diarrhea yet?" Nicoletta says. She and Rosiella giggle.

"Excuse me?" I must have heard them wrong. It must be the drink affecting my hearing.

"Every tourist who comes to Indo for the first time will get food poisoning for sure," Nicoletta says.

"I'm not a tourist," I say, hating how defensive my voice sounds.

"Actually, Sharlot's mom is Indo," George says.

Rosiella rolls her eyes. "Yeah, but you grew up in the States, right?"

I nod.

"So you've got a bule stomach. Easily poisoned."

I shake my head. "No, not poisoned yet." I don't tell them it's because I've spent most of my time cooped up in Kiki's house, eating home-cooked meals like the world's most boring tourist. I can't believe that I'm standing here defending, of all things, my freaking bowels.

"Dude, it's nothing to be ashamed of," Rosiella says. "When I first came back to Jakarta after my first year at Oxford, my stomach had become so weak from all that clean British food that I had to go to the hospital after eating my favorite roadside nasi goreng."

"Holy shit," I say.

"I had to go to the hospital after eating clam kway teow," Dicky says with a deep laugh. "You know, from that place in PIK?"

Nicoletta nods.

"So worth it, though," Dicky says.

Nicoletta and Rosiella both nod while saying, "Mm-mm."

I can't believe they're actually saying a trip to the hospital is worth a plate of kway teow. It's just rice noodles, for crying out loud.

"It's not actually that big of a deal," George says. "Pretty sure we've all had to go to the hospital at some point for food poisoning."

"WHAT?"

George shrugs. "Yeah, you just go in, get an IV drip and some clay or charcoal pills and you'll be fine within the hour."

"And then you can go home and eat more delicious, dirty food," Nicoletta says, and the others all nod.

I'm gaping at them like a guppy. "I've never known anyone who has had to go to the hospital for food poisoning."

Rosiella and Nicoletta laugh at me. "Don't be surprised if it happens to you here."

I look down at my drink, suddenly feeling ill.

"Oh, I think Eighth Aunt wants to talk to us," George says. We say bye to his cousins and depart from the increasingly raucous group. Once we're out of earshot, I breathe a sigh of relief.

"Does Eighth Aunt really want to talk to us?" I say, looking around.

"No, but she's the matriarch, so I'm just using her as a way to get us out of uncomfortable conversations." George grins at me. "You okay?"

"What's not to be okay about? I can talk about diarrhea all day long," I say drily, despite evidence to the contrary. But George must see through my BS, because instead of walking back inside the restaurant where the throng is, we somehow find ourselves meandering toward the beach, where the crowd is thinner. I take in a deep breath of the sea-heavy air, trying to calm my racing mind. I've never felt so out of place before, so horribly different from everyone, so alien. And it doesn't help that I'm with a guy who thinks I'm someone I'm not. I take a mouthful of my drink which I'm inexplicably still carrying and belatedly recall how strong it is.

"I'm sorry about my family," George says.

"It's fine. They're . . ." I try to search for the right word, one that won't be super offensive.

"A lot?" he says.

"Yeah." I laugh a little. "How are you doing?"

He shrugs. "Okay, I guess. Given the whole situation. Hey, thanks again. For being so awesome during the interviews. I totally choked and you saved my ass."

Huh. I definitely wasn't expecting that. "It's fine. But what did happen back there? I was under the impression that you get interviewed like every week."

George gives a bashful smile that's more adorable than I was prepared for. "Yeah, I guess it was just . . . everything, you know? There's us, and then there's the app." He runs his fingers through his hair and shakes his head. "I'm kind of sort of nervous about the app?" He releases his breath in a long sigh. "Wow, I haven't told that to anyone before. My family only cares about how the app would make the company look, but I actually want it to do okay. I know, it's a super-crowded market and everything, but I actually think it might do some good. I don't know, sorry, I'm just rambling now."

Despite myself, my heart goes out to George. I wasn't expecting to see his vulnerable side, and it's disarming in its sincerity. I know how he feels, the fear of failure looming large and heavy over him. But George has it even worse, because if he does fail, it'll happen publicly. Yeesh, what a position to be in. It strikes me that I never connected with Bradley on a deeper level, not like this. Hell, I don't even know what Bradley's fears and dreams are, aside from that he wants to be an architect. Before I can second-guess myself, I reach out and put my hand on George's arm. He startles, and I snatch my hand back. Okay, that was a mistake.

Cheeks burning, I take another sip of my drink and regret it immediately. I need to put this stupid thing down because I keep taking sips without meaning to. My head feels a bit fuzzy, like my brain's grown fur. Does that thought make any sense? "I kind of hate all of this. I'm sorry we met." Wow, I can't believe I just said that out loud.

George's face is unreadable, or maybe it's that I'm too tipsy to read anything, whether they be faces or words. After a while, he says, "I understand if things aren't, um, as expected. To be honest, you're kind of not what I was expecting either."

Ouch. That's a bit of a kick in the gut. Anger surges through my veins, lighting up my senses. I'm a disappointment to him because I don't fulfill his idea of the perfect Chinese-Indo girlfriend. Not obedient enough, probably. "Yeah, you're not the only one who's disappointed," I snark back.

He actually winces like I've hit him. "Um, okay." He looks down at his feet and I gnaw on my lower lip and wish the sand would part and bury me alive. "Anyway, I get that neither of us wants any of this to happen, but since it is, let's just try to get through this weekend and then we can go our separate ways."

"Yep."

"Yep."

"Yep." I just have to get through the next few days as the fake girlfriend of someone I don't like, who doesn't like me back. That's totally fine. That's very doable. What can possibly go wrong?

CHAPTER 16

George

I wake up to a sight no one should ever wake up to—Papa, Eighth Aunt, Nainai, and Eleanor sitting on Eleanor's bed, staring at me. I jerk upright, going from drowsy slumber straight to adrenaline-pumped alertness in a single second.

"What—what happened? Everything okay?" Dread lurches up my throat, bitter and sharp. Somebody must've died. One of our family members. Maybe an aunt or an uncle. Maybe even a cousin.

"George, how was it last night, introducing Sharlot to the family?" Eighth Aunt says, not bothering with any greetings.

"Wha—" I rub my face with both hands. "Why are you all here in my room?"

"Technically it's also my room," Eleanor pipes up. "I gave them permission to come in. Not that any of you needed any permission, since you are all my elders and I respect you with every shred of my being." She grins up at them and is rewarded with a pet on the head from Nainai and a smile that is 100 percent gooey affection from Papa. Ugh, why haven't they seen through her act yet?

"Yes, very true, meimei," Nainai says in her wobbly old-person voice. "You shouldn't be demanding permission from your elders to enter your room, Ming Fa. Unless you have something to hide." Her numerous wrinkles rearrange into a frown.

"No, I wasn't demanding, I was just—" I sigh. "Never mind. What can I do for you?"

Nainai's wrinkles shift back into her usual genial expression. "There's a good boy. Tell Nainai how was your evening with Shi Jun?"

It takes a beat for me to recall that Shi Jun is Sharlot's Chinese name. "Um. It was okay, I guess? We were at dinner with all of you."

"I saw you two going down to the beach, maybe having a romantic moment?" Nainai grins at me. They're all wearing Cheshire cat grins now, actually.

I shrink back from them. "No, actually. I—uh—I get the feeling that Sharlot—I mean, Shi Jun—doesn't like me that much. I think we're probably better off as friends once this whole event is done, so please don't get your hopes up, Nainai," I say as gently as I can. The only other person that Eighth Aunt has told the truth to is Nainai, but Nainai still seems to harbor hope that we might actually end up dating for real. The probability of that happening is less than nil, but try telling that to Nainai.

In reply, they all talk in low voices among themselves, as though I'm not right here in front of them and can hear every single word they're saying.

Papa: "You're right, he's hopeless."

Eleanor: "Told you."

Nainai: "He'll be celibate his whole life. No one will continue the family name."

"Can I just point out that Indonesia has over two hundred million people? Plenty of families share our surname. It's hardly as though the Tanuwijaya name will end with me. Plus, it's not even our real family name." When my grandparents immigrated to Indonesia eons ago, they changed their Chinese family names to Indonesian ones to better integrate with the local population. "Remember? Our real surname is Lin, and there are probably about a gazillion people on the planet with the same surname, so. Crisis averted."

They ignore me and continue speaking among themselves. Then they sit back and Eighth Aunt says, "George."

"Eighth Aunt."

"We all agree that you are . . . mm, how shall we say it?"

"Is it loser?" Papa whispers in English. Or at least he thinks he's whispering. People all the way in the next villa can probably hear his "whispers."

"Thanks, Pa."

"I say with love, son," he says.

"I really don't think you can call your kid a loser with love."

He frowns. "Of course I can. I love you, so everything I say come out with much love."

"Just." I pinch the bridge of my nose. "Carry on, Eighth Aunt. So, you all agree I'm hopeless."

"Well, you see, the thing is, George, our publicity team has done such a great job all these years of painting this amazing picture of you. Turning you into one of the region's most sought-after boys. You know how hard that was to achieve? There's a lot more that goes into it than just being good-looking, George," Eighth Aunt says. "The public expects a certain image from you. Strong, assertive, manly."

"An image of toxic masculinity," I say.

"No, no. We're modern. We don't want you to be aggressive or to treat women badly, of course."

"Right, of course."

"But you also can't show weaknesses. You see what I'm talking about?" Eighth Aunt says, leaning closer to me. Then she grimaces and leans back. "Ugh, your morning breath is awful."

I cover my mouth, feeling even more self-conscious than before. "Sorry. Um, right. I have to be strong but pliant, assertive but accommodating, manly but vulnerable. Gotcha."

"Exactly!" Eighth Aunt cries, choosing to completely ignore the sarcasm in my voice. "See? I knew our little George Clooney would get it."

"Yeah, I mean, I've got the perfect speech all lined up for the event. You don't have to worry—"

"No, George," Eighth Aunt says. "We're not talking about the event, although of course that's also very important. But see, the thing is, publicity about you and Sharlot has sort of, ah . . . blown up."

"You're trending," Eleanor says.

Eighth Aunt nods, digging her phone from her handbag. She opens up ShareIt before handing me the phone.

I have to lean back a little to be able to focus on the screen, and when I do, my heart skips a beat. Eleanor's right. #GeorgeIsTaken is indeed trending in Indonesia. I don't even know how I feel about that. A bit nauseated. I chew my lip, reminding myself that this will pass within a few hours. Trends on ShareIt never last long.

"We're going to have to make sure this lasts as long as possible," Eighth Aunt says.

"What? Why?" Stupid question. The moment the words flop out of my mouth I know the answer: because of OneLiner. Because of our company. Because, of course, everything we do is about boosting the company's image and therefore the company's profits.

"It's increasing awareness about OneLiner," Papa says. "George, I have taught you about brand awareness for years, come on, son, keep up."

"Right, of course. Sorry, I just haven't had my coffee. But look, Eighth Aunt, if it's publicity you want, I have so many more ideas for OneLiner that I know would increase its visibility, and—"

Eighth Aunt puts a hand up. "No, George. You have some good ideas, yes, but publicity like this can't be bought. It happens organically. It's a marketing dream come true!"

"So, um, what does this mean, exactly?"

"It means that we've given a carefully vetted journalist permission to shadow you and Sharlot for the whole of today," Eighth Aunt says. "She and her crew will be filming you on your day adventuring around the island."

"Make the footage good, Ming Fa," Nainai says. "Don't make us lose face."

"Wait, I don't—" My head is spinning. "You can't have reporters following me and Sharlot around. That'll ruin everything. It'll be so awkward!"

"Nonsense," Nainai tuts. "I was only sixteen when I married your yeye, and I knew how to put on a good front for the reporters. You kids nowadays grow up with cameras all around you. You take photos and videos of yourselves and post them everywhere for everyone to see! What's one more camera?"

"It's different, Nainai. Plus, this is such an intrusion on Sharlot. We can't make decisions that affect her without asking her first."

"We did," Eighth Aunt says, "she's agreed to it. On the condition that her cousin Kiki comes along for moral support."

"But no worries, gege," Eleanor says, "because I'll come along too!"

"Oh god." I rub my temples again. "So I'm going to have a romantic day with Sharlot . . . along with reporters, Kiki, and my little sister."

"Yes," Eighth Aunt says with a smile.

"And none of you sees anything wrong with that?" I say.

They look blankly at me. "When I was courting your mother," Papa says after a beat, "we always went in a group with our friends or relatives. It's how it's done in our culture. How else would we show that you're not doing anything *bu san bu si?*"

Bu san bu si literally translates to "neither three nor four."

It's Mandarin for "up to no good." Indonesia's a pretty conservative country when measured up against Western standards, but the Chinese-Indonesian community is even more conservative. It's not even about religion; it's a really weird thing where I feel like a large part of the Chinese-Indonesian culture is based around olden-day Chinese customs that most people in China have moved on from, but we never got the memo because we left China. Dating is very much one of these things. We don't do arranged marriages anymore, but we've got something worse: chaperones.

While Chinese people in China *and* Native Indonesians in Indonesia date as per Western standards now, we Chinese-Indonesians are still stuck with chaperones. You will often hear of two consenting adults going on "dates" accompanied by various family members—aunts, uncles, cousins, siblings, parents, etc. The chaperones will judge the date and often, if they don't approve (i.e., if the other party isn't as rich as they'd hoped), the couple's parents are told and the couple will be pressured to split up. If they don't, the families pull all sorts of telenovela-worthy stunts to convince them. The stunts vary from "You will bring shame and make us all lose face!" to "I will literally DIE if you don't do as I say. LITERALLY."

"Yes, we need to show everyone that you are a proper gentleman, courting Sharlot in a proper manner," Eighth Aunt says. "Let's go over the rules: Hold her hand whenever you can, but do not touch her anywhere else, you hear me?"

"Oh my god," I mutter.

"Kissing: forehead and cheek only. No mouths. And definitely no tongue. And nowhere else on the body, obviously."

"Please stop."

She goes on for a while, giving me an entire list of rules. Although I'm already aware of all these rules, hearing her list them aloud is overwhelming. By the time she's done, I feel ready to burrow back into bed and sleep away the whole day.

"One last thing, George," she says.

"There's more?" I groan.

"You need to make Sharlot fall in love with you."

I stop grimacing and stare at her. Everything else she's said up to this point has been bad enough. But this feels like crossing a line.

"These reporters, they're seasoned experts. If they see that Shi Jun is about to dump you, imagine how terrible that would look," Nainai says. "Aiya, my only grandson getting dumped! Why anyone would want to do that is beyond me. You are perfect."

My heart hammers so hard I feel it pounding in my head. "This feels really wrong. Sharlot is a person, for god's sake, not a trophy—"

"You're a good kid, George," Eighth Aunt says. "I know the circumstances behind your meeting aren't great . . ." She narrows her eyes at Papa, who shrinks back guiltily. "But that doesn't matter as much. Focus on the here and now. Treat her well, be kind to her, and trust that she'll like you for who you are."

"Oh, Ming Fa, she'll love you," Nainai says, reaching over with a wobbly hand and pinching my cheek. "How can she not?

Look at my little George Clooney. You look exactly like him, you know. But more handsome because you're Chinese."

I pretend not to hear Eleanor's snort. I excuse myself to go to the bathroom. Inside, I stare at the mirror for a long time, wondering what the hell I'm going to do.

CHAPTER 17

Sharlot

The day starts off way too early for civility, but of course, Kiki's already dressed in an extremely Instagrammable outfit. Or maybe I should say a ShareIt-able outfit, since we are in Indonesia after all. Locally sourced cream-colored cotton pants that show off the curve of her butt, check. Pristine white shirt knotted round the waist that shows off her flat belly, check. Floppy sunhat, check. Fierce sunglasses, check.

"Come on, get your arse out of bed or we're going to be late."

I blink blearily at the bright sunlight streaming in through our floor-to-ceiling window and groan. After being told by Fauzi last night that we're going to have Rina following us around today, I'd stayed up way too late last night drawing on my trusty tablet to help calm myself down at the thought of today's "date" with George. The last thing I want to do is spend the day with my fake boyfriend while being tailed by a reporter, but I suppose I don't really have a choice.

While I brush my teeth, Kiki patters back and forth from the room to the bathroom and then tells me she's laid out an outfit for me in the walk-in closet.

This morning, Kiki has chosen to dress me in a mauve sundress with a yellow-parrot print. It's an off-shoulder piece that ends just above my knees and makes me look sweet and ultra-feminine.

"Wow," I mumble, dragging a brush through the tangled mess atop my head that calls itself hair. "I never would've picked this dress, but it actually works."

"I know, I'm talented like that," Kiki says. "Here, I've made you some decaf."

"Decaf?" I groan, taking a sip of the tepid espresso anyway.

"Bali has got some of the best coffee Indonesia has to offer. We're not going to amp ourselves up on shitty coffee. We have to make a pit stop at a proper café, hence the decaf for now."

God, she's really thought of everything.

"Stop whatever you think you're doing," Kiki orders. She plucks the hair brush out of my hands, spritzes something that smells of oranges into my hair, and runs her fingers through the mess. Somehow, she manages to finger-comb my hair into a manageable tousle before pulling it into an intricate side braid. Then she slaps some BB cream onto my face, dabs some lip stain on my mouth and cheeks, and when I next look in the mirror at the two of us, side by side, it's near impossible to look away. We look like we've just walked out of a photo shoot.

"I hate to say it, but you really are talented."

Kiki smirks, and we make our way out of the bedroom and

into the shared living room. Immediately my chest tightens at the anticipation of seeing Mama again after our barbed words yesterday. But the living room's empty.

"I think she's still sleeping," Kiki says, reading my mind. "I heard her come back pretty late last night."

I nod without saying a word, still feeling the guilt lancing through my stomach. Why can't Mama and I, for once, just have a conversation where neither one of us is trying to hurt the other? And hold up, she came back late last night? The thought of her dating George's dad once again worms through my gut. Surely not. That would just be way too weird for the both of us, right? Right. Still, I resolve to have a talk with Mama as soon as I come back this evening.

Once we get outside of the villa, the vise around my chest loosens. This early in the day, the air is damn near magical: cool and fragrant with jungle dew and ocean salt. I close my eyes and breathe in deep. I swear I can practically feel it cleansing my lungs.

"You know," Kiki says, falling into step beside me, "your mum's a lot cooler than you think she is."

"You don't know my mom." I bite my lip. I hadn't meant it to come out quite so acidic.

Kiki shrugs. "I know, but it's just—she's so much better than my mum." She scoffs a little, and I glance at her from the corner of my eye. It's the first time I notice a shade of vulnerability on her flawless features.

"Your mom's pretty strict, huh?"

"It's not about her being strict," Kiki says with a sigh. "She's such a social climber. Like, she was so insistent on having me come on this trip with you, not because she gives a shit about you or your mum—no offense—but because she wants me to hang out with the konglo, you know?"

"What's konglo?"

"It's short for konglomerat." She pronounces it kong-lo-*mer*-rut.

"You mean conglomerate?"

Kiki's mouth twitches into a small smile. "Yeah. We Indos like to bastardize English words. Anyway, *konglo* is what we call the uber wealthy here—families that own multinational corporations and so on. Basically, your boyfriend and his lot."

"George is not my boyfriend," I say instinctively.

"Seriously, dude, get used to referring to him as your boyfriend. The entire country thinks you're his girlfriend, might as well ride this wave. You know how many people would kill to be in your position right now? Like my mum, for example, would definitely throw you under a literal bus if she thought that meant that I would get to be George's girlfriend. Again, no offense."

"You do realize that saying 'no offense' doesn't mean you then get to say offensive things?" Still, I can't help but smile at Kiki. She's reminding me of Michie in the best possible way—all honesty, no bullshit. "And you are free to take my place as George's fake girlfriend."

Kiki tilts her head and gives me a knowing sideways look that makes me want to pinch her really hard. "Anyway, I'm just saying, all in all, your mum could be worse."

I purse my lips, hating that she's right. Luckily, Kiki soon loses interest in the subject and starts talking about something else—her jet skiing adventures with Eleanor yesterday evening and how she wishes she had a younger sister just like Eleanor, and did I know that Eleanor's name is actually Eleanor Roosevelt?

When we get to the hotel lobby, I gulp at the sight of Rina and her camera guy. "God, here goes," I mutter.

"Get used to it, Meghan Markle." All sympathy, this one. "And stop fussing with your hair. You're going to ruin the braid."

I hurriedly swing my hands down to my side.

"Dude, don't march either. What is wrong with you?" Kiki hisses. "Walk like a normal human girl."

Somehow, I manage to tell my legs to keep moving instead of melting into a puddle.

"Morning," George says, walking over to meet us halfway. I hate to say it, but he looks banging. Button-down shirt that shows off his broad shoulders and biceps and khaki shorts that show off his calves. I never thought I was a calf girl, but here I am ogling his calves like some weird calf-obsessed person. Wow, how many times can a person think the word *calves* in the space of two seconds? I swallow and wave back, reminding myself to smile. I think I manage to smile instead of stretching my mouth into a rictus grin. I pretend not to notice that the huge camera is pointing right at my face.

Then he's right in front of me and he's leaning in for a— a kiss? A hug? My mind short-circuits, because apparently I, Sharlot Citra, do not know how to human. As he puts his face toward mine, I turn my head and turn what was supposed to be a chaste cheek-to-cheek kiss into me kissing him on his cheek. *Aaah.*

George springs back, his cheeks practically neon red. I swear I can practically see my lips branded on his cheek. Quickly, I take my thumb and try to wipe the lipstick off his cheek, but I only smear it.

"It's fine," George says with a sheepish smile, his cheeks still burning red.

It was just a peck on the cheek, I want to scream at the universe. I've French-kissed a heck of a lot of guys—okay, not a lot, but a very respectable handful—and somehow, this feels like a much bigger deal. The cameraman seems to think so too; he's adjusting the lens to zoom right at our faces. I turn away, but not before catching the look on Rina's face. It says: Ooh, stupid cameraman better have gotten *that*!

Okay, it probably doesn't say that, I'm not an expert at figuring out what faces are saying, but Rina looks pleased. Like the cat that caught the mouse or squirrel or whatever it is that cats like to catch.

"Hi, future sis-in-law!" Eleanor says, bounding over and giving me a huge hug. She's got her hair in two buns and is wearing a bright-yellow top and a short denim skirt and she looks like the human version of sunshine.

"Uh, er." I have no idea what to say or do, aside from awkwardly patting her on the shoulder.

"Eleanor," George hisses through gritted teeth.

"What? You should be so lucky, gege," Eleanor says.

"I mean, I don't disagree that he'd be lucky." The words slither out before I can stop them, and for a split second, I stare at them, horrified at what I just said.

Then George grins the same time as Eleanor laughs, and I breathe a sigh of relief. Okay, luckily they didn't take that badly, but come on, mouth. Don't do me like that.

Eleanor goes over to Kiki and says, "Ci Kiki! You look ah-mazing. You know, I wish instead of gege I could have you as an older sibling."

"Oh, sweetie. You have no idea how much I wish I had you as a younger sister." Kiki slings her arm around Eleanor's thin shoulders and they start walking toward the entrance, where another ginormous Alphard awaits.

"Shall we?" George says, holding out his hand.

I gulp, and I honestly can't tell if I'm nervous because of the fake dating or the cameras. Then I catch his small smile, the expectant look in his eyes, and I realize that he's just as nervous as I am. The realization warms me and I exhale as I put my hand in his, noting with some surprise that his hand is significantly bigger than mine.

"Let's go," I say with a lot more confidence than I feel.

Of course, the first stop we make, as predicted by Kiki, is a café. I like cafés just as much as the next person, but in Indonesia, I'm finding that coffee isn't so much a pastime as its own religion. The Alphard drops us off in front of a place called Sejuk Coffee Studio, which on the outside looks like a small, slightly rundown building. But once we walk inside, I go, "Whoa."

The place is one of those magical buildings where the inside is a lot bigger than the outside looks. Inside, Sejuk Coffee Studio is a completely modern-looking space that reminds me more of a swanky art gallery in LA than a café. I'm realizing that a lot of places in Indonesia are like this: unassuming and sad-looking on the outside, disarmingly stunning on the inside.

"Good choice," Kiki says to George. "I've been wanting to check out this place since they started working together with 5758 Coffee Lab."

"Same."

"Excuse me, not to be rude, but why are we here?" Eleanor says. "Coffee is so overrated."

"They also have chocolate drinks," George says, smiling down at his little sister. "They roast their own cocoa beans too."

Eleanor grunts, mollified but not entirely happy.

"And we're here not just for breakfast and coffee, but to have a quick lesson in how to do latte art," he says, turning to me too.

Eleanor's mouth drops open. "Ooh! Can we learn to make those foam teddy bears and stuff?"

George looks up at the barista who's come out from behind the counter to greet us. "Yes, of course," the barista says. "Hi, guys, my name's Lukmi. It's great to finally meet all of you. Come round here, I've got everything ready for you."

Lukmi leads us through the beautiful café and to the bar, where as promised, there are various cups and pourers laid out in anticipation for our lesson. I'm not normally passionate about coffee, but it's impossible to not get carried away by the whole vibe of the place. It's so obvious how much pride they take in it. Lukmi tells us about how throughout history, coffee has become yet another colonized commodity, and how at one point, it got so bad that those who grew the beans couldn't afford to drink the fruits of their labor.

"The problem with the huge, multinational coffee companies," Lukmi says, "is that they buy their beans from everywhere—Indonesia, Colombia, Brazil and so on. And then they mixed them up, so you couldn't even tell which is what coffee." He says *mixed* like it's a bad word, which I guess in this case it is. "They'd import the beans to their processing plants, and then export them back to Indonesia and sell it to us at a hundred times the original price. It took a lot of time, effort, and policy change to make sure Indonesian farmers are protected. Actually, George, your family's company was one of the ones that pushed hard for changes to be made to the industry."

George nods. "Yeah, my dad was the one who spearheaded that project."

His smile is so full of pride that I find myself smiling slightly myself. It's next to impossible not to.

"He's a real fan of independent coffee shops like this one," George says to me. "I got my love of coffee from him." His smile wanes a little. "My dad said he got it from my mom, who was obsessed with coffee. Her favorite was Toraja coffee."

"Ah, she had good taste then, your mother," Lukmi says. "Toraja is naturally sweet and spicy. We buy ours straight from Sulawesi and process the beans ourselves."

I had no idea how fraught the coffee industry is. Listening to Lukmi talk about their heritage—my heritage—I'm torn between pride and shame. Pride that I am connected by blood to this rich, complex culture that has so passionately fought for the rights of its people. Shame because I'd been so ignorant. How many times have I gone to Starbucks and ordered a tall latte without considering the effects the corporate giant has on farmers all over the world? Who knew I would learn so much about Indonesia through coffee?

"We only brew local coffees here," Lukmi says, "and trust me when I say Indonesia's got the best coffee in the world. We swept the awards at the 2019 Agence pour la Valorisation des Produits Agricoles in France."

"That's amazing," I say, and realize that I do mean it. I truly am amazed. I recall the coffee I'd had in Kopi-Kopi and how rich in flavor it had been compared with my usual latte.

Smiling, Lukmi starts the coffee grinder and makes us each a kopi susu with Toraja beans—a plain coffee with milk sourced from a local dairy farm. I take a cautious sip, unsure what to expect—usually I load my lattes with sugar—and oh . . . wow. This drink.

"My god," I whisper to Kiki, who's taking a deep inhale of hers like she's trying to infuse her lungs with the rich, deep fragrance.

"I know," she says. She takes a sip and closes her eyes, savoring the taste.

I'm no coffee connoisseur, but even I recognize how complex this coffee is. It doesn't need any sugar. It would be a shame to cover up this incredible taste with any sweetener. In fact, the thought of anyone adding anything else to this cup of coffee annoys me, and I realize now why people get so heated up about their coffee.

    With a start, I realize George is watching me. "Do you like it?" he says.

    "Yeah. It's amazing. Your mom had good taste."

    He gives me a smile that's so bright and unabashed that I feel my cheeks warming. "She really did," he says, then leans in and lowers his voice, "but she would put sugar in her coffee, so I don't know that Lukmi would approve."

    I laugh and George puts a finger to his lips like this tiny little tidbit about his mother is our secret.

    Now that we've had our caffeine shot, Lukmi starts the latte art class. He talks to us about correctly steaming the milk to get the perfect texture and taste, then gives us each a pourer full of steamed, foamy milk and tells us to follow him. We watch as he pours milk into a waiting cup of coffee, jiggling the pourer with expert ease until he forms a graceful swan on the latte.

    "Now, you try it," he says.

    I do as he says, trying to remember everything he's instructed, pouring as carefully as I can. I step back and admire my handiwork.

    "Not bad," George murmurs, looking over at my cup. "I've always wanted a blob fish on my latte."

    I glare at him. "Let's see yours then."

    George takes a dramatically slow breath and starts pouring. He wiggles his hand as naturally as though he's done this a dozen times before and manages to make semi-decent circles on his coffee. The circles are misshapen of course, but at least they're not a shapeless glop like mine is.

Kiki and Eleanor have gotten spoons and are totally cheating by spooning the foam onto their cups instead of pouring them in. Kiki is making—oh god, of course she's making boobs. And Eleanor is trying to make a snowman. Or a foam man, I guess.

"Kiki," I hiss, "stop making boobs! We're being filmed."

She looks at me innocently. "Excuse you, this is a teddy bear. Can I help it if that's where your perverted mind goes?"

"Oh." I frown down at her cup. "Sorry, I didn't realize—"

"Nah, I'm just kidding, they're totally boobs."

George bursts out laughing, and though I try my best to stop myself, I can't help but cackle as well. Lukmi just rolls his eyes at the camera, like he's seen this about a hundred times.

"C'mere, you two," Lukmi says to George and me. "Latte art can be fun"—he gives a wry nod toward Kiki and Eleanor, who are now sporting milk-foam mustaches—"but it can also be romantic." He winks at us.

"Oh, er . . ." Whatever I'm about to say, I manage to swallow it down. I'm supposed to be George's girlfriend. I should be excited at the thought of doing a romantic activity with him.

"Right," Lukmi says. "Sharlot, you hold this." He hands me a milk pourer filled with foamed milk. "And now, George, you hold her hand—uh-oh, what's going on?" he says as George touches my hand gingerly and I fumble and nearly let the pourer fall.

"Sorry," George mumbles.

"It's okay, really." I give him a small smile. He puts his hand over mine, engulfing it with his warm, firm grip. My heart skips a beat. Despite everything about our situation, my traitorous hormones won't stop reminding me that there's a very good-looking guy holding my hand.

"Now, pour together and I'll read your milk foam."

"Sorry, read our milk foam?" I say.

"You know, like reading tea leaves?" Lukmi grins. "It's just for fun, but people have said my milk-foam readings are very accurate."

I turn to George to give him a can-you-believe-this-guy look, but find him standing so close to me that I immediately change my mind and turn away, my whole face flaming. The nearness of him is overwhelming.

Together, we guide the little pot over the big cup of coffee that Lukmi has prepared for us. The cameraman guides his lens to zoom in on our hands. George is so close behind me that I can sense the warmth radiating from him, and as he moves, I feel his chest—his pecs, oh my god—lightly bumping the back of my shoulders. I valiantly try to focus on the latte. Our hands move together and we start pouring the foamed milk into the cup. I'm not sure who's leading whom. George's hand is gentle over mine, and we pour with a lot more confidence than I'm feeling.

A whole bunch of concentric circles appear. Excitement unfurls inside me. We're doing it. I'm getting the hang of the wobbling movement needed to make the circles, and when the latte reaches the brim of the cup, George gives my hand a small tug and I let him lead the pourer down the middle of the circles. It's only when we lift the pourer that I realize he's turned the circles into a heart. He grins down at me, and my breath catches for a second.

"We did well," he says in a voice so low it's clear the words are only meant for me. His mouth is close to my forehead and I feel his whisper caress my skin, sending an electric current down my entire length. Seriously, please stop messing with me, hormones. I look away quickly and blink at the cameraman, who's trained his lens at our faces. I wonder how we must look, how guilty *I* must look. I don't even know why I'm feeling guilty.

We all watch Lukmi as he peers closely at our cup and walks around the table, inspecting it from all angles. He's a total showman, completely at ease with the camera and our attention. He straightens up and says, solemnly, "Mm. You two are a strong couple."

Kiki whistles and Eleanor giggles. With flames licking my cheeks, I don't even dare look up at anyone, least of all George.

"See, these lines tell me that you two have very strong feelings for each other. Ah, I remember what it was like to be a teen and be in love."

I swallow the urge to correct him and tell him we are most definitely not in love.

Lukmi peers at the cup again. "But this line says your relationship is very new."

My heart thumps wildly, my stomach twisting and turning like a wet shirt being wrung dry. I can't believe our lie is being called out by a freaking latte-art reading.

"Probably because they've been dating long-distance and have only just started seeing each other in person," Kiki pipes up.

I shoot her a grateful look.

"Oh yeah, that'll explain it," he says. "This shows mutual respect, a deepening friendship, and . . . oooh." He grins straight into the camera. "A strong physical attraction."

Everyone whistles and hoots. George turns lipstick red. I'm pretty sure my whole face is on fire. Because, goddammit, despite the fact that I don't believe in any of this woo-woo BS, there is definitely a "strong physical attraction" on my part. And I feel very, very exposed.

Lukmi laughs at our obvious embarrassment and says, "I'm just messing with you. Come on, latte-art class is done. Let's have some breakfast, ya?"

He leads us to a table where we're served more cups of coffee as well as nasi bakar—fragrant rice stuffed with roast pork and wrapped in banana leaves before being grilled. The nasi bakar is topped with sambal matah, which is Balinese chili made of shallots, lemongrass, and chilies, chopped and soaked in coconut oil. The grilled rice is delicious, but the sambal matah is to die for. When I run out of nasi bakar, I end up eating the sambal matah with a spoon.

"You might want to be careful with that," George says.

"I know I'm half bule, but I can handle spice."

"I know, but remember last night's conversation with my cousins?"

For a second, I stare at him uncomprehendingly. Then I recall his cousins asking me if I've been poisoned yet. "Ah," I say with a nod. "Gotcha."

"Here, you should probably take a charcoal pill, just to be safe." He hands me a tube of activated charcoal pills called Norit.

"Thanks." I wonder if he brought this tube of charcoal pills just for me. The thought is a surprisingly nice one and I find myself smiling at George as we walk out of the café and into the Alphard.

"Next up on the itinerary: white water rafting at the Ayung River!" Eleanor crows. "I can't wait. Have you ever gone rafting before, sis-in-law? I've been twice, and both times were *so* fun. Don't worry, I'll help you if you don't know how to do it."

George gives me a look, then leans over and mutters, "Shouldn't have given her any coffee."

I bite back my grin. It's impossible not to love George's bouncy little sister. "Actually, yeah, I've been once, in LA. But we went at the wrong time—there had been a drought, so the water level was really low and there was no current. In fact, we ended up having to paddle downriver because the wind kept blowing us upriver."

Kiki laughs. "Okay, that is definitely not going to be an issue at Ayung."

She's right. When we get to the rafting place and I see the river in person, I'm filled with uncertainty. It looks . . . really fucking fast. I look back at everyone else and notice with some relief that Rina is also looking uncertain. She's saying something to the cameraman, who's also looking worried.

". . . gear get wet," he's saying.

Ah, of course. It makes sense that he'd be worried about his camera getting drenched.

"No worries," the rafting shop owner calls out. "Leave your gear here. We've got just the thing for the occasion." He comes around from behind the counter carrying a large box.

A camera drone. Great. Just what I need—a high-def cam to catch every single terrified expression on my face.

CHAPTER 18

George

The problem with white water rafting is that it seems a lot more fun than it actually is. Like, I'd see photos and videos of my friends on social media rafting down the Ayung River, accompanied by dramatic splashes of water, and I'd think, Huh, that looks like fun. And then I'd remember that I did it once or twice before, when I was about Eleanor's age, and I'd remember the adrenaline rush and how it had indeed been fun.

But what I completely failed to remember is also the un-fun parts—how crazy wet it is, and how the water often splashes right into your face and up your nose and blinds you, and also how terrifying the whole thing can be. Of course, with the camera drone flying over us, I have to make my best efforts to appear to be having fun. I can just hear Eighth Aunt and Papa discussing how the family company shares plummeted after a video of me shrieking in terror down the Ayung River went viral.

Our guide, Sita, is in her mid-twenties. Her muscled arms are covered with intricate traditional Balinese tattoos and she speaks with the authority that comes with the knowledge that she's the best person for the job. After giving us a short lecture on safety regulations—keep our life jackets and helmets on at all times, don't freaking stand up and so on and so forth—she helps us into the raft.

Here's the other thing I've forgotten about white water rafting: It's really hard keeping your balance on the rubber raft. It wobbles from side to side and every move you make on it makes this horribly loud, screeching rubber sound. I have never felt as large and lumbering as I do on a raft. Of course, Eleanor, trained by years of gymnastics, practically cartwheels into the raft, stepping lightly and easily and taking her seat in the middle. Kiki struts in as though she were walking the runway, followed by Sharlot, who for the record is looking as uncertain as I feel. Sharlot navigates her way onto the raft with far less grace than the other two, which makes me feel a bit better. Thank god we're both equally clumsy and uncoordinated. Without thinking, I hold out my hand to her. She takes it, and then the next second, the raft wobbles and she crashes into my arms. I smell her shampoo first, the scent of it filling my senses, and the next moment my mind reminds me that I'm holding a very attractive girl in my arms. Well, this is awkward. Somehow, my hands are around her waist. As soon as I realize this, I whip them away and help her up before sitting down on the side of the raft. Neither of us can look at each other, though I am painfully aware of the way that Eleanor and Kiki are leering at us.

Rina and the camera guy get on as well; he's got a smaller camera that's been wrapped up in a waterproof bag, because of course. With everyone on board, we're off.

The Ayung River is the longest river in Bali and runs almost seventy kilometers. It flows down the northern mountain ranges, passing by the farmlands of Gianyar before hitting Denpasar, which is where we start. The Ayung River has class II and class III rapids, which in terms of rafting difficulty means it's got some tricky parts but isn't considered dangerous.

Of course, "isn't considered dangerous" doesn't mean crap as soon as we hit the first rocky conditions and the waves crest white. Our raft swerves here and there, guided with expert ease by Sita, and we all scream as we go over a drop-off.

"HOLY SHIT!" Kiki shrieks. "That was a fucking waterfall! We just went over a waterfall!"

Up to this point, I had been clutching my paddle like a—ha!—life raft—but the drop-off undid something inside me, and suddenly, I remember why I loved rafting. Because it feels like flying. I glance over to my side and meet Sharlot's eyes.

Her entire face is shining. She's grinning so wide, her eyes bright and filled with life. I'm pretty sure I'm wearing the same expression, that realization that I love this thing I thought I would absolutely hate. Our bodies shift, and the way we grip our paddles changes. Before, it had been a thing we'd clutched out of fear. Now, it's something we wield as we slice our way through the water. Behind us, Kiki and Eleanor are continuously shrieking—I think they're doing it just to annoy Rina and the cameraman, who aren't looking at all impressed.

Sharlot and I plunge our paddles into the water with a whoop. The raft flies and bounces and careens over the river, my heart racing. Water splashes all over me and I cry out with joy. This is what being alive feels like. I've forgotten what it's like to be so present—to not be thinking about the future or ruminating about the past—there's just me and the Ayung River and Sharlot next to me, and I am one hundred percent here. I thought playing *Warfront Heroes* made me feel alive, but it all pales in comparison with this heart-thumping, stomach-kicking wild ride. I never want it to end.

Next to me, Sharlot glances over and grins right before a huge wave of water drenches us both. She laughs unabashedly, and I feel as though I'm finally seeing the real her—so different from the girl Papa and Eleanor chatted with on ShareIt. It's almost impossible to reconcile the Sharlot in person and the Sharlot online.

The rocky part of the river is followed by a stretch of relatively calm water. "You guys can relax for a bit," Sita says. "I'll let you know when things are about to get exciting again." We all sigh happily and sit back, paddling at a slower pace. The raft floats along the river and I half listen to the chatter among Kiki, Eleanor, and Rina, who seem to have become friends. They're arguing over whether Millie Bobby Brown was better in *Stranger Things* or *Enola Holmes*. One thing they can all agree on: MBB is amazing in general and needs to be in more things. I nod to myself, thinking of how good both shows were, though *Enola Holmes* was a bit too painful for me to enjoy because of the way the mother had just abandoned Enola. I didn't care how big her reason was, I had been so upset by her leaving that I spent most of the show with my stomach puckering up and twisting here and there. I'd kept glancing over at Eleanor to make sure she was okay, that Enola's mother's disappearance wasn't triggering any dire emotions inside her, but Eleanor's made of sturdier stuff than I am. She just kept cramming caramel popcorn into her mouth while going, "Duh, not the real chrysanthemums, Enola, the ones your mom painted!"

"You okay?" Sharlot says, snapping me out of my *Enola Holmes* reverie.

"Oh yeah." I glance over at her. She's completely soaking wet, her braid hanging heavily down her back. Her cheeks are flushed with color and she's smiling a smile so unguarded it makes my heart stutter. I quickly look away, pretending to focus on paddling. "Are you okay?" I say, more to the paddle than to Sharlot.

Sharlot laughs. "Yes. This is amazingly fun! After my first time, I just assumed that white water rafting would be super boring, so I never bothered going again. I didn't think it could be like this."

I never thought it could be like this either, I want to say. In a K-drama, this is totally what the guy would say, while looking deep into the heroine's eyes so she understands that he's not, in fact, talking about rafting. But this is not a K-drama and I definitely can't pull off such dramatic statements. Eleanor is likely to overhear and make gagging noises. Plus, that's going a bit far. I don't know Sharlot that well.

"It gets even wilder during the rainy season," I say instead. "Then the difficulty rating goes up from Class II to, like, Class IV."

"Wow. That sounds hard-core." Her grin widens. "But it also sounds *fun*."

Again, this strange incongruity between in-person Sharlot

and online Sharlot. I can't help blurting out: "You're so different from your online messages."

Belatedly, I recall that saying this always seems to sour things between us, so I hurriedly add, "I mean in a really great way. Like, everything about you has been a surprise in the best possible way."

The corners of her mouth lift slightly. "I guess I could say the same about you."

"Really?" I'm surprised by that, especially given how eager and happy she was in her chat messages. She called me "perfect," even. But somehow, in-person me is better than perfect. Muaha-ha-ha!

She shrugs, leaning over and lowering her voice. We're close enough for me to see tiny water droplets on her eyelashes, and I have to resist the urge to touch her face. "Yeah, I do. I prefer this version of you."

My god. I have no idea what to say to that, so I say the most unsexy, Papa-like thing ever: "You must be thirsty. Do you want some water?" Clearly I deserve to be put down.

Sharlot laughs. "Nah, dude. You know how much river water I've swallowed? I forgot to close my mouth in between screams."

"Me too. Except in my case it wasn't screams but, like, manly shouts. More like roars, really."

"Oh yeah, totally. I definitely did not notice you shrieking like a toddler."

"Whaaat? Me? Never." We grin at each other.

Then Sharlot spots something in the distance and her eyes widen. She clutches at my arm and I look to where she's pointing, half wondering if we're about to go over an actual waterfall. Instead, what I see is a small boy at the riverbank, squatting with his back to the river and his bare bottom over the water.

He's literally shitting into the water. The water that's being splashed all over us. The water that we just admitted to drinking loads of.

Sharlot and I meet each other's eyes and we completely lose it. We double over, laughing madly, and though Kiki and Eleanor keep shouting, "What? What's so funny?" neither Sharlot nor I can draw in enough breath to tell them.

CHAPTER 19

Sharlot

By the time we get to the end of the rafting course, two hours have passed and we're all exhausted, our teeth chattering from being drenched over and over again. Even in the tropical heat, the river water, flowing fresh from the northern mountains, is surprisingly cold. Back on dry land, we're met by an assistant who's somehow procured our belongings and dry clothes. I grab one of the fluffy towels they provide us, my sundress, and go inside the women's bathroom, where there are showers to rinse off in. Toweling myself dry is simply heaven, and then Kiki and I spend some time brushing the tangles out of Eleanor's hair.

Eleanor stares at us in the mirror with her wise-little-girl smirk as we fuss over her thick, long hair. "I love both of you so much," she declares. "You're the older sisters I always wished for. I mean, no offense to George, but boys are just so clueless. I'm a sophisticated creature; I need more than my bumbling older brother and father to help guide me into becoming a lady."

I bite back my smile, feeling slightly sorry for George. He's so outmatched by Eleanor. Hell, I'm outmatched by Eleanor. Then

I realize what Eleanor meant. I recall that her mom had passed away years ago, and that this wonderful girl only has her dad and older brother with her. I wrap my arms around her tiny frame and give her a tight hug.

"You're wonderful, Eleanor."

"I know," she says simply, and Kiki and I laugh. "Although now that you're both practically family, you should call me by my real name: Eleanor Roosevelt."

"It's a good name."

"Yeah. I like it. Gives me something to strive for. Though if you asked me, there are much better role models my parents could've gone for. Like Ching Shih, the lady pirate who amassed more ships that Davy Jones. I would've liked being named after a pirate."

I snort at the thought. "You would've made the best pirate. You would've been a scourge of the seas."

Eleanor nods solemnly, side-eyeing me through the mirror. "What?"

"There's something bothering me, sis-in-law."

I don't bother correcting her. "Hmm?"

"How is your personality so different in real life from your ShareIt personality?"

My fingers freeze in her hair, and I glance up and meet Kiki's eyes. They widen for a second. A warning: Step carefully.

"Oh, um. Well, that's actually very common. People are rarely what they seem online. Something to watch out for when you're old enough to talk to people online. You're not doing that yet, are you?"

"Don't change the subject, sis-in-law."

Damn it, this kid is way too smart.

"See," Eleanor says, "I know that people are different online, but most of the time the difference is, like, based on looks. Like, they edit their photos to make themselves look cuter or whatever. Or they sound really bubbly and outgoing online, but in real life they're a lot shyer. But with you, it's the other way around. Online you're kind of uppity, and in real life you're . . ." She gestures at me.

Kiki and I stare wordlessly at Eleanor. I can't believe that after all this, my cover's getting blown by a thirteen-year-old savant. "Eleanor—"

"It's okay," she says. "I like this version of you much better. And you don't have to explain yourself to me. I'm just saying, I'm glad you know that people aren't always honest online."

Huh.

I meet Kiki's eyes again and both of us give each other a tiny shrug, like what the hell was that about? She's glad I know that people aren't always honest online? Is Eleanor trying to tell me something?

"Eleanor—" I begin.

"I'm starving," she moans, clutching her stomach. "Let's go have lunch. My hair is sufficiently gorgeous."

"Uh. Okay," I say.

Eleanor skips out of the changing room and into the blinding sunlight, leaving me and Kiki behind to exchange curious glances.

When I walk outside of the changing room, I nearly bump

into Rina, who's standing right outside the door with a calculating expression on her face. My heart rate thunders into a gallop again. Shit, did she hear what Eleanor said? But Rina is busy tapping on her phone and barely glances up at me. Maybe she didn't hear it after all. One can hope.

The next stop is lunch. This time, we go to a place called Bebek Tepi Sawah, which translates to "ducks at a rice field." The restaurant is literally in the middle of a rice field, and it is one of the most beautiful places I've been to. The place consists of open-air villas with traditional thatched roofs surrounded by serene rice fields and a small river dotted with lily pads and flowers. It looks more like a swanky spa than a restaurant, and yet there's a simplicity in the design that keeps it from looking like a pretentious LA spa.

Apparently, they've been expecting us, because upon arrival, we're led to a private villa where we take off our shoes before climbing up and sitting down cross-legged on the soft, woven rattan floor. Minutes later, our drinks arrive—whole coconuts with the tops freshly chopped off. I take a sip, but it turns into a gulp and another and another, and before I know it, I've finished off all the coconut water in my coconut. Oops.

"Do you want another?" George asks. He's sitting adjacent to me. I give a sheepish smile when I realize that he's been watching me inhale the coconut water like a barbarian.

"No." I mean, I kind of do, but that seems greedy.

He leans close and says, "I inhaled mine too and I want another drink but I don't want to appear greedy, so you have to order another drink as well."

I bite back my smile. Ever since the white water rafting, I feel as though something has shifted. The air between us is no longer as thick, no longer as charged. And all it took was seeing a kid shitting into the Ayung River. Who would've thought?

"Okay, but only because you insist."

"Cool," he says. "Or should I say, rad."

I wrinkle my nose and laugh. "Rad? What are you, a sixty-year-old man?"

A frown creases his forehead. "You were the one who used it first, remember? Over chat?"

Oh shit. I swear I can practically feel the insides of my stomach hurling to my feet. The chat messages between Mama and George. Why did I not bother to read through them carefully? I'd only read the first few and then skimmed the rest in a rage. Argh!

A couple seats away, Rina is watching us with eagle-sharp eyes. I can practically see her ears pricking up at this awkward exchange.

I quickly say, "Right, yeah. I did. Totally rad. Very rad." I try for a laugh, but it sounds hollow.

George smiles, and I search desperately for signs that he's on to me, but as usual, his smile is guileless. Which makes me feel even worse somehow.

He leans in, making my skin break out into gooseflesh, and says, "Do you want to try my favorite drink in the entire world?"

Thank god, I guess he hadn't caught on to the suspicious

vibes of Radgate. My muscles turn to water and I let my breath out. "Like I can say no to that."

He raises a hand. A waiter immediately appears and George orders a drink called soda gembira for us. Eleanor asks for a chocolate milkshake, Kiki orders an avocado coffee, and Rina and the cameraman ask for black coffee because they're clearly the spawn of the devil. I have no idea how Kiki, Rina, and the cameraman could possibly have more caffeine; I'm still feeling the buzz from the Sejuk kopi susu.

I turn to George. "Did you just order a drink called 'happy soda'?"

"Yeah." He leans a little closer to me. "I was about four when my mom first let me have a sip of it at a restaurant. She called it the happiest drink in the world. It tasted like a rose garden to me, and I've always associated it with my mom ever since."

My heart twists at this small glimpse of his past with his mother. "I love that she called it the happiest drink in the world. Like Disney World in a cup. She sounds like such an awesome person."

"The best."

"Don't you think it's a bit of a girly drink to have?" Rina says. She's got this look on her face that I've mentally dubbed the "Reporter Trying to Get a Reaction."

George shrugs easily, and I'm reminded of how used to all of this he is, how comfortable he is being filmed and prodded with stupid questions designed to get a rise out of him. "I never really thought of it. Are guys not allowed to have delicious drinks?" he says, laughing.

"I thought we were past this kind of gendered bullshit," I snap at Rina. Because unlike George, I'm not comfortable with baiting questions, even when they're not directed at me. Plus, this kind of sexism, especially coming from another woman, is the kind of thing that rakes my skin.

Instead of being flustered like I half expected her to be, Rina's mouth quirks a little, an amused look crossing her face. Then she shifts her attention to me. A live one, her expression reads. Ah shit.

"You're right, Sharlot," she says. "I'm sorry, I should've known better than to say such things. Have you always been an activist for gender equality?"

Okay, that's going a bit far. My insides are squirming, because though I slap down instances of sexism and racism and other kinds of prejudice when I come across them, I'm not exactly an activist. And somehow, being questioned like this makes me feel like a complete hypocrite. Well, more of a hypocrite than I already am, that is.

I shrug. "I don't know that I'd call myself an activist."

"Ah, I'm sure you must be so busy with school and everything," Rina says, nodding. Then she turns to George. "It must have been such a surprise to meet Sharlot in person and realize that she's so different from her online persona?"

George's practiced polite smile freezes. "Sorry, how do you mean?"

"Oh, I've heard that Sharlot online is very different, more . . . ha, I was going to say prudish, but I realize that's probably a sexist term"—Rina laughs apologetically—"let's say . . . more traditional? Much more traditional than she is in person?"

Oh my god. She did hear the conversation in the bathroom after all. She knows something is off. I feel sick. My insides twist like eels, knotting painfully.

George frowns, not understanding what she's getting at. "Well, um, I think everyone's slightly different from their online personas, right? I know I am."

"Sure, but most of the time, the differences go the other way around. People are usually much more open online and more guarded in person. I think it's interesting that in Sharlot's case, it's the opposite. Is it possible that Sharlot isn't who she says she is?" Her smile widens.

My skin is radioactive, buzzing with anxiety and fear. I need to say something. Something to defend myself. Or maybe something that would distract her? Anything at all would be better than just sitting here gaping at her like a fish on land!

Kiki and Eleanor must have overheard, because they're looking at us with worried frowns etched on their foreheads. Come on, guys, I mentally will at them, say something. Pipe up with one of your witty comebacks!

"Well, that makes sense," George says. "Is any of us ever a hundred percent who we say we are online? Actually, we should all be more careful online, because online is forever."

"Yeah, exactly," Kiki finally pipes up. "Once you say something over the internet, it's there forever. You could delete a dumb tweet, but chances are someone's screencapped it so it's never actually gone."

"Yep," I say. "That's why I'm more guarded online. I think the consequences of what we say and do online are even bigger than the ones in person." My mind tries to catch up with the words falling out of my mouth, parsing through them to figure out if what I said made sense, and huh. I think it actually does make a bit of sense.

"That's a really good point, Shar," George says. He reaches out and gives my hand a small squeeze, right in front of the camera. I can practically feel the lens zooming in on our hands. It works; the attention shifts from the fraught topic of online personalities, and Rina smiles and says, "Aww. You two are adorable."

Just then the drinks arrive, and all of us lean back in our seats. I exhale and sag with relief, thankful that the weird, tense moment with Rina is done. She's been so quiet and unobtrusive this entire morning that part of me forgot she's here as a reporter. But after that exchange, my hackles are up and my instincts are all screaming to watch out for her.

George meets my eye and gives me a small smile. *Okay?* he mouths.

I nod, feeling really grateful for his intervention. He really did his best to save that prickly moment without speaking for me, and I'm seeing him in a whole new light.

Then I realize that I'm still holding his hand. Ack. I snatch my hand away as though it'd just caught fire. I swear the entirety of my arm is burning. George looks just as embarrassed as I feel. Of course, as soon as I do that, I realize I should've continued holding his hand because that's what a normal couple would do. I steal glances at Rina, wondering if she noticed. But again, she's busy tapping on her phone. Okay, let's hope she didn't catch that.

My soda gembira is placed in front of me. It's a beautiful drink, with white and pink layers and strips of fresh coconut.

George perks up at the sight of it. "The white layer is condensed milk," he says, mixing his soda gembira up. "And the pink is a mixture of soda water and rose syrup."

I mix mine up until it's all a uniform light pink and take a sip, and aah. It's the most appropriately named drink ever, because it's impossible to drink this bubbly, fizzy rose-flavored drink and not feel delighted by how refreshing and indulgently sweet it is.

"Oh my god, this is *delightful*." I laugh and take another sip. "Hands down the best fucking drink ever."

I glance at George and find him watching me with an expression so soft, so unguarded, that it makes my insides feel all melty. He smiles. "Yeah, it really is. Even the smell reminds me of her."

Together, we smell our drinks, and my eyes flutter closed at the sweetness of it. It smells like the color pink.

"I once read that scent is the one thing that can take us back in time," I say, and he nods.

"Whenever I smell rose syrup, I can practically see her." He sips his drink. It's near impossible to tear my eyes from him. He looks so happy, like a little kid who's been told Christmas came early. It's getting strangely harder to hate him, and honestly, I don't hate not hating him. It's a weird feeling, learning that I do actually like George as a person. I've never felt this way before. Back in LA, I was attracted to Bradley, sure, because who wouldn't be? But I never really connected with him on a deeper level than that. I didn't think too hard about it, I just assumed that was how most relationships are—you're either into the other person for their looks or for their personalities. And now, I'm looking at George and he's not only hot, but he's also funny and kind and smart, so freaking smart, and holy crap, what a lethal combo that makes.

Fortunately, our food arrives then. A welcome distraction from this strange new sensation spreading throughout my body. We've obscenely over-ordered.

There's deep-fried duck served with seasoned rice and three different chilies, including more of the addictive sambal matah. A huge plate layered with banana leaves is piled high with sate lilit—minced, seasoned chicken meat wrapped around stalks of lemongrass and grilled to charred perfection. There's also a dish called bebek betutu, which is a whole duck seasoned with a thick spice paste and wrapped in plantain leaves before being roasted. Unlike the fried duck, whose meat is satisfyingly chewy, the bebek betutu is so tender that I can't even eat it with a fork as the meat keeps sagging off. My mouth is burning from all the different Balinese chilies, but I can't stop eating.

By the end of the meal, we're all defeated, sagging back in our seats and rubbing our bellies with glazed expressions. Kiki summons a waiter and orders us all a round of avocado coffee and an avocado chocolate for Eleanor.

"I can't eat another bite," I protest, but she tells me I need it. Like, *need* it. "Plus, haven't you had enough coffee?" I grouse. "If I cut you, I bet you'll bleed coffee."

She laughs. "You're probably right about that."

When the drinks arrive, they're as beautiful as expected. The glasses are smeared with thick chocolate syrup before being filled with creamy, blended avocado and topped with a shot of espresso. The drink is so thick that I have to eat it with a spoon, more dessert than drink. And it's delicious. I can't imagine going back to American coffee after what I've sampled here in Indonesia.

Just as Kiki had predicted, the avocado coffees revive us—it's impossible for Indonesian coffee to not revive anyone, even a corpse—and we leave the restaurant ready for our next adventure.

The next stop is the Mandala Suci Wenara Wana, better known as the Sacred Monkey Forest Sanctuary in Ubud.

"Is it a zoo?" I say as we alight from the minivan. George shakes his head.

"It's a Hindu temple that also doubles as a natural habitat for monkeys. It's kind of the opposite of a zoo."

And he's right. The first thing I see as I step outside is a monkey on the side of the road, drinking out of a plastic water bottle. It's such a jarring sight to see that I stand there for a second, unmoving. The monkey is so close to me I could reach out and poke its tail. This is surreal. As though noticing my attention, the monkey looks up and I'm met with a disturbingly human gaze. I swear this monkey knows exactly what I'm thinking. It looks me up and down and then goes back to drinking out of its bottle.

"I guess you're not interesting enough for it," George murmurs.

I laugh. My god, this place. This entire island! It's like walking into a magical place where every part of the island is imbued with thousand-year-old secrets. Before entering the sacred monkey forest, I'm given colorful pieces of cloth to tie around my waist and shoulders because my off-shoulder dress is considered too short and revealing to be respectful toward the Hindu religion. Normally, I would've bristled at this, but something about the place eases me. Most people around, both male and female, are wearing the bright yellow-and-purple cloths in some way, whether as skirts or as shawls to cover bare shoulders. It's a humbling sight. I tie on both pieces of cloth securely, and once I'm ready, we all go through the entrance and into the forest.

The sanctuary is like a national park, with numerous trails going through the heavily forested area. All around us, climbing and jumping from tree to tree, are monkeys of all sizes. I spot little baby ones clinging to their mothers' backs and can't help but point them out with all the delight of a little kid. I should probably be cooler about this—I mean, even Eleanor isn't being as gung ho as I am—but it's as though the magic of the place has infected me. Or maybe it's the sugar and caffeine I had at lunch.

As we walk, I take photos and send them to Michie. But by now, it's two in the morning in LA and she's probably asleep. I send her photo after photo anyway. She'll see them when she wakes up and I can't wait to hear what she has to say about this incredible place.

When a baby monkey detaches from its mother and walks toward me, I stop in my tracks and giggle out loud. Without warning, it springs up. I don't even have time to shriek, never mind duck, before the little paws dig into my hair and snatch at my sunglasses before jumping off my shoulder and slithering up a nearby tree.

"Holy shit! Did you guys see that? Oh my god!"

Kiki and Eleanor double over with laughter. Seriously?

"Filled with empathy as usual," I snap at them while rubbing gingerly at my head.

"Are you okay?" George says, stepping so he's in front of me, looking closely at my head. "Let me see." He lifts his hand and touches the side of my face so gently that my mouth goes dry.

Somehow, I manage to find my voice and say, "I'm fine."

George tucks my hair behind my ear, his fingers leaving a trail of flames on the side of my head. "Yeah, I think you are," he says, and I can't bear the expression he's wearing, like I'm the only person in the world worth paying any attention to, everything around us disappearing into silence until there's just me and him on this entire island. Okay, please cool it, hormones.

"We should probably get those sunglasses back," Kiki says. "They're Gucci, you know."

George and I blink and step back from each other. "Yeah, of course," he says. "I know just the trick." He reaches into his pocket and takes out—of all things—a small banana.

"Is that a banana in your pocket or are you just happy to see me?" I say. Oh my god, why, mouth?

Eleanor shrieks with laughter as George's cheeks turn red.

"Sorry, I couldn't resist. Because, seriously, why do you have a banana in your pocket?"

"Because I knew we were coming here!" He shakes his head at us. "God, you bunch of toddlers. Now my banana is about to save the day." He turns and looks up at the top of the tree, where the baby monkey is sitting. It has placed the sunglasses on its face, but they're too big for it and keep slipping off. He raises the banana and calls out to the baby monkey, who perks up, the oversize glasses slipping down onto its shoulders. "Give me the sunglasses," George shouts out slowly, enunciating each syllable, "and you'll get a banana. Mm-mmm, banana. Yum."

The baby monkey descends slowly, cautiously, and George waves the banana at it. But just as the baby monkey reaches the lowest branch, there's a rustle from a nearby bush. A huge monkey leaps out, grabs the banana, and darts up another tree. I don't know if I'll ever be able to stop laughing at the perfect mix of shock and horror on George's face.

CHAPTER 20

George

We've been walking the forest trail for about ten minutes, chatting amicably with one another, Eleanor and Sharlot still giggling over my monkey mishap, when Eleanor says in an extra-loud voice, "And then I overheard Herry—you know, Herry Kusuma? He was talking about how he's really going to miss us all when his entire family moves to Sweden."

You could see Rina's entire body perk up; I swear, even her ears straighten up. I bet the hairs on her nape are pinpricks. "Herry Kusuma?" she says, gesturing at the camera guy to follow this conversation from a few paces away, probably to keep from spooking Eleanor.

I have no idea what Eleanor's trying to pull. Herry Kusuma is the youngest son of the owner of Sanu Group, our biggest corporate rivals.

Eleanor says. "We're classmates. We both go to Xingfa School. You know, I heard that Herry had been waitlisted because he failed the entrance exam, and his family had to "donate" to the school. Did you know that?"

Rina frowns. "Do you have anything to corroborate this claim?"

Eleanor studies her fingernails. "Hmm, I'll have to think about that. So anyway, Sweden . . ."

Next to Eleanor, Kiki's viciously biting her lip like me, probably to keep from smiling. I turn around to look at Sharlot's reaction and find that she's not paying attention to Eleanor and Rina. Instead, she's too busy taking photos of the monkeys, trying to catch their attention as she snaps away.

"You're really into these monkeys, huh?" I say. Then I wince inwardly. Did that come out sounding as lame as it did in my head?

She takes another picture of a beleaguered-looking mother monkey with a baby monkey swinging from her tail. "Yeah, I can't wait to draw them. Their muscle tone and the lines of their bodies—it's amazing."

"Huh. I didn't know you drew."

She glances at me before looking down at her phone. "A little."

"That's really cool. Is that what you're planning on majoring in when you go to college?"

This time, the glance she gives me lasts a bit longer and no longer has any barbs. One corner of her mouth quirks up.

"What?" I say.

She shrugs. "Nothing. It's just—you didn't assume it was a hobby like most people do."

"Oh. Yeah, I guess it's the way you said 'muscle tone'? Kind of intense and creepy. So I figured it's more than a hobby."

She laughs. "Intense and creepy, huh? Nice." We fall into step and she starts talking about art. "Yeah, I've been drawing ever since I could hold a crayon. But honestly, it's a bit of a crapshoot because artists are so notoriously underpaid. We're always being expected to work for exposure, which just means work for free. So my mom is really against it. She wants me to major in something more reliable like pre-law or pre-med."

"Ah, the usual Asian-American dream jobs," I say.

"You guys don't get that here?" she says, looking quizzically at me.

I shrug. "Not so much lawyers and doctors, because they're not the highest earners in Indonesia. It's mostly business. We're all raised to take over the family companies here."

She nods slowly. "Oh yeah, you mentioned in your messages."

Argh. My chest tightens. My so-called messages where Eleanor and Papa had droned on and on about how much I adore finance. "Yeah, about that." I take a deep breath. Time to give her at least a glimpse of the real me. "I may have been, uh, trying to impress you." Oh god, this is painful. But somehow, I forge ahead. "To be honest, I'm not that passionate about the family company."

"Oh?" She side-eyes me before snapping another photo of a nearby monkey.

"Yeah. I never really thought about what I wanted to do in life. Because my cousins and I were always told we'd just go into the family business. Sorry, I didn't mean that to sound quite so bratty. I know I'm very privileged," I add quickly. "And I'm grateful for all of it."

"No, I get it. I mean, to a certain extent. I don't know what it's like to be a billionaire," she says with a wry smile, "but I know what you mean about feeling meh."

"Yeah. Feeling 'meh' describes it perfectly. Until OneLiner, actually."

She cocks an eyebrow at me. "The app about treating girls like 'precious things'?"

Oh god. How the hell Eleanor let Papa say that about girls, I will never understand. "I definitely do not want to treat girls or anyone as precious things. Sorry, I'm really bad at interacting over chat."

Sharlot nods slowly. "Yeah, I'm starting to get that impression."

"OneLiner is more about guys than it is about girls. It's more about tackling toxic masculinity and not letting guys get off the hook with all that boys-will-be-boys bullshit. There's still a lot of toxicity when it comes to the concept of masculinity here in Indo. Like, you'd hear parents tell their sons not to cry because 'boys don't cry' and stuff like that." I shove my hands in my pockets, feeling awkward and vulnerable at revealing this to Sharlot. "I just—when I started working on OneLiner, for the first time ever, I felt invested in the family business. Like, wow, I think I might actually be making a difference? I don't know, it probably sounds dumb."

"No, actually." Sharlot stops walking and turns to face me. "It doesn't sound dumb at all. In fact, it might be the first un-dumb thing you've said to me."

My mouth opens and closes, but no words come out. There

are way too many emotions churning inside me. Before I can reply, a small shape whips past my head and plucks Sharlot's phone right out of her hand.

"Not again!" she screams.

We run after the monkey. I take out another banana and wave at it, shouting, "Pisang! Pisang!" I figure it's a better bet to shout "banana" in Indonesian, since the monkeys here are more likely to understand Indonesian words. At some point as we run, something breaks loose within us and we start laughing as we dart through the forest.

Sharlot is giggling so hard that her cheeks have turned red, and her hair has come loose from her hair band and is wreathed around her face in crazy waves. She looks the way I feel—warm and alive and invincible. Monkeys scream and chatter all around us, flying from tree to tree, and I laugh again. We're flying along with them.

We burst out of the darkness of the trees and into sudden sunlight and Sharlot gasps at the sight before us. We've come to the side of a temple, one that overlooks a cliff. Below us, the sea slides into the rocks, and ahead of us, the horizon is endless, the water a silky sapphire blanket. Monkeys and tourists alike stand at the edge of the stone balcony, chilling, enjoying the sight. Everyone is happy, as though the peacefulness of the temple has infused our spirits.

Our monkey has climbed up the stone balcony with Sharlot's phone wrapped in its tail. It turns its head and gives us a mischievous look, which makes Sharlot laugh. I hold out the banana to it, approaching as slowly as I can. I swear the monkey actually rolls its eyes at me before flicking its tail up. The phone swings through the air in a graceful arc. Time stops, everything moving in slow motion. I reach up for it, stretching my arms as far as they'll go . . .

The phone lands in my hands with a neat little plop.

"Holy shit!" Sharlot cries. We stare at each other for a moment. The monkey chitters impatiently and I realize I'm still holding its banana. I throw the banana gently at it and it catches it with easy grace before sashaying away.

Sharlot and I double over laughing. "Oh my god, I can't believe that actually happened," I gasp in between laughter. I hand the phone back to Sharlot, ignoring the spark when my fingertips graze her hand, and she slips it into her pocket.

"This place," Sharlot murmurs, wiping away her tears of mirth. She walks slowly and leans over the stone ledge, gazing into the far-off horizon.

Would it be sensible of me to try holding her hand right now? Maybe not. But that's the thing, I don't want to be sensible anymore. For once, I want to be like Papa's side of the family— led fully by my emotions, all big romantic gestures and follow your dreams.

Sharlot turns to me, and her expression is soft and so open that my heart cracks open along with it. "I can't believe I didn't want to come here." She looks back out onto the water. "I was so smug, I just thought—god. I thought that Indonesia's a Third World country. I know how that must make me sound."

I nod. Something about the rawness in her voice makes me

think I shouldn't reply, that I should let her talk because she needs to get this out there.

"I looked down on it, you know? I snorted every time my mom talked about Indo. I'd roll my eyes. And I'd just think of, like, I don't know, huts?" She laughs mirthlessly. "I'm such an asshole."

"You're not," I say automatically. Sharlot shakes her head.

"I am. I'm no better than those obnoxious Americans who insist that America's the best country in the world when they've never been outside of it." She releases her breath. "You have no idea how shitty I feel about how I've treated my mom this whole time, especially when it comes to anything that has to do with Indonesia."

The expression on her face is so raw, so unguarded, that I have an inexplicable urge to wrap my arms around her shoulders. I have to fight to keep my hands still. "To tell you the truth, I haven't exactly been the best son either." I think of Papa and how hard he's tried to mold me into a better kid, and it fills me with so many conflicting emotions, all of them confusing. "Ever since my mom passed away, my dad's been trying so hard to—I don't know—make sure that I'm okay? He went to therapy with me for a while, which is really rare here. There's still a whole stigma about seeking help for mental health, especially back then, so to have him go with me was like, whoa." I cringe at the memory of the media fallout that had caused.

"Oh shit, that sounds awful, George."

"Yeah, it was pretty bad. The news sites were filled with stories about how my dad must be emotionally unstable and what did that mean for the family company?"

"God, that must have been so hard."

"I actually don't remember much of this. I only found out because I Googled my name a few years ago and found all these news articles about it."

"That's terrible!"

"It's okay, my dad and I had a long talk about it. I think he did the best he could. Good thing the family had his back. Especially Eighth Aunt. She took over everything for a while. It gave us the time we needed to—well, fall apart, basically."

Sharlot nods. "Not to compare it to what you went through, obviously, because that was a million times worse, but yeah, I feel like I need some time and space to fall apart a little."

"Is there a reason why you need to fall apart?" I'm trying to be careful with my words, because I sense that we're circling some huge issue that she's too scared to tell me, and I want to be there for her.

"So many," Sharlot snorts. "The whole reason we came here was—uh." She hesitates, her forehead scrunching up, then she quickly says, "Never mind, it's stupid. I'll tell you next time. All you need to know is that I messed up, and here I am. And it's just been this constant whirlwind and I wish I had some time to stop and just . . . breathe. I guess it's partly why I've been so horrible toward my mom."

"I think, at the end of the day, our folks know we're trying our best, just like they are."

"I haven't, though. I haven't tried at all with my mom. Back home, I'm always just yelling at her over the smallest stuff." She snorts and grimaces. "I even yelled at her over juice, can you believe that? Juice!"

I think of all the things I've freaked out at Papa over. "That sounds ridiculous, but it's the exact sort of thing that my dad and I argue over, so yeah, I believe it."

She laughs. "I can't imagine you arguing with your dad over anything."

"Oh, trust me, we definitely do."

Smiling, we stare out at the view before us, watching the waves crash into the cliffs. I watch Sharlot from the corner of my eye and marvel at how strong of a bond I feel toward her now, after just a day of talking to her. She's been one of the best surprises of my life.

After some time, she gives a relieved sigh. "Thanks for letting me thought-vomit all over you. I hadn't realized how much that stuff with my mom has been weighing me down."

"Anytime."

We look at each other and it's like the final wall has finally crumbled and I'm seeing all of Sharlot for the first time. She's flawed and broken and more beautiful than ever. My throat goes dry. Everything stops. The world stops spinning on its axis, pausing to hold its breath for us. Expectation clings to the air, making it heavy on my skin. Both of our hands are resting on the short stone wall. I inch mine forward and she moves hers just a tad closer as well. Another centimeter, and the tips of our fingers are touching. Such a small, innocent touch, but it sets my whole body on fire. My heart is thumping so ferociously that I'm sure she can feel it on my fingertips. And then—miracle of miracles—Sharlot takes my hand, interlacing our fingers together. She glances up at me with a shy smile before looking back at the horizon, and we stand there for a long time, not saying a word but somehow communicating so much more than we ever did before.

After a while, we walk along the cliff side, still holding hands, and it feels as though something has opened up between us. Our conversation flows so smoothly that I can barely keep up with everything that I want to say to her. I tell her everything, about Mama and how much I miss her, about how guilty I feel that I'm not more like the male heir my family has always wanted.

Well, almost everything.

Everything except the one thing that matters the most, the truth about how she and I met. The very beginning, the foundation of our friendship. I should tell her. I feel it wriggling in my head like a pale worm, its bristles scraping against my skull, itching to be told. It's only a matter of time before I cave, and why not now? Something tells me that she'll be receptive to it, that she'll understand how overbearing Papa and Eleanor are, especially when they join forces against me. She'll know it wasn't done with malicious intent.

"Shar, I need to tell you something."

The words bypass my brain and come out sounding like they're being said by someone else. I don't even recognize my voice.

Sharlot stops walking and turns to me, the sun at her back and casting a glow around her. She looks so incredibly beautiful. I take a mental picture of her, trying to memorize everything about this moment that I'm about to ruin with my shameful lie. I clear my throat.

"What is it?" she says after a pregnant pause, smiling up at me. It hurts, that she's not expecting anything bad. It hurts knowing that I'm about to hurt her.

"Um. You know how we met on ShareIt?"

Her little smile freezes for a second. "Yeah?"

"Um. Like, how I messaged you out of the blue and stuff?"

Her gaze skitters away from mine and she looks out onto the sea, then back toward the forest. Then her eyebrows raise and she waves madly. "Hey! Hey, guys! We're here!"

Sure enough, walking out of the shade of the trees is the rest of our group. Eleanor and Kiki laugh and jog toward us, Rina and the camera guy walking briskly behind them, looking very grumpy.

"What happened back there?" Rina says through clenched teeth. "We've been looking for you two."

"Oh!" Shar says. "I'm sorry, I was taking pictures of the monkeys and I didn't realize we'd gotten separated."

"We would've called," Rina says, teeth still clenched into a smile so angry it looks more like her just baring her teeth, "except Kiki and Eleanor don't have their phones with them, and I don't have your personal cell numbers."

"Yeah, sorry, I left my phone in the car because I didn't want the monkeys to get at them," Kiki pipes up.

"And I'm thirteen, so I don't have a cell phone," Eleanor says, smirking.

Rina narrows her eyes at them. Like me, she probably doesn't believe for a second that Kiki would leave her phone in the car. I realize that Sharlot and I are no longer holding hands. Did I let her hands go, or did she pull them away when the rest of the group found us? And come to think of it, the rest of the group didn't find us so much as Sharlot led them to us. A knot of worry forms in my stomach; why had Sharlot been so eager to get the group back? We were having a good time without them, right? Or have I just really, really misread the moment and she was actually squirming to get away from me? The knot in my stomach turns into a rock, all-consuming and impossible to get around, weighing everything down. That must be it. She must've found me unbearable.

As though to prove my point, the rest of the way back to the car Sharlot pointedly walks with Kiki and Eleanor, winding her arms through theirs so there's no chance I could walk next to her or anything. I put my hands in my pockets, my cheeks burning with shame. I wish I could disappear; I wish I could just hide in my room and pretend this whole day never happened. How did I miscalculate it so badly? I thought we'd been having a great time, that we were actually connecting with each other.

You're bad with girls, a little voice in my head says. *You're a nerd; you spend all your free time gaming. Face it, George, you're not the kind of dude who'd get girls, aside from ones who are after the family wealth.*

God, I really want a hole for me to disappear into. I'm quiet the whole way back to the car, not bothering to strike up a conversation with anyone. Kiki and Eleanor regale Sharlot with stories about their hike, and I notice Rina gesturing at the camera guy to focus in on me; I guess I'm looking visibly down. With some effort, I look straight ahead instead of down at my feet as I walk, trying not to look like my entire world is crumbling.

Okay, so maybe I do have melodrama running through my veins after all.

Once inside the car, I pretend to doze off, leaning my head against the headrest and closing my eyes. I even let my mouth fall open slightly, just to make it even more convincing. The others talk among themselves for a few minutes, chattering about how fun the monkey forest was, but after a while they all quiet down, probably absorbed by their various phones (minus the phoneless Eleanor, who's probably taking the quiet time as a chance to work on her plans for world domination). Now I totally empathize with Papa wailing and running away flailing every time he gets upset because I definitely am feeling the urge to do a bit of wailing myself.

Finally, *finally*, we get back to the hotel. I practically scramble out of the minivan as soon as it stops. Then I catch myself and stand there in a very gentlemanly fashion and help the others out. My heart squeezes painfully when Sharlot, upon seeing my outstretched hand, bites her lip and touches it for the barest second as she climbs out. The moment her feet touch the ground, she lets go of my hand, as though it burned her to touch me.

Why?

Or something less whiny and dramatic. In other whys: Why has the dramatic flair that's apparently been lying dormant inside me chosen this particular time to erupt?

We thank Rina and the cameraman for their hard work and then the four of us walk in painful silence toward the villas. Eleanor looks up at me and widens her eyes meaningfully. *What the hell did you do, gege?*

I raise my eyebrows and shrug. *Nothing, I swear!*

Behind her glasses, her big eyes narrow. *Yeah, right. When we get back to our villa, I am going to dissect every moment you spent with her and we will find out exactly where you messed up, because you definitely messed up.*

We stop in front of Sharlot and Kiki's villa, and Eleanor says, "We'll see you at tonight's dinner!"

"Looking forward to it," Kiki replies with an affectionate grin at Eleanor. The two of them really get along as thick as thieves.

Meanwhile, Sharlot and I are standing in front of each other in what is quite possibly the most awkward moment known to humankind. Case in point, we're each staring at our feet. Even our feet are embarrassed; since we're both wearing sandals, I can see how our toes are curling in, as though they don't want to be part of this awkward time.

"Um, so I'll see you later," I say finally. The air around us is so thick it feels like I've just talked underwater, my words fighting through sludgy air to get to her.

She nods, her gaze flicking up at me for a split second before darting away again. "Yeah. Later."

I turn to leave. I know when I'm not wanted, and I'm not one of those guys who think no is a challenge to press harder.

"George!"

There's so much urgency in her voice that I whip back around, my heart hammering so hard I can feel its thuds in my hands. "Yeah?" I hate the naked hope that leaps into my mouth, making my yeah so desperate and raw.

Sharlot meets my eye, and the expression on her face is a mirror of all the things I'm feeling. I'm sure of it. She feels the same way about me. She likes me too, I can see it plain as day, but something holds her back.

"I—" She gnaws on her lower lip, then says, "I had a great time today. Really."

My hand twitches, wanting so badly to reach out for hers. But I hold myself back. "Thanks for saying that. I had a great time too."

Her lips quirk into a small smile. "And, um." She hesitates for a second before shaking her head. "Anyway. Yeah. I'll see you at the dinner tonight."

Is that it? Was that everything she wanted to say? I get the feeling that there's more, but I've misread Sharlot so many times that I don't dare push. I just nod and walk away.

CHAPTER 21

Sharlot

The moment the door closes behind us, Kiki whirls around and shouts, "WHAT THE HELL, SHAR?"

I pretend not to know what she's talking about and walk past her, grateful for the air-conditioned villa air that refreshes my flushed skin. I go to the minibar, fill a glass with ice cubes and bottled water, and drink it all. Heaven. I refill it and sip the second glass slowly while my mess of a mind tries to knit the scramble of thoughts in my head into a coherent order.

"Hello?" Kiki says, standing right in my face, her hands on her hips.

"What?"

She throws her hands up. "Don't give me that act, Shar. You know what I'm talking about. What happened between you and George? Things were going so well, and then we get separated for like an hour and when we came back, you were awkward as hell!" She sighs and softens her voice. "Did you two kiss? Was he a bad kisser? All teeth and tongue?"

"What?" That shocks a laugh out of me. "No, it was nothing like that. We were just . . . talking." And holding hands. But I don't tell her that. And anyway, who the hell gets excited over holding hands? Even though it was the most intense hand-holding in the history of hand-holding.

She grins at me and rests her elbows on the bar, placing her chin on her hands. "Oh? Tell me about the heart-to-heart."

And despite myself, despite all of the bad stuff swirling and knotting inside me, there's more than a small part of me that does want to spill it all over a giggling-fest. And so I do. I tell her about how we connected on an even deeper level than just kissing, how we shared with each other our pasts, how he had told me so openly about his mother.

"And then he was about to tell me something big. Something—I don't know—he said he had to tell me something, and I thought he was going to ask me why I'm so different from online. I thought he might've figured it out, and I kind of freaked out."

Kiki frowns. "Uh-oh. Freaked out how?"

"I saw you guys in the distance and that was when I called out to you."

"Ah." She nods. "Yeah, you were really eager to catch our attention. I remember wondering why you were waving so hard. But as far as freak-outs go, that wasn't too bad."

I groan and slump across the bar, resting my flushed face against the cool marble. "It was bad. You should've seen the look on his face. Like I'd strangled his puppy with my bare hands or something."

"I like how you went straight for a puppy-killing analogy. That's not at all weird or disturbing."

Despite myself, I snort a little at this. I rest my chin on the bar and peer up at her. "You know what is weird and disturbing?"

"You're going to say something mean like, your face, aren't you?"

"No! God, you have such a low opinion of me."

Kiki sighs. "Fine, what's weird and disturbing?"

"Aside from your face?"

She groans and we both laugh. "Sorry, I couldn't resist. But seriously, what *is* weird is how much I don't hate this." I gesture between the two of us.

Kiki's eyes soften. "Yeah."

"I mean, when we first met, you were a *lot.*"

"Me?" she cries. "What about you? Miss I'm-too-amazing-for-this-place."

"I was not!"

"Oh my god, this was you when you first arrived." Kiki jumps off the bar stool and stands up straight, lifting her chin and looking around her with a slight sneer curving her upper lip. She wrinkles her nose and says in a thick American accent, "Ew, do people, like, actually live in this hovel? Like, gross."

"Oh, well, this was *you* when we first met." I stand up as well and look down my nose in the most exaggerated way possible. I lift my right arm, letting my hand flop down lazily. Then I adopt a faux British accent. "Oh, dah-ling, do American rednecks know how to use proper cutlery or do you eat straight off the plate like the dreadful beasts that you are?"

"Like, in America, which is the center of the world, like, you get given a free puppy at like, every street corner."

"Do you not have a chandelier in every room? My word! You peasant!"

By now, we're both laughing so hard I'm actually having to press my legs together to keep from peeing myself.

"I was not like that!"

"Yep, you totally were."

"So were you!"

We flop over the sofa, still laughing, and Kiki opens a carved wooden box that's been placed neatly at the center of the coffee table. Inside are fancy chocolate bonbons, and we go "Ooh!" and pore over the selection. When I bite into mine, the hard chocolate shell gives way to a creamy coffee center. "Oh my god, this is so good," I moan, settling back into the comfortable sofa.

Kiki nods with her mouth full; she's popped two whole bonbons into her mouth and looks like a hamster who's shoveled too much food into its cheeks. I grin at her, and she winks back. When she's finally swallowed her chocolate, she says, "You're right, you know. I . . . I don't hate this too. I wasn't sure what to expect when Mum and Dad told me you were coming to visit. I was really nervous."

"You? Nervous?" I gape at her.

"Yeah, of course! You're American!"

"So?"

"We're always watching American shows and reading American books, and they always make American teens seem so cool. And I was really sure that you'd arrive and look down on everything. I don't know." She takes another piece of chocolate, nibbling on it this time. "I thought for sure you'd find me uncool and be extremely bitchy about it all. To be fair, when you first arrived, you definitely gave that impression."

"Only because I was so intimidated!" I say.

Kiki lifts her eyebrows at me.

"You were like, ultra-fashionable—"

She flips her hair behind her shoulder and wiggles her eyebrows at me. "Obviously."

I roll my eyes. "Everything about you is so classy and grown-up, and there I was in my ripped jeans and shirt. I felt so, so"—I search for the right word—"dowdy."

"Ha! I was thinking the opposite. I felt so dumb in my tailored clothes and I thought you looked amazingly cool in an effortless, rule-breaking way. I guess that's kind of how we've always viewed American teens—like, we're so boring and predictable here, but you Americans are different. You're daring and you color outside the lines and you break all the rules."

I pop the rest of the candy in my mouth and think about our first meeting, seeing it in a new light. How weird that while I'd cocooned myself in my insecurities and envied Kiki's composure, she'd been doing the exact same thing. When we meet each other's eyes, we smile.

"I'm really glad you came for a visit," she says.

And despite the circumstances of my visit, I realize that I am glad too. "Yeah. I'm glad I got to meet some of my family members."

"Anyway, so back to George . . ." She pauses to take another bite of chocolate. "Ooh, this one's raspberry. Mmm. So you were saying, he looked like you killed his puppy?"

"Oh god. Yeah." A flash of George's disappointed, hurt face slashes through my mind, making me wince. "I don't blame him, I mean, there he was about to say something important, and I went ahead and ruined everything. But I just couldn't do it, I couldn't stand there and let him share his secrets with me when I'm lying to him this entire time."

Kiki nods. "What do you think he was about to tell you?"

"I don't know, but it felt big."

"Ooh, he was probably going to tell you he really likes you."

Heat rushes to my cheeks. "No. No way. It's way too soon." My stomach is doing advanced yoga. "No. We've only known each other for like, *days*."

"Well, technically, he thinks you've been chatting constantly for a week leading up to your coffee date," Kiki says, helpful as ever.

I groan. "That's exactly why I couldn't let him go on with whatever he was going to tell me. This whole thing is a sham! Plus, he liked that version of me that my mom cooked up. That awful, sexist, judgmental, boring—"

"I think he likes this version just fine," Kiki says.

My mouth snaps shut. Because George had said that he likes the real me too. But I just can't let go of the fact that he also liked Mama's version. Ugh, it's all so confusing. And it doesn't matter which version he likes anyway. If he ever finds out the truth, he'll hate me. All of me.

"Actually, that's not the worst part," I add. "The worst part is that I like him. I like this George, the one I spent the whole of today with, the one who laughed when we saw some kid shitting in the Ayung River, the one who snuck away in the monkey forest."

"Wait, go back," Kiki says. "You saw some kid shitting in the river? The river we were just rafting in?"

"That's your takeaway from all this?"

She shudders. "You know how much river water I swallowed?"

"Same."

"Oh god." She shudders again. "And George found it funny?"

I nod. "We were laughing so hard about it." I sigh. "He's so different from all his chat messages. I really thought I was going to hate him, that I had no skin in the game, you know? I thought I'd meet up with him, be bored out of my mind, and then go home. And even after we got invited to Bali, I just thought I'd put up with him for the weekend and then go home and forget all about him. I never thought I was in any danger of falling for him—" I clap my hands over my mouth with a gasp.

Kiki's staring at me, her mouth open. "Did you just say 'falling for him'?"

"No?"

"Yes, you did."

"No, I meant, like, falling as in a crush, sort of thing."

"Right, because that's what people mean when they say falling for someone." Kiki frowns at me. "Are you going to be okay? I don't want to see you get hurt."

I quirk the corner of my mouth at her. "That's really nice of you to say."

"You'd be so unbearable, can you even imagine?" she says, then laughs when I throw my snot-filled tissue at her. "But really,

Shar, I'm sorry about all of this. I never thought it would be like this either. When I read those chat messages between George and your mum . . . I mean, yeah, he sounded like such a basic bitch."

"Right? From his messages, he seemed like he would totally be the kind of asshole who narcs on his classmates if they, like, I don't know, wore their uniforms wrong or something."

Kiki laughs, nodding. "Totally." Then she leans forward. "So what are you gonna do?"

I shrug. "What is there to do? I just have to keep going, just survive this weekend and then go home and forget about everything."

"What?" she cries. "No way! You can't do that!"

"Why not? Plus, did you forget that I'm only here for the summer? I'll be gone in six weeks, and who knows when I'll be coming back here, if ever?"

Kiki stares at me. "Don't say that. I hate the thought that I might never see you again."

That stops me short. I didn't even think of that, which makes me feel guilty as hell. But isn't that exactly what I've been doing my whole life? It's my knee-jerk reaction whenever things get tough—I run. Just like my mom, I guess. When things get too real, the walls come slamming down and off she goes, sprinting away as fast as she can from her problems. The realization that I'm guilty of the exact same thing that I've judged Mama so harshly for is sobering. And here I am, wanting to run away again, go back to LA and forget that all of this ever happened. Disappear from George's life for good. Take zero responsibility for my own mistakes. The same thing I did to Bradley—cut him off, ghosted him, pretended there never was an us. I'm no better than Mama.

Guilt makes my voice thick as I say, "Yeah, I do too." And I mean it, truly. "We'll see each other again for sure. I'll make my mom bring me here again next summer."

"I could come visit over Christmas, maybe?" Kiki says, suddenly looking shy. "We could go to Disneyland, watch the Christmas fireworks."

"I would love that. You could meet Michie. You'd love her." Or maybe they'd hate each other and tear out each other's throats, that's also a very likely possibility. I remember Bradley, and the twinge of guilt twinges harder. Bradley would like Kiki. He likes everybody. He's too good for me, I see that now. Sure, I realize that besides being extremely attracted to him, we didn't have that much in common, but I still owe him at least the courtesy of telling him I'm fine instead of just disappearing completely from his life. He's been nothing but decent toward me. After this weekend, when all the madness has died down, I will message him and apologize for having been such a jerk.

"Okay, so now that we're both agreed that you and I are okay and that we'll definitely see each other again, what about you and George? I don't think that burying your head in the sand and planning on not seeing him ever again is wise."

"Why not?"

"Because you like him. And he likes you too, it's so obvious, Shar. It's really gross, the way you two looked at each other this entire day. Like you're barely restraining yourselves from jumping each other. Ugh. I felt really bad for Eleanor. It must've been hard for her to witness that."

"We were not!"

"Trust me, I know lovey-dovey eyes when I see them. And the look that George was giving you? Textbook. He likes you. The you in person. The real you. I mean, sure, maybe he likes the fake you too, but who cares? You guys are hitting it off in person, so that trumps the online stuff, right?"

I want her to be right so badly. I let the words wash around me, but they keep snagging on the chat messages my mom had exchanged with George. How enthusiastic he had sounded with each terrible lie my mother told. When she told him *I* liked to cook because a woman's place is in the kitchen. He'd said I would make the perfect wife. That's not something I can just forget.

"I need to tell him the truth," I blurt out. Kiki and I stare at each other for a second. I can't believe I just said that out loud, but now that I have, I realize it's true. I do need to tell him the truth.

"Seriously?" Kiki snorts. "No, dude, what would you even say?"

I shrug. "I don't know, the truth! I'll tell him that my mom's—you know, the way that she is—and that she freaked out because, uh—" I falter when I get to the why of the situation, because I can't imagine a reality where I tell George about Bradley and how I'd been so keen on losing my virginity. Oh god, just the thought of it is mortifying. I bury my face in my hands, not quite understanding why I feel mortified, because I'm not ashamed of my sexuality. I guess I'm ashamed of the way everything happened. The way I freaked out, the way I broke up with Bradley because I couldn't swallow my pride, the awful mess I'd left behind me.

But for the first time, I don't want to just run away from my mess again. I want to face it. If not to fix it, then at least to acknowledge that it's happened, and the part that I've played in making it happen. I like George. Really like him. And I want to be honest. But wanting to be honest is one thing. Having to actually do it is quite another.

"Okay, so I'll just tell him that Mama was very keen on having me make friends in Jakarta, so she started chatting with him. That doesn't sound at all weird or inappropriate." My voice is shrill with desperation.

"So he'll find out all that time, he was chatting with your mom," Kiki muses. "Yeah, that's not at all weird or inappropriate. It's definitely not going to scare him off and get us thrown out of Bali."

I throw my head back and groan out loud. "Forget it. I'm gonna go for a walk and clear my head before dinner." I can't stomach the thought of seeing George at dinner, having him be nice to me, knowing that I'm lying to his face.

"You do that. I'm going to have a long, hot soak in the tub."

Like I said, all empathy, this one.

CHAPTER 22

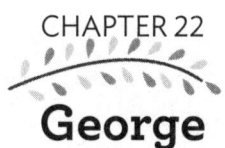

George

Eleanor and I come back to the villa to see Papa, Fauzi, and two other employees sitting in the living room surrounded by a mess of papers and laptops on the coffee table. Of course Papa's spending his time at this gorgeous resort working.

"Hi, Pa. Hi, everyone. Everything going okay?" I say. Eleanor gives Pa a kiss on the top of his head before going to the bar and getting herself a cold bottled water.

"Yes, just going over last-minute details for the event tomorrow." Pa glances up at me and seems to only just recall that I spent my day with Sharlot. He perks up and says to his employees, "Break for five minutes." They nod and leave the villa. As soon as they're out, Papa grins at me. "How was your day, George?"

I don't know what it is, but something about the day I've just had with Sharlot has lit a fire under me. I would normally tell Pa it was fine before retiring to my room, but for the first time, I don't want to just do that. I want him to take me seriously. I don't want to just be another small cog in the family company, blithely following the instructions of what to do and where to go. I want to make my voice heard. I swallow the lump in my throat. Go for it, self. This is it! Listen to Nike and just do it. "It was okay but, Pa, listen, I was just thinking about the app, and I have so many ideas for it. I was thinking we could have a sharing function—"

"Tch," Papa tuts, waving at me, still smiling. "Not about that, George. Tell me the important stuff, eh? How did your date with Sharlot go?"

"It was good, but can we please talk about OneLiner? I really think I have some good ideas—"

Papa's face grows somber. "Listen, George," he says with a heavy sigh. "I understand you're excited because it's your first app. But it's just a publicity thing, yes? Once it's launched, it'll get swallowed up by the millions and millions of other apps in the store and it'll disappear forever. We never really expected it to have staying power, you knew that. Don't get distracted from the actual purpose of the app. It's mostly there to boost our company profile."

My insides knot. I did know that, but did it have to be like that? I know the market is supercompetitive, but can't the app have some staying power, at least? Can't it stand on its own merits instead of being just another advertisement for the family company? "I know that, Pa, but we can at least do it well."

Papa shakes his head. "You'll learn as you get older what really makes a difference to the company. This—spending too much time tinkering around and perfecting the app—isn't it. But increasing your profile by having the romance of the year with Sharlot, now that is good publicity." He smiles at me and switches to English. "Wait, I get Nainai, she want to hear this."

"Why are we speaking English?" I mutter, but he's already scampered outside to find Nainai, who's dozing next to the private pool. I follow Papa outside and try to push the disappointment deep, deep down.

"Come out, is nice day, very nice out here!" Papa calls out in a voice loud enough to wake the—well, Nainai.

She startles awake and looks around, blinking owlishly for a second. I walk through the sliding doors and take a big lungful of the clean Bali air, savoring the pristine sight of the private pool and garden. Eleanor plops down on the lounger and hands Nainai a glass of orange juice. I have no idea how Eleanor does this; she always knows just what our elders need before they even realize it. It's one of the many reasons she's so adored by them. Nainai accepts the juice with her wrinkled, pale hands and smiles at Eleanor.

"Did you kids have fun?" she says, sipping the juice.

"George and Sharlot snuck off together!" Eleanor cries.

The effect is immediate.

I jerk up. "What? No, we didn't. We got separated—"

"And they held hands," Eleanor says in a dramatic voice.

Papa gasps audibly, his eyes wide.

Nainai sits up so fast the juice slops over her hand. "Aiya!" Papa and Eleanor fuss around Nainai, wiping up the juice with her beach towel.

"My little grandbaby!" Nainai cries, waving Papa and Eleanor away and reaching for me.

I gingerly crouch down so that Nainai can put her arms around me and give me a sort of hug. "Uh, it's really not a big deal, Nainai."

She pets my head like I'm a good dog. "Oh, my little grandson, you held hands! With a girl. You know, I was convinced you were a gay."

I pinch the bridge of my nose. "Nainai, we've talked about this before. It's the twenty-first century, you can't say stuff like that."

She waves me away and holds her arms out to Eleanor, who doesn't hesitate before laying her head on Nainai's lap. I wonder if Eleanor will ever grow too old to do that. How does she carry off being everyone's baby?

"And anyway, it wasn't the first time I've ever held someone's hand. You know, I've made out with other girls before," I mutter. Not that it matters; Nainai and Papa are enthralled with Eleanor as she regales them with an overly dramatized account of our day.

"And then," Eleanor says, "gege helped Sharlot onto the raft—it was very wobbly and Sharlot was very scared—gege was a total gentleman and held her hand like this—"

"I really don't remember Sharlot being very scared," I say, but Papa shushes me. "You know, given it's about me and Shar, don't you think I should be the one telling this story?"

They all look at me like I've just started speaking German before turning back to look at Eleanor, who continues talking. "And the Ayung River was so fast, oh my gosh, it was *so* scary, Pa, I can't believe that you let me go on it, I could've died!"

"My baby," Papa gasps, while Nainai wails and hugs Eleanor tight.

"Seriously?" I say. "That's not even close to being true."

"You are such a brave little warrior," Nainai says, cupping Eleanor's chin. "You're like Mulan."

Eleanor nods proudly and smirks.

"Why didn't you protect your little sister?" Nainai snaps at me.

I gesture wildly. "You just told her she's like Mulan!"

"She could have died!"

"Okay, first of all, the river was really mild. Second of all, we had a perfectly seasoned guide and we were all wearing life jackets. Thirdly, I don't even know why I'm having this conversation." What I really want to say is how the hell do they turn everything—even something as small as holding hands—into something huge and dramatic? But I can't be bothered, so I just say, "I'm going to take a shower."

"Wait!" Papa says. "Tell us about Sharlot and this magical date."

"Just speak Indo, Pa," I say. I close my eyes and sigh. "It was good."

Groans all around. "It was good?" Eleanor says. "This is why nobody ever asks you to tell stories, gege."

"He's hopeless," Nainai says.

"Hey! That's not nice." I sigh again. "I mean, it's kind of weird describing it to, uh, to my grandmother, my father, and my little sister."

They stare uncomprehendingly. "George Clooney," Papa says after a while. "We are family. This what family do."

"I'm pretty sure it's not what families do." By now, I feel so tired that I'm ready to tell them the truth. "Okay. It was—even with Eleanor and Kiki and the reporters there—it was the best date I've ever been on."

Papa and Eleanor squeal. "I knew it!" Eleanor cries. "I knew she's going to be my sister-in-law!"

"That's quite a leap." But my voice is drowned by their excited flapping. I've completely lost them now. Shrugging, I open the sliding door and step back inside the villa. I go to the bar and take out a cold ginger ale. It feels amazing sliding down my throat, spicy and refreshing. I hold the can to my forehead and close my eyes.

"So, why do you look so down about it all?" Eleanor says, suddenly materializing next to me.

"Jesus!" I jump back and nearly drop the can. Papa is standing behind Eleanor. My loud, flappy, overly dramatic family can also move as quietly as a ghost when they put their minds to it.

"Did Sharlot reject you because she realized you're super boring and also into badgers?" Eleanor says.

I gape at them, opening and closing my mouth. "I don't—I—what? I don't know! I don't think so. Look, she didn't reject me, okay? I just—I'm feeling bad because I feel terrible lying to her about how we met online. All those chats we had, she thinks they were with me, but they weren't. They were with you and you." I point an accusatory finger at Pa and at Eleanor. "Thing One and Thing Two."

At least they have the good grace to look slightly abashed about it. Which doesn't last long, obviously. Eleanor is the first to rally. "It doesn't matter, gege! It's just chat messages. I bet she doesn't even remember what was said."

"She does. And the point is, what you two said is so different from the real me that I don't know which version she likes."

At this, Papa starts laughing.

"What's so funny?"

"Oh, son. Obviously she like proper version. The one Eleanor and I come up with. That one is very good version, every girl will fall for."

"Thanks, Pa."

"That version is good catch," he continues. "Like to do calculus, want to provide for family, is good husband material."

I glare at Eleanor. Of course Papa would think that's the ideal guy, but Eleanor should know better. But all she does is shrug and say, "Don't look at me, gege. I tried telling Papa that times have changed, but I am but a powerless, innocent child."

"Mm-hmm. Okay. I'm gonna go for a walk." Actually, what I really want is to take a long shower. But knowing my family, they'll all be waiting outside of the bathroom the entire time.

Outside, I wave at Fauzi and the other employees, who are all smoking, and begin walking. I'm not really sure where I'm headed, except I know I don't want to run into anyone I know, so I walk away from the main resort building. I guess I should be grateful that Eighth Aunt wasn't at the villa to join in the interrogation. Kind of weird, that. She's usually around, especially when Papa's going over the details for tomorrow's launch. That's Eighth Aunt's jam. I shrug and exhale. Who cares about that right now? Why am I even thinking of Eighth Aunt?

I follow the winding path until I hit the boundary of the resort, which is bordered by a tall wall, then I start going down the steps toward the beach. The resort boasts several kilometers of beachfront, and at this hour, there are still quite a few people out on the sand and lounging in the cabanas. I take off my sandals and walk to the waterline, relishing how the sand feels between my toes, and look out onto the water, feeling like my insides have been carved out, leaving me an empty husk. Okay, that sounds really dramatic. I guess I do have some of my dad's side of the family's flair after all.

It has been a day. I close my eyes and breathe in the salty air. In my mind's eye, I see Sharlot's face again. The way she'd looked at me as we revealed things about ourselves to each other. Real things, not surface bullshit. The way her hand had felt in mine, an utterly perfect fit. And then the desperation on her face when I told her I needed to reveal something. My chest twinges like my entire being is cringing with embarrassment. She had been so eager to get away from me. Have I misread everything? I'd thought that maybe she felt the same way I did. I sift through everything that happened today. The latte-art class, when Lukmi had asked me to put my arms around Sharlot. I could've sworn she'd leaned into me then, pressing her back up against my chest. I can still smell the fresh, tropical-flower scent of her hair. Or had I just imagined it? Maybe I was the one pressing up against her like some creep, and she'd been inwardly screaming?! Oh god, I can totally see guys doing this kind of shit and thinking it's romantic while girls either roll their eyes or make panicky faces at their friends to come rescue them. How did I become one of these assholes? What else have I misread? When I held her hand, was she actually dying to get away from me? AAAAHHH.

I'm this close to running down the beach while wailing, Papa-style, when a familiar voice says, "Oh, hey." I look up and who do I see, but Sharlot herself.

Great. Oh man. My mind has just chosen to implode about her, and here she is in the flesh. Why is she here? Chinese-Indos don't tend to go for the beach in Bali, because we're obsessed with not getting a tan. Then it hits me that she's more American than Indonesian, and if the movies are anywhere near accurate, she's probably all about getting a tan. Or maybe my mind needs to stop churning a mile a minute and give my mouth something to say instead of staring at her like some creepy creep?

"Uh." I should probably say something a little bit more cerebral than "uh," but my mind is drawing blank after blank.

"You okay?" Sharlot says, tucking her hair behind an ear. It's immediately blown loose by the sea breeze. I find myself reaching out to tuck it back in for one horrifying second before my mind manages to catch up with my hand and wrestle it back down to my side.

Snap. Out. Of. It.

I give myself a little shake of the head. "Yeah, I'm okay. Just wanted to, uh, take a little walk before dinner. Clear my head." Speaking of heads, I lower mine and then start walking, because the last thing I want to do is make Sharlot uncomfortable again.

"What's for dinner tonight?" she says, falling into step beside me.

My mind's knitting itself into the most elaborate knots,

trying to come up with explanations as to why Sharlot is choosing to walk with me. I mean, I haven't asked her or anything, she's the one who chose to join me. So maybe I haven't misread everything after all? You wouldn't join a guy you found repulsive on a walk on the beach, right?

"I think we're having a Japanese-Balinese infusion thing here, uh, at the hotel. I don't know."

"Wow, Japanese-infused Balinese food. That sounds yummy."

"Sure, yeah." My stomach's puckered into the size of a walnut and the thought of food is unbearable right now.

She glances at me before looking off into the horizon. I remind myself not to stare.

"Um, why are you out here? You must be tired after today." Did that sound as awkward out loud as it did in my head? How have I forgotten how to converse in the space of a few minutes?

"I'm still pretty keyed up, actually. I blame it on the coffee. I'm not used to the stuff you guys have here. They're so strong. I swear they're laced with cocaine or something."

I laugh at that. "I guess if you've only grown up drinking Starbucks . . ."

"Wow, okay, coffee snob," she shoots back without any barb. She takes a deep inhale and stretches her arms over her head. "But yeah, I did grow up drinking Starbucks and thinking that was real coffee. I've got no problem admitting I was wrong about that. I . . . I've been wrong about a lot of things recently."

Is it just me or is the look she gives me just then a particularly meaningful one? I need to take a class on how to decipher looks from girls.

"I've been wrong about a lot of things too," I say. What I really want to do is elaborate and tell her I was wrong to judge her based on our chat messages, but what if I wasn't wrong?

She takes a sudden long breath and says, "Um, so at the monkey forest, you were about to tell me something?"

Oh crap. Everything in my mind is obliterated. I try to think back to that moment, when I had decided in a hot rush of emotions to tell her the truth. "Er. Yeah, it was just—um, yeah, um." She had looked so panicked then. What did she think I was about to tell her? Anyway, it doesn't matter. I don't know what I was thinking. I can't possibly tell her before the launch of OneLiner. I don't know how she might react, but it's probably not going to be a happy reaction. I mean, sure, she's amazing in person, but her chat messages are all about righteousness, and what I did was definitely not righteous in the least. She might choose to blow up the entire thing, tell the world that I tricked her, that my family deceived her. Done right before the launch, it might undo us all.

"It's nothing," I say, after a terrible silence.

She looks disappointed, but then her eyes widen and she grabs my arm and yanks me to hide behind a nearby cabana.

"What is it?"

She shushes me and points in the distance, where I spot two figures on the beach. Two women. I frown at their silhouettes. Are they supposed to mean something to me?

"Wha—"

"That's my mom," Sharlot hisses. I don't know why she bothers trying to speak in a low voice; we're far enough away that they can't possibly hear us.

As though she hears what I'm thinking, she gestures for me to follow her. Still crouched low, we make our way toward the two figures as stealthily as we can, which is probably not at all stealthy. Fortunately, Shar's mom and her friend don't notice us. The crashing waves mask any sound of approach, and soon we're about as close as we can be while still remaining hidden. We stand behind a large rock and I rake my hair out of my face as Sharlot peers out from behind the rock. Why are we even hiding? Next to me, Sharlot suddenly stiffens and lets out a small gasp. Curiosity overcomes me and I peer out above her head.

Oh.

Shar's mom is kissing the other woman.

"Ah. Uh." I have no idea what to say. I take a deep breath and hold it for the longest time. The kiss continues for an eternity. Civilizations are built and crumble back into dust and are replaced by the time they emerge for air. And when they do, my mind short-circuits, because I get a glimpse of the other woman's face.

It's Eighth Aunt.

CHAPTER 23

Sharlot

George catches my hand and I realize I've been whispering, "Oh my god," out loud and am getting louder. I clap a hand over my mouth and stare, wide-eyed and wild-eyed, at George. He goggles back at me, his mouth gaping open. We gesture frantically at each other, shouting soundlessly behind our rock. No words come out, but I think the conversation is somewhere along the lines of:

Holy shit?!

I know!

What the hell?

I KNOW!

WHAT DO WE DO?

I DON'T KNOW!

AAAAAHHHHH!

AAHGSFHGASJSH!

At some point, we decide we can't possibly get caught by Mama and George's Eighth Aunt, so we rush from the beach, clambering up the stone steps back to the main resort building.

Once we're far enough away from the beach that we can no longer see even a glimpse of sand, we stop and catch our breaths.

It's only then that I realize we're holding hands. When and how did that happen? Who caught whose hand? George seems to realize it at the same time and snatches his hand away like my fingers have turned into snakes, which is very flattering. Not. I try not to show how much that bothers me. And anyway, we've got a more pressing issue here.

"Oh my god," I say again. I feel like I should probably say something more intelligent than that, but seriously, oh my god.

"Did you know your mum's, uh—?"

Something about the way he falters rakes at my skin. "You can say 'lesbian,' George. Or bisexual." The words come out so much more caustic than I meant them to that I almost apologize. Almost.

He grimaces. "Sorry, I didn't mean to—I mean, I'm just. I don't—um."

He looks so sorry that I deflate a little. "It's fine. No, I didn't know. I've always assumed that my mother's straight." The words burn me with guilt. Why had I assumed that Mama was straight? Now that I stop to think about it, it feels like a serious oversight, an assumption I made because I'm heterosexual and therefore everyone else is too. A lazy, harmful assumption. I mean, I even assumed she was into George's dad! Why do I have to make a heteronormative assumption about everyone? This is definitely something I need to work on. I squeeze my eyes shut. Somehow, this realization has changed everything. When I think back to my interactions with Mama, they're all colored differently, all of them reframed with a different meaning.

George is looking as shaken as I feel, and it hits me then that he must be pretty surprised too, since it wasn't just Mama on the beach. "You good?" I say.

He gapes at me. "I mean, yeah. Just a bit shell-shocked." He pauses, looking thoughtful. "It's stupid, but I'm just looking back at everything I thought I knew about Eighth Aunt and realizing that I knew nothing about her. She never married, you know. I always thought it was because she never met any man good enough for her."

"Well, I mean, that's also probably true," I say.

He laughs. "Yeah." He hesitates. "I guess I'm really happy for her, but also really sad."

"Why sad?" I immediately bristle again. Is he sad because he thinks any sexual orientation aside from hetero is less than legit?

"Because it's not allowed here, Shar," he says softly. "It's not as bad in places like Bali and Jakarta, but in the more provincial areas like Aceh, it could get you like, caned. And even in Jakarta, people are mostly not accepting of it. If they were found out, they'd become social pariahs."

Oh. A small star implodes inside me, shattering everything. Was this why Mama hadn't wanted to come back to Indonesia all these years? I think of how judgmental I'd been toward her for keeping things from me, for not wanting to talk about Indonesia, and I feel nauseated at how cruel I'd been. I'd just assumed that she didn't want to come back here because she felt the place isn't good enough for her. I was so wrong. I have no idea, absolutely none, what it's like to live in a place and know that who you are could land you in prison. The suffocating weight of it.

The truth is, Mama isn't just my mom, she's a whole person in her own right. How did it take me so long to see that? I've always just seen her as my mother, the person whose life revolves around mine. What a selfish, bratty way to think of another human being. She has a story of her own, one that doesn't involve me at all. One that's heartbreaking.

"Oh god." I sink down onto the ground and bury my face in my hands. Dimly, I feel George's hand on my shoulder, and the weight of it is so reassuring that before I can stop myself, I lean into him, resting my head on his shoulder. He stiffens. For an awful moment I wonder if he's about to push me away, but then he puts his arm around my shoulders and I let myself fall apart, just a little.

"She's been carrying this weight with her all this time," I whisper.

"Yeah," George says quietly. "They both have."

"Do you think that maybe that's why she left Indonesia and never wanted to come back?" My voice is raw with desperation. I can't help but think of every thoughtless comment I've thrown at her, every barb I've stabbed into her armor because I was so angry about her unwillingness to tell me about Indonesia.

"Maybe? Probably? I don't know, I can't pretend to know what it's like to live in a place that doesn't accept—" His words break off in a ragged sigh. "God, all this while, Eighth Aunt..."

"I've been so horrible to her, I've been so shitty," I moan over and over again, and George nods and holds me tighter and tells me it's okay, there's time for me to make it up to Mama, that she knows I didn't mean to hurt her, and so on and so forth. The whole time I'm falling, George holds me together, his arms tight around me, not letting me crash into a thousand pieces. He murmurs things to me. "It's okay" and "You'll be okay" and a dozen other words that mean nothing and everything in this moment.

"I wish I could do something. Show her that I know and I still love her and that I'm sorry. I wish I could know what they went through when they were younger. She said they were best friends. Did they—did someone find out, and my mom had to leave?" Every single possibility is horrifying. Mama, just a teenager at the time, having to flee the only home she'd ever known. Having to leave her girlfriend behind. And yet, despite all of that, she was able to make a good life for herself and for me. From the depths of this awful realization, a newfound feeling emerges—admiration. My mom is sort of a badass.

It feels as though hours have passed by the time I stop freaking out and am able to lift my head to face the world again. I'm a mess. I feel like a little kid who needs her mom. I turn to look at George and realize that our faces are only inches apart. Everything inside me is so raw that I nearly start crying again at the sight of him, because here is a guy I've been doing nothing but lying to, and it's so impossibly hard to look at him when he's this close to me, when I can see how his eyes aren't black like I thought they were, but the deepest, warmest brown. When I can see the tiniest freckles dusted across his nose, when I can see a small scar just below his left eyebrow. It's like reading his life story on his face, and it's too much. This close, I can't bring myself to hate him, and maybe I don't hate him, not even when I think of our chat messages, not even then.

It takes a lot of effort to look away. I do anyway because it's all too much. "I . . . uh." My voice is raw and jagged and I barely recognize it. I clear my throat and try again. "I should go get ready for dinner. You should too."

You should too. Can I possibly sound more naggy?

He nods and gives me a small smile. "Yeah." We're still holding hands as we stand up. I start to pull my hand away, but stop. Because . . . I don't want to. I want to keep holding hands with him, which is very weird and not at all the way things are supposed to be.

I guess George is too much of a gentleman to let go of my hand when I'm so obviously holding on, so we walk back toward the villas hand in hand. My heart is thudding so hard I'm pretty sure he can feel my hand pulsing in his, but he doesn't say anything. I steal glances at him, wondering what he's thinking, wondering what I should say to Mama, wondering at how much things can change in a single day.

"Are you going to say anything to your aunt?"

George looks thoughtful. "I don't think so," he says finally. "It's not really my secret to reveal, and I don't know how comfortable she'd be talking about it with me. I do want her to know that I would support her if she were to come out, but I don't know how to do that, so. Yeah. What about you?"

"I'm really torn. I know what you mean about it not being my secret to reveal, but I know my mom. If I don't bring it up, she'll never bring it up herself, and the thought of her keeping it to herself is . . ." My breath releases in a shuddery sigh and my eyes fill with tears. "I don't think I can go to the big dinner tonight." The thought of having to face his cousins and aunts and uncles is exhausting.

I'm expecting George to tell me that I have to, that people will wonder why I'm not there, but instead he says, "Yeah, me neither."

"Shall I tell everyone that I finally got the food poisoning that they've all been waiting for me to get?"

George laughs. "Okay. How about we both have runny tummies—"

"Runny tummy?" I have to chomp down viciously on my bottom lip to keep from grinning.

"It's nicer than saying diarrhea!" George cries. "Anyway, I'll tell everyone we're a bit run-down after today's activities and we want to be fresh and perky for tomorrow so we're giving tonight's dinner a miss. And then . . ." He takes a deep breath. "How about you and I go have some real Balinese food? Just the two of us. No cameras. No cousin or pesky little sister."

"That sounds great." The words slip out before I realize what I'm saying. And I mean them. Oh god, how I mean them. Nothing sounds better than a quiet dinner with George right now. His smile covers his entire face, making him look all of five years old. It's so endearing I almost kiss him. Almost.

"Okay, I'll arrange for a driver and tell my dad we won't be joining for dinner and see you back here in ten minutes?"

I nod.

He gives my hand a squeeze. "You're gonna be fine, Shar."

I love the way he says my name, turning it soft and sweet in his mouth. And when we arrive at my villa, something overcomes all the questions and voices in my head and I stand on tiptoes and kiss him on the cheek before I can second-guess myself. The look of surprise on his face is such a delight to see that I can't help but smile. Then I say, "See you later!" and slip inside my villa. I lean against the door and take a deep breath. God, what a day.

"You're grinning as wide as the Joker," Kiki says from the living room couch, where she's channel surfing. "My guess is that it has something to do with Prince George, am I right?"

I wrestle the smile off my face and pointedly ignore Kiki as I make my way to the bathroom to take a shower and get ready for my evening with George.

CHAPTER 24

Sharlot

I don't know what I was expecting when George said local Balinese food, but whatever it was, it doesn't come anywhere close to the reality. The restaurant he takes me to, Warung Babi Guling Pak Malen, is a swelteringly hot warehouse-like shack packed full of people. It's still really early—barely six o'clock, but the place is heaving. We grab seats at a long table with five other people who are too busy talking among themselves to pay us any attention, and George asks if I'm okay with him ordering the food. I nod, grateful that he's going to be doing the ordering. I don't want to sound like a total princess, but I'm kind of out of my element here.

As George puts in an order for what sounds like an obscene amount of food, there are shouts of *Awas!* which means "Watch out!" and four men walk through the restaurant carrying an entire roast pig skewered on a spit. Holy shit. I watch, open-mouthed, as they lug the humongous thing to the back of the restaurant, where a group of women chop it up into various parts with startling efficiency.

The food arrives just minutes after George puts in our order—plates of rice piled high with juicy chunks of pork, fried green beans, crunchy pork crackling, crispy golden-brown pork skin, pork satay, and of course, Pak Malen's special house blend of chili. Two icy bottles filled with a dark-brown drink are placed alongside the dishes. George has even ordered an extra plate of the pork meat and crackling on the side.

I'm melting in this heat, so I take one of the bottles. The label reads Teh Botol, which literally translates to "bottled tea." What a boring name. I take a sip, and whoa. I've honestly never tasted tea this good. It's knock-your-socks-off strong, delightfully sweet, and so fragrant that it feels like drinking a bottle of jasmine flowers.

George must've noticed my expression because he laughs and says, "I know, right? Teh Botol is the best. I have no idea what they put in it."

I take a small spoonful of rice and cut off a bit of pork and put it in my mouth. Holy crap, my toes have curled up tight out of sheer deliciousness, and I'm clenching my spoon and fork so tightly that the edges are digging painfully into my palms.

"Good, huh?"

"*So* good." I take a bite of the pork skin and it's as crispy as a potato chip, savory and sweet all at once. "My god."

"They continuously brush the pig with coconut water as it roasts, which is why the skin is sweet."

I close my eyes and take a deep inhale. Sure enough, I can smell the scent of caramelized coconut along with the meaty juices of the pork. I'm glad George has thought to order an extra plate of the stuff, because now I'm just popping them like chips. It's only after my plate is completely cleaned that I stop gorging myself long enough to have a conversation with George.

"Sorry about that. I'm usually more ladylike when I eat."

"You mean you don't usually eat like a bear who's just come out of hibernation?"

"Uhh, look who's talking," I shoot back, glancing at his own empty plate. "You finished your food before I did."

"Well yeah, see, I actually do eat like a bear who's just come out of hibernation. It's part and parcel of being a healthy, growing boy."

A plate of pork crackling is placed between us. "Freshly fried," the server says. "For George Tanuwijaya and his first love." He winks at us and leaves before I can say anything.

For a second, neither of us speaks. Then I shrug and pop a piece of crackling into my mouth. Immediately I'm filled with regret, because holy crap, that's hot. "Ow, ow, ow." I bite it between my teeth and blow in and out while covering my mouth with my hand.

"Very ladylike," George says, grinning.

When it's finally cool enough, I put it back in my mouth. Savory, porky umami fills my entire mouth. "Wow. Okay, I changed my mind. The skin isn't the best part about this meal. The crackling definitely is."

George nods as he chews on a piece. "Did you know that pork crackling has zero carbs and is actually pretty high in protein?"

I can't help snorting out loud.

"And pork fat has been found to be good for brain development. It's high in DHA—the omega-3 fatty acid that they recommend pregnant women to have in large doses."

"George," I say, leaning close to him.

His face turns serious and he leans close too.

"That is so sexy. Talk to me some more about omega-3 fatty acids."

There's a beat of silence, and then he laughs. He laughs like I've never seen him laugh before. His entire demeanor changes, his broad shoulders shaking, his whole face lighting up like a sunrise. I'm surprised by how difficult I find it to look away from him right now. It's probably just all the endorphins from the food and the sugary drinks.

After paying, we go back to the car and George asks the driver to go back to the hotel. I think about going back to the villa and being alone while everyone else is still mingling at the huge family dinner and my insides clench. "Actually, can we go someplace else?" I say.

George turns to me with a puzzled frown. "Really? We've got an early morning tomorrow. What're you thinking of doing?"

"I don't know. I just—I'm not ready to go back."

He must've noticed something raw in my expression because he asks the driver to take us someplace else. It strikes me that it may not be a good idea to let a boy I've sort of kind of just started to know take me somewhere I don't know while I'm in a foreign country, and I pat my messenger bag to assure myself that my can of deodorant's still in there. In a pinch, it'll make for an excellent pepper spray substitute.

After about a twenty-minute drive, the car stops at the front of what looks like a garage.

"Um . . ." Okay, now I'm really starting to question my life choices. The shop sign says: ULUWATU SCOOTER & MOTOR BIKE HIRE. A grin spreads across my face. I would never have thought of doing anything like this. Come to think of it, I never would've thought that George—born and raised in the city and chauffeured around his entire life—would want to ride a scooter around Bali either. I mean, his "hobby" consists of doing *math*, for god's sake.

We walk inside and George speaks rapid Indonesian to the shopkeeper before turning back to me. "He's asking if you've ever ridden a scooter or motor bike before."

"Oh. Um. No." I know it's dumb, but saying it feels like I'm admitting a character flaw or something. Definitely minus cool points for me.

The shopkeeper gives me a once-over and then says in English, "Sorry, miss, you not eighteen yet, you not drive scooter. You two just hire one, okay?"

"What?" I snap. "No way, not okay. Why the hell can't I ride a scooter on my own?"

"Sorry, no rental to foreign teens. You get hurt, my business get sue. I rent to him only."

By now, I'm way too full of carbs and sugar and pork crackling to do anything but shrug and say, "Fine."

We're given a helmet each, and like a total noob, I struggle to clasp mine. George steps toward me and says, "May I?"

May I.

My heart gives the tiniest bit of a squeeze at how old-fashioned he sounds. I nod wordlessly and he takes the straps of my helmet. His face is so close to mine that I have no idea where to look. I keep glancing away and then glancing back, trying not to be so obvious about admiring his face. Up close, he's even better looking than he has any right to be. His eyebrows are thick and straight, making him look slightly stern, slightly older. And his jawline is so strong. Very Captain America–ish. Except, you know, Asian.

The clasp clicks into place, shocking me out of my lecherous thoughts. I practically jump away from him as though I've been burned. George looks a bit taken aback by that—who can blame him?—so I busy myself by looking everywhere around me but at him.

It's only after George pays and an assistant wheels out a scooter that I realize something really, really awkward: I'm going to have to put my arms around his waist.

Uh-oh. The realization's like a supernova inside me. Suddenly, every part of me is burning, from deep in my belly all the way to my fingertips. I'm sure my usually pale cheeks are now neon red.

Stop that, Shar. He's just some kid. Okay, so technically he's your age and therefore not a kid. But look at him! He's so—so kidlike with his clean-shaven chin and those big teddy bear eyes of his, and that neat haircut and those surprisingly broad swimmer's shoulders and his angular, muscled arms and—hmm. Okay, so technically he's not at all kidlike. But he's still a nerd. He legit talked about DHA omega-3 fatty acids as dinnertime conversation. You're going to be hugging a nerd.

A hot nerd.

Argh, this is hopeless. Oh, wait, I know what this is. It's my stupid teenage hormones again. Right. I don't actually like George. It's just glandular.

I ease my breath out slowly. Dear glands: Please stop glanding. Okay. I've got it under control. All it took was to identify the problem, i.e., my hormones, and now that I'm aware of it, I can totally ignore it.

"You okay?" George says, climbing onto the seat. He turns the key and the scooter starts up with a rumble.

A small whisper-moan slips out of me. He looks sexy AF on that thing. STOP IT, GLANDS.

He must've misread my hesitation because he gives me a reassuring smile and says, "Don't worry, I'm a safe driver."

Which should not be sexy, but somehow is. This is hopeless. I take another big gulp of air and slowly make my way to the scooter. When I swing my leg over the back seat, I swallow so loudly I bet George can hear it over the sound of the engine. WTF? What part of *be cool* did my body not get? Stop salivating/sweating/doing anything that involves any secretions!

We sit there for a moment, and then George turns around and says, "Um. You should hang on to me."

"Right." I have to consciously instruct my arms to lift up and go around his waist. How far should I go? I fail to come up with an answer, so I go all the way around and link my fingers together at his front. Great, now my entire body is pressed up against his back. My next inhale is so shaky it makes me cough. George shifts, and I swear I can feel every muscle on his back moving, his skin hot and very much *there*.

"Let's go," he says, and swings us out of the garage.

The moment we hit the road, all thoughts of how awkwardly close to George I am sitting whip out of my head. The salty seaside air blows into my face, and for a few moments, I close my eyes and allow myself to just enjoy the sensations of everything. The thrum of the scooter, the feel of the wind in my hair, the sensation of speed, the hardness of George's abs—

No. Bad brain. Bad.

I open my eyes again and find that George has taken us off the main road and we're now on a small road that goes alongside the cliffs overlooking a pristine beach. Wow. This time, my entire body relaxes. It's impossible not to when I'm presented with this incredible view—the fine sand so yellow it looks like something a child might have drawn, the water a deep sapphire, all the robust tropical jungle around us. So different from the beaches of California. So much more untamed and magical.

I don't know how long we ride for—I've lost myself entirely in this moment. But when we finally do stop, I realize with a start that I've rested my head on George's back. Oops. I jerk away as soon as the engine's cut and practically scramble off the scooter. When I stand, I brush invisible lint off my clothes to avoid meeting George's eye.

"We're here," he says, taking off his helmet.

"What's here?"

"The Uluwatu Temple." He points to the distance, where the cliffs curve into a bracket. At the very tip of the cliffs right above the crashing waves is a pagoda.

"Wow." Talk about magical. This is right out of a fantasy novel.

"It's my favorite part of Bali," George says, leaning against the railing and gazing at the temple. "We could go closer, but there's always a huge crowd there. They've turned the surroundings into a tourist spot with restaurants and kecak dance shows."

"What's a kecak dance?"

"It's the Balinese fire dance. I think there's supposed to be one at the launch tomorrow."

"Cool, I can't wait to watch it." And I actually do mean it, with zero sarcasm, which surprises even me. There's just something about Bali. I glance at George, who's gazing at the temple, the brilliant orange sunset painting his face a fiery red, before gazing back out at the incredible scenery before me. Something overcomes me and I take my tablet out of my bag. "Is it okay if I sketch for a bit?"

George looks pleasantly surprised. "Yeah, of course."

We find a nearby bench and sit down. I make myself as comfortable as I can, sitting cross-legged so I can rest my tablet on my lap. At first, I think it's going to be awkward to have George watch me do this, but as soon as I draw my first stroke, I leave behind all of my hesitation and lose myself in the blank page. As I sketch, George and I chat about nothing and everything. I'm only half listening, but somehow it's so soothing to hear him talk about random stuff—how over the top his family is; how he's learning to cook from his grandmother; how excited Eleanor is about getting a phone, though he's not sure the internet is ready for Eleanor. I laugh at some things and murmur sympathetically at others and I tell him everything as well.

"I never got along with Mama," I say, and it's surprising how effortlessly the words come out. "When I was little, I'd ask her all these questions about Indo, and she never wanted to answer them. It made me so angry that I decided to shut her out. I never really stopped to think why she didn't want to talk about Indonesia." I sigh and look up from my sketchbook, but George is smiling a little as he watches me, and I feel my cheeks growing warm. "What?"

"Well, we've been focusing on the bad, which is understandable, given there's so much bad about the whole situation and lack of LGBTQ rights here, but there's also a lot of good. I mean, if you think about it, it's sort of . . . really freaking sweet. Your mom and Eighth Aunt were in love as teens, and they carried that with them for like, ever. They're, what, in their late thirties now?"

"Ancient," I say.

"Yeah, total dinosaurs. And yet they're still in love with each other. I mean, isn't that romantic? Their story has a happy ending, Shar. Despite everything else working against them. They did it. They found each other again, after all this time."

Warmth floods my heart and envelops my entire being. Tears rush into my eyes. He's right. I've been so focused on the bad that I forgot the most important thing, which is that Mama and

Eighth Aunt have managed to find each other again. That kiss they shared today . . . I smile as I think about all the history behind it. Who would've thought that my strict, overprotective mother could have this insanely romantic, defiant, fearless love story behind her?

The sun has set when I finish my drawing and we both look at it wordlessly. I hadn't been sure about what I was going to draw until it's drawn, and now here it is. A boy and girl at the beach, holding hands before a blazing sunset. I watch him look at my drawing and then George looks at me and we close the electric distance between us. Our mouths meet in a soft rush, his lips yielding to mine. The good, clean scent of him enfolds me, and I twine my hands around the back of his neck, needing to feel more of him against me. Our mouths move against each other's in sync with the waves crashing against the cliff side, and I know then that no matter what happens, this isn't something I am going to be able to move on from so easily, not even from all the way on the other side of the world.

PART THREE

CHAPTER 25

Sharlot

When I wake up the next morning, our villa is swarming with people. Hair and makeup and nail artists and someone's assistant who's rattling off instructions to Mama. There's also someone who's come by to deliver boxes of food, because of course multiple people have arranged for food to be delivered so every available surface is covered with various foods and makeup and hair equipment and papers that are probably itineraries for the day. Kiki is getting her hair done. When she spots me creeping into the living room, she says something to one of the makeup people and immediately I'm led to a chair next to hers and pushed into it.

"Ah, the girlfriend," someone who's presumably a makeup artist says.

"It's the twenty-first century, we're still referring to people as 'the girlfriend'?" I snap very snappishly. I did not manage to get much sleep last night, not after that incredible kiss.

"Oh, I'm sorry, dear," she says, not at all looking sorry. "But that is what you are known as. It'll be a while yet before people learn to see you as your own person." She tilts my face this way and that and says, "Beautiful. I know just the look for you."

"I mean, I can do my own makeup—"

"Not like this, you can't, sweetie," the makeup person says, already dabbing primer onto my face.

"Trust me, you're gonna want to get your makeup professionally done," Kiki mutters. "Otherwise, you'll look so drab in the photos. There's just something about pro makeup that I can't get right, no matter how many times I try."

I catch Mama's eye in the mirror as she walks past and she pauses to plant a kiss on the top of my head. I almost jump out of my chair and hug her. I want to tell her I know, and that we should talk about everything.

"Morning, dear. Feeling better this morning?" she says.

It takes a moment to recall that I supposedly had food poisoning last night. "Oh yeah. Loads. I took those activated charcoal pills and they worked wonders."

Mama smiles at me. "Good!" She starts to walk off, but I call out to her and she turns her head and looks at me expectantly.

I can't ask her any of the things I want to ask her now, not with everyone around, so after a pregnant pause, I shrug and say, "Nothing. You look great."

She beams and walks off. She really does look great. Younger, more vibrant. More present, as though the last few years she'd just been a ghost of her real self and now she's coming back to life. Truly, I have missed out on so much of her. There's so much for us to talk about. But later, not now.

"Don't frown, dear," the makeup artist says. "Smooth out your forehead, please."

I try not to glower at her intrusion. My phone beeps.

George [08:12AM]: Breakfast? ☺

My whole body blushes.

George [08:12AM]: They've got made-to-order waffles at the breakfast buffet.

Sharlot [08:13AM]: Gah, so tempting, but I can't. I was ambushed by a battalion of makeup artists

George [08:14AM]: Oh yeah. I forgot about that. El has gone to Eighth Aunt's villa to get her makeup done as well.

Sharlot [08:15AM]: You're lucky you don't have to gel your hair and makeup done 'cause you're a boy

George [08:15AM]: You mean because I'm naturally gorgeous?

Sharlot [08:16AM]: Eh

George [08:16AM]: Harsh.

"Stop smiling, please," the makeup artist says, sounding markedly grumpy. "Just—keep your face neutral, okay?"

I didn't know I was smiling until she pointed it out, and when I try to follow her instruction about keeping my face neutral, it takes a surprising amount of effort to wrestle the smile off my face. What the hell?

With a start, I realize that I hadn't even thought twice before replying to him. Since when did it become second nature to chat with George?

"Let me guess," Kiki says, leaning closer and peering at my phone, "texting CuriousGeorge?"

I tilt my phone away so she can't see the screen, suddenly feeling self-conscious. I'm glad that by now I have about three hundred layers of product on my face to hide the blush that's surely creeping up my cheeks.

"You don't have to look so guilty about texting your boyfriend," Kiki says, laughing.

I swear my entire face is made out of molten lava. Texting my boyfriend. How natural that sounds. How *weirdly* natural. Fortunately, Kiki goes back to tapping on her own phone and leaves me to my own jumbled thoughts. My phone beeps again.

George [08:32AM]: Ta-da!

He's sent me a photo of waffles with slices of pork and pork crackling on the side.

George [08:32AM]: The Balinese version of chicken and waffles.

Sharlot [08:33AM]: Thanks for making me jealous

George [08:33AM]: ... look again at the picture, doofus.

Frowning, I do as he says. And this time, I see that the food's inside a takeaway box. How did I miss that before? My heart swells up like a balloon. I feel as though my entire body is made out of heart. I bite my lip to keep from grinning and the makeup artist tuts again, so I hurriedly fight to rearrange my features into something more acceptable.

Sharlot [08:34AM]: Thank you. You didn't have to do that

George [08:35AM]: Do you want anything else from the buffet table?

He sends me a handful of pictures, this time of the buffet display.

"Is that the breakfast buffet?" Kiki says. I hadn't realized she's yet again snooping, but I'm not surprised.

"Yes," I mumble.

"Why's he sending you photos of the buff—ohhh." She looks at me, grinning like a loon. "Aww, Shar, that is so sweet!" She turns to the makeup and hair people and says, "He's getting her food from the breakfast buffet. Isn't that so sweet?"

They both nod, smiling for the first time. "Ah, young love," my makeup artist says.

"Girl, that is definitely sweet," Kiki's hair person says. "Any boy who remembers to bring you food is a keeper."

"Stop it," I groan.

"Tell him I want sushi with extra salmon roe and sea urchin egg custard," Kiki says. "And I also want some honeycomb—this hotel is known for having actual honeycomb."

"How do you know what they have?" I mutter as I rush through her order.

"Instagram," is all Kiki would say. Then she rattles off more food and drink that she wants.

Sharlot [08:39AM]: Kiki wants sushi with extra salmon roe, sea urchin egg custard, honeycomb, tenderloin tacos, coconut ice cream with caramelized palm sugar syrup, bacon pancakes, cappuccino, and a jamu

George [08:40AM]: Oh.

George [08:40AM]: My.

George [08:40AM]: God.

Sharlot [08:41AM]: Sorryyyy

George [08:41AM]: [Shocked face emoji]

Sharlot [08:42AM]: I can tell her we can't get her those things

George [08:42AM]: And suffer her wrath?? I'll get them. I can do this. I am a valiant warrior.

Honestly, mouth, please stop smiling like that.

Sharlot [08:43AM]: My knight in shining armor

George [08:43AM]: That is literally me.

Sharlot [08:44AM]: Oh, and Kiki says make sure it's the turmeric jamu and not the fermented rice one

George [08:45AM]: What's the difference??

Sharlot [08:45AM]: Apparently the turmeric one helps curb your appetite and the fermented rice one increases your appetite

George [08:46AM]: Does she realize how much food she's just asked me to get her?

Sharlot [08:46AM]: Yes, George, of course I realize it. I'm not stupid. The turmeric jamu also has slimming properties, which will negate all the calories from the food you're supposed to be getting us

George [08:47AM]: Hi, Kiki.

Sharlot [08:47AM]: Hi. Stop chatting and start gathering my food, k thanks.

George [08:48AM]: Ok. Does Sharlot want anything else?

Sharlot [08:48AM]: Yoasd&24@

George [08:49AM]: . . . You okay?

Sharlot [08:50AM]: Hi! Yes, I'm okay. Just had to wrestle the phone from Kiki. Thanks for getting the food!

George [08:50AM]: Np!

I glare at Kiki, breathing hard and clutching my phone to my chest. "I can't believe you were about to type *you*."

She shrugs, not looking sorry in the slightest. "I'm just being romantic."

"Stop fooling around, please," my makeup artist says. She hadn't been impressed when Kiki and I battled over my phone. I glance up at the mirror and pause.

"Whoa." Kiki was right about getting my makeup professionally done. I've never seen my skin look so glowy before. It looks poreless and dewy, like a K-pop star. And she's done some shading on strategic parts of my face so that my nose looks more defined and my cheekbones are popping. Speaking of popping, my eyes look incredible—huge and alluring and impossible not to stare at. "Wow, thank you," I manage to say after a while.

"Stop talking," she murmurs as she paints my lips. She narrows her eyes at me. "You'll have to take small bites when you eat so you don't spoil my handiwork."

I widen my eyes at Kiki, who's shaking with silent laughter.

The hairdresser, in the meantime, has swept my hair into a complicated side braid twined with ribbons and flowers. Once my hair and makeup is done, I'm squeezed into a dress that Kiki's prepared for me—a floor-length lilac gown made of the softest chiffon. The waist is cinched with a beautiful traditional jeweled belt and the skirt flows down as smooth as a waterfall. When I walk, the chiffon moves silkily, brushing my skin like a soft cloud. I feel like a fairy princess come to life.

When George arrives, I answer the door and am rewarded with the sight of George standing there, openmouthed as he takes me in.

"Hi." My voice comes out small and foreign. I don't recognize the sound.

"Shar—"

The click of a picture being taken distracts us both, and I turn around to see Kiki taking photos of us with her phone.

"Look, I got his expression," she says, scrolling through the photos. "Ah, if this isn't love, I don't—ow, ow, ow!"

I shove her while pinching until she stomps away, yelling, "I just wanted to help!"

"Oh, here's the food." George hands me a stupidly heavy bag

filled with takeaway boxes. Kiki rushes back, snatches the bag from me, and scampers away, yelling, "Thanks, Prince George!"

"Sorry," I say, desperately searching for an excuse. "She's just . . . she's. Yeah."

One corner of George's mouth lifts into a wry smile. "I could get used to being called Prince George."

I roll my eyes, and just like that, we're back to our usual selves. Though I can't help but notice that George is stealing a lot more glances at me than before, which makes me self-conscious as hell. I touch my face lightly, feeling how crazy smooth my skin is. "Does it look okay? I've never had my makeup professionally done."

George hurriedly nods. "Yeah, I mean. Yeah, you look good. Really good." He scratches the back of his neck and glances away, but not before I catch the blush coloring his cheeks. "Anyway, I should get going. We're having a rehearsal for the launch, and uh. Yeah."

"Oh yeah." I hadn't thought of how busy his day must be, given he's the face of the new app and everything. "Sorry, if I had known you're so busy today, I wouldn't have asked you to get me and Kiki breakfast."

He shrugs. "It was nothing." He turns to go, but changes his mind at the last minute and turns back to face me.

My heart goes, "AAAAH," or maybe it's my mind? Well, some part of me is going, "AAAAH," anyway. When I swallow, my mouth is bone-dry. What does that even mean, bone-dry? And why am I thinking about things like *bone-dry* now? What is it about George that makes my thoughts zip around like they're caught in a hurricane and my heart pound like . . . uh, like a mallet being pounded into a vat of glutinous rice to make mochi? Okay, clearly I need to work on my analogies.

"Yeah?" I squeak. I didn't mean to squeak. I'm not the type of person who squeaks.

"I—um." He licks his lips quickly, like his mouth is as dry as mine. "I have something to tell you."

"Oh?" I squeak again in the squeakiest squeak that ever was squeaked.

"It's just—you know how we met? Online?"

Oh shit. Oh god. Oh no. All the butterflies that were fluttering inside me just a second ago turn into lead and drop dead with a heavy thump. He's going to tell me that he knows all about my lie. He's found out somehow. Maybe he's figured it out. He's not stupid, he would've figured it out at some point. "George, I'm so sor—"

"I didn't think I'd like you, but I do," he blurts out.

"—what?"

"I really, really like you, Sharlot," he says, and his voice is so earnest that it makes tears spring into my eyes.

"I really like you too," I whisper in a hoarse voice. This moment is both beautiful and terrible. How can one heart be filled with so many emotions at once? I'm torn between spinning and laughing with giddy joy and curling up and crying with crushing guilt.

The relief on his face is palpable. Since when did his face become one that I'm so fond of? How did that happen? I reach out for his hand and practically smile with my entire body when he catches it. The feel of his fingers around mine is at once comforting and familiar, like our hands are meant to hold each other's.

"After the event, can we talk?" he says, taking a step toward me. He's so close that I can't breathe without taking in the scent of him, a heady smell of freshly roasted coffee and crushed jasmine flowers.

I just about manage a nod. My entire body aches to step closer so that we are pressed up against each other, so that I can feel the reassuring warmth of him against me. I take a small step and now there's only a single, lonely inch separating us. "Yeah, I would like that."

He dips his head slowly, gently, and I raise mine to meet his. When our lips finally touch, it's soft and sweet and utterly intoxicating. But the truth still holds me back, its presence a stumbling block in my mind. Tonight. After the event. I'll tell him the truth, and it'll be okay. We like each other. Really like each other. And I'll explain to him that I didn't have much of a choice in the matter, and that Mama didn't mean any harm, and he'll understand. Maybe he'll even find it funny.

He's not going to find it funny. What was I thinking? There's nothing funny about finding out that you were being swindled by your girlfriend's mother.

Girlfriend.

I hate that the word makes my heart flip, that it makes me want to squeal and laugh. Part of me, anyway.

And also, I won't remain his girlfriend, fake or not, for long. Not after I tell him the truth. Which I will, tonight. I can't have it festering inside me for much longer.

Backstage, I pace around restlessly. I can't believe I'm actually here at the launch of OneLiner. George's family has really gone all out for the event; they've erected a giant stage right smack in the middle of the resort at the end of the infinity pool. There are colored spotlights everywhere and what looks like thousands of lanterns strung up above the pool, their light reflecting beautifully on the water, making it look like a pool full of stars. Huge cameras have been set up in front of the stage to live-stream the event to various TV channels and all over social media, and there are over a thousand guests seated in Tiffany chairs in front of the stage, fanning themselves and sipping signature cocktails.

"Hey," George says, coming up the stairs. He's a sight to behold. In his tux, with his hair mussed up just so, he's devastatingly handsome. I have to remind myself to not stare. I force a smile.

"Hey, you look good."

He flips imaginary long hair behind his shoulder. "Thank you, I know."

I laugh, groaning.

"You look beautiful," he says, his voice turning serious, and I stop laughing because now I'm melting into a puddle. Stop that, self.

"Um, so." I have no idea how to accept compliments. "Are you ready for, um." I gesture at everything around us—all of the crew rushing around backstage and calling out cues and giving instructions.

He shrugs. "No? But I don't think that matters. The show must go on, or whatever." He gives me a rueful smile that makes him look so boyish and adorable. Gah, stop that, stop admiring his smiles and his stupidly good-looking face and his very broad shoulders and his hair and—

"Ladies and gentlemeeeeeen!" the MC's voice booms across the stage and the audience, which has been murmuring and chatting up to this point, quiets down. "Welcome to the exciting launch of OneLiner!"

George half smiles, half grimaces, and we both turn to look at one of the screens backstage that allows us a view of the audience out there. With a start, I realize that we're holding hands. When did that happen? How the hell did we become one of those couples to whom holding hands is so natural that I don't even notice when he takes mine? Or maybe I was the one who sought his hand out. I give myself a little shake. Whatever, it's just holding hands, sheesh. Stop freaking out, please, self.

"We are so honored to have all of you here tonight to celebrate the first ever app designed by our own George Tanuwijaya," the MC says. "And after the presentation, you will get to meet the girl who has captured George's heart!"

Even from backstage, we can hear the appreciative applause and hoots from the audience. George's palm turns slightly moist and I squeeze his hand as reassuringly as I can, even though my own insides have turned to water.

"You'll do great."

He nods, looking like a terrified kid. But before he can reply, one of the backstage techs strides over and attaches a small mic to the lapel of George's tux. Next to the tech is Fauzi, scrolling through his tablet and looking very harassed.

Fauzi glances up at us, seems to only just notice my presence, and says, "Oh, you're back here. Perfect."

"Uh. Perfect?" I say.

"Yeah, I was just looking for you. Rina requested your presence backstage because she has a surprise for you."

"We do not like surprises," Eighth Aunt says, appearing suddenly, surrounded by a battalion of personal assistants.

Fauzi bows his head slightly. "I—yes."

"What's the surprise?" Eighth Aunt says, her gaze piercing into Fauzi. He visibly wilts, and I don't blame him in the slightest.

"I—uh—I'll find out."

"Good." She turns to me and George as Fauzi rushes off, and brushes invisible lint off George's shoulder. "George, are you ready? Well, I suppose it doesn't matter. I trust that you are, anyway." She glances at me. "Sharlot, you look presentable."

I get the feeling that it's high praise, coming from Eighth Aunt. Something about her makes me feel like I should be dropping into a curtsy. Instead, I bow my head the way Fauzi did and say, "Thank you, Eighth Aunt." I can't believe this is the woman I had seen Mama kissing just yesterday. She's so formidable now. Come to think of it, I can't believe this is the woman George and I had run into at the café back in Jakarta. She'd been loud and friendly then, but tonight she's donned her CEO mask and she looks like she could conquer the entire world if she wished.

Fauzi returns, looking visibly more panicky than before. "I seem to be having some difficulty getting hold of Rina, but please don't worry, everything is going as planned."

Eighth Aunt turns her laser gaze back on him just for a moment, and in that single look, the displeasure is so obvious on her face that we all shrink back. Then, without taking her eyes off Fauzi, she says to one of her personal assistants, "Find her." One assistant peels off from the entourage.

"Is this normal?" I whisper to George.

He shrugs. "Sort of? We like to err on the side of caution."

"And we do not trust reporters," Eighth Aunt says, making both of us jump. God, she really doesn't miss anything. "Especially ones who say they have a surprise for us. Surprises are rarely good, my dears, unless we are the ones who set them." She winks at me and I catch a glimpse of the woman I had seen with Mama. It's impossible not to like Eighth Aunt; she is magnificent with her many roles—businesswoman, know-it-all auntie, and now a . . . girlfriend? To Mama. I wish I could sit down with her and talk about everything. Everything I've ever wanted to know about Mama.

The MC is getting the audience hyped up about some lucky draw. There is a huge cheer and the sound of trumpets blaring, and he reveals the grand prize for the night: a McLaren 570G. My eyes widen. I don't know anything about the particular number, but even I know that a McLaren is expensive as hell.

"Can I enter the lucky draw?" I say.

Eighth Aunt laughs. Fauzi leans over and says, "Okay, three minutes until you're up, George. You've got your speech ready?"

George nods, looking markedly paler than usual. I squeeze his hand again and he shoots me a grateful look. "Uh, actually, can I have a moment with Shar?" he says.

The others nod and walk a few paces away, giving us a tiny bit of privacy. I turn to face George, clasping both his hands in mine. "You're going to be great. I know it." I mean, I don't actually know that he's going to be great; if it were me, I would most definitely freak out and tank the entire thing, but I think it's what you're supposed to say to someone before they go onstage in front of a live audience.

"Yeah?" he squeaks. Oh my god, it's too adorable.

I stand up on tiptoes and kiss him lightly on the cheek. "Yeah. You've got this."

"I'm glad you're here," he murmurs.

The look he gives me melts me all the way to my toes, and god, how is it possible to like this boy so much when I've only just gotten to know him? Seeing him feels springtime, my whole being waking up after a long hibernation. I like him so, so much, without any restraint, without any cynicism, and I'm so invested in this, in everything about George, including this app that he's so obviously into. I clap loudly as he walks onstage and will him to do well with all of my being.

CHAPTER 26

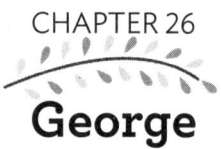

George

Music blares, the spotlights swing, and suddenly, I find myself in the center of the stage. My mind is a complete mess, my thoughts scrambling over themselves. Has the stage always been this huge? It feels endless. I could've sworn it was a lot smaller when we had the rehearsal this afternoon. I glance at the audience and nearly freeze. My god, there're so many people here. And even more watching online. There are two, three, no, four giant cameras aimed at me, their lenses capturing my every moment, swallowing me whole to be spat out at viewers across the whole country.

This is fine, I'm totally fine. I'm okay. I can do this. I'm a Tanuwijaya, this is what we do. Most of my older cousins have had to do this at some point in their lives and they've all done great, even Nicoletta. I can't be the first Tanuwijaya to fail the clan. I shove everything Sharlot-related out of my mind and focus on the present. Smile. Remember to smile. Right. I plaster on a grin, which feels more like a grimace, as I shake the MC's hand.

"George, how are you tonight?" he booms.

I turn to face the audience and spread my arms out, as rehearsed, before saying, "I'm feeling great, Yohannes. Good evening, everyone!"

Cheers and whistles ring out from the audience, and my stomach unknots a little. I'm not exactly in my element, but I've been trained endlessly for events like tonight. Haven't I spent years being coached on how to behave at business meetings, at public events, at both friendly and heated negotiations? As the MC says some more things about me and OneLiner, I take the chance to inhale slowly and find my grounding. I run through my lines mentally and am relieved to find that I can still remember them. This evening's going to be a breeze. Okay, it isn't, but it's not going to be a disaster, at least. Phew.

The audience claps appreciatively. I give the signal for the huge screen behind me to light up with my presentation. The screen comes to life, and the sight of the beautiful, sleek app that I've spent the last year or so helping to coax to fruition soothes my nerves. My spine straightens. The MC hands the stage to me and I launch into my speech without hesitation, the words tumbling out of my mouth as rehearsed.

"I'm so honored to be able to stand before all of you and present OneLiner. This application means everything to me, because for too long there's been a lot of . . . let's say, less-than-stellar behavior from boys my age. All around the world, the way we treat girls needs to be improved."

I think of the past few days with Sharlot. How they've flown by, simply because I spent them with her. How complicated and smart and sharp she is, and how it feels when I finally manage to get her to laugh. I wonder what she'll think of the app. I don't know why I haven't shown it to her. I guess like everything else I've done in my life, I feel self-conscious about it and assume the worst. But I want Sharlot to approve of it.

"One of the most important ways that OneLiner will help is through communication. We want to encourage parents to talk to their sons, not just place the focus on telling daughters how to behave." I glance up at the screen, avoiding looking out at the audience because it'll definitely throw me off, and the sight of the familiar slides gives me more confidence. "The responsibility lies on us boys, and educating ourselves is the first step forward. For so long, we have shirked our responsibility by giving excuses like 'Boys will be boys' when we behave badly. OneLiner is going to tackle these harmful mentalities by showing the logical fallacy behind them and how they affect everyone." As I continue my presentation, going into the statistics and the long-term effects of toxic masculinity, I can see that the audience is absorbed, and I can't believe that my message is being listened to without interruption. Without anyone telling me that this is just a publicity stunt. I think I might actually be making a difference.

I try to look for Sharlot in the wings but can't see much, what with all these spotlights glaring down on me. Regardless, I can't stop grinning as I walk them through each facet of the app, as though I'm a little kid showing Papa my art project. In the front row, Papa and Eleanor are clapping and beaming so hard at me that I get a little teary-eyed. Here it is, over a year of hard work from the family, the tech team, our employees, all to bring this to life. It's a surreal feeling, getting to present it to the public. I understand now why so many of my cousins so passionately dive into the family business once they finish college. It's in this moment that I know for sure, I want to go into the family business too. Maybe not in the way that Papa expected. I don't want to just be on the board, to just see the company as nothing more than moving numbers. I want to dive into the nitty-gritty of it, to create new products that will actually make a difference, if not in the world, then at least in my own country. Too soon, the presentation is done, and on cue, the stage fireworks go off. The audience oohs and aahs, and the MC bounds back onstage, congratulating me and shaking my hand with obvious relief. Oh my god, I did it. My head is buzzing—hell, my entire body is buzzing. I feel both energized and noodly with relief. Dimly, I sense Eleanor running up to the stage and throwing her arms around me, shouting, "gege, you did it!" The audience is clapping hard, and from the wings, Eighth Aunt is clapping and nodding with a look of pride. I could so get used to this. Why had I dreaded it so much? Why was I always so sure that I'd fail the company and disappoint my family?

Sharlot rushes onstage as well, and god, it feels so good to see her right now. She's such a huge part of this clarity I feel, and I'm so glad that I have her next to me. I stride toward her and in front of everyone, I hug her tight. There's a huge "Aww" from the audience, and Sharlot and I break apart, our faces on fire, but we're both smiling and everything is perfect.

Then someone says something into the mic. It takes a moment for me to notice it; in fact, I only notice when the noise around me suddenly recedes. I turn and see Rina on the other side of the stage, her cameraman standing next to her with his camera aimed and ready.

"Excuse me," she says with a smile. "I'm Rina from *Asian Wealth*, and I'd like to applaud George for such a wonderful presentation."

Eighth Aunt and Papa are looking at Rina with puzzled expressions on their faces. Well, Papa looks puzzled. Eighth Aunt is frowning, obviously displeased.

"I'd like to follow up with a presentation of my own." She nods to someone backstage, and the screen behind her changes from the final slide in the OneLiner presentation to a collage of photos. I blink, all thoughts inside my head scrambled and confused. Because the photos are of Sharlot . . . and some blond guy.

"Oh my god," Sharlot gasps next to me.

Rina zooms in on one of the pictures, where Sharlot is kissing the boy. "This is Sharlot, George's girlfriend. She's right here, standing next to George. Hi, Sharlot!"

All eyes turn to Sharlot. She gapes back with open horror.

"See, I was trying to figure out who is the girl who's managed to capture the heart of one of the most sought-after teenage heartthrobs of our country. George is such an important member of the Chinese-Indonesian community. I look at him as my younger brother, so maybe I'm slightly protective," she says with a laugh. "I took it upon myself to do some research into George's first girlfriend, since he's all about respecting girls and so on, and one would hope that his girlfriend would feel the same way about being . . . well, respectable. But as it turns out, Sharlot is anything but respectable." She zooms in on another picture, of

Sharlot in a bikini, sitting on that same blond guy's lap, grinning with her tongue out.

In a country as conservative as Indonesia, the picture is shocking. Sure enough, when I look back at the audience, many of them are sneering at Sharlot.

"Boo!" someone in the audience shouts. "Slut."

The word unfreezes me—why the hell had I just been standing there, frozen for so long? There's a sour taste at the back of my mouth that makes me want to retch. "Stop this now," I say.

Instead, Rina continues speaking. "I wouldn't be surprised if Sharlot and Bradley here have gone all the way, if you know what I mean."

I look at Shar. Her face is a picture of utter shame and sorrow and it breaks me entirely. I turn to Rina, my blood boiling throughout my whole body, pounding an enraged rhythm. I grab the camera. I want to fling it aside, but the cameraman is ready for me and tightens his grip on it. "Stop filming!" I shout. "Is this what you want? To attack a girl on live TV?"

Rina lifts her chin. "I want to seek the truth. It's my job. And I'm trying to protect our community. We're an ethnic minority here, it's important for us to uphold a good reputation."

Something about it cracks me. I can't think straight. My thoughts are a boiling mess of anger and panic. Indonesia is a conservative country that still shames women for premarital sex. If this were to be the big news of the night, Sharlot is never going to live it down. She'll be radioactive for life. I need to make things right. There's only one thing I can do to salvage the situation. "You want the truth?" I say, my voice coming out soft and poisonous. "The truth is *I'm* the liar. I was the one who misled Sharlot into dating me."

"George!" Eighth Aunt barks from the side, but for once in my life, I ignore her.

"I lied to her all this time. All the chat messages that were sent to her from my profile, they weren't from me. They were from—" Too late, I realize I'm about to throw Eleanor and Papa under the bus too. Shit. "They were from someone else," I mumble vaguely.

"From who?" Rina says, her nostrils flaring, probably because she smells blood and is going in for the kill.

"Just—someone."

"Are you saying your account got hacked?" she says with a little sneer that makes it obvious she doesn't believe me.

"They were from me!" Eleanor cries.

Everybody gasps and turns to look at her, and she shrinks back for a second before straightening up. "What? I'm thirteen, I don't know any better. And I just wanted George to be happy."

"And me," Papa says. Everyone gasps even louder. Eighth Aunt's eyebrows are practically hovering above her head by now. He hangs his head. "It was—I thought I was doing something a father should do. Push his son to grow up, be a man. I'm so very sorry, Sharlot."

"Those messages weren't from you?" Sharlot says in a dreamlike voice. She gapes at me, as though seeing me in a wholly different light. I can't blame her.

"I'm so sorry, Shar—"

"So, George Clooney Tanuwijaya," Rina says, "the face of the app to teach boys how to treat girls right, lied all this time to his own girlfriend. Let his little sister and his father pretend to be him so he could fool an innocent girl into dating him."

An innocent girl. I breathe a small sigh of relief. At least the heat's off Shar.

Rina snorts. "I say 'innocent girl,' but of course, the twist is that the girl he was fooling isn't innocent at all."

There's a furious "Aiya!" and before any of us can react, Shar's mom strides toward us with all the commanding air of an army general. She snatches Rina's mic and flings it away. It crashes to the ground with a horrible screech. Everyone goes silent.

"How dare you?" Shar's mom hisses at Rina. "What kind of journalist are you, preying on underaged teens for a scoop? Disgusting." She spits at Rina's shoes. "I was the one who started chatting with George. It was all me. Sharlot not want any part of it, so do not blame her for any of this. And while we're on topic? Slut-shaming my daughter? Fuck. You." She turns to Sharlot and puts her arm around her. "Come, we going home." The two of them start to walk away, but Sharlot's mom turns around and points a finger in Rina's face. "You little shit, come anywhere near my daughter again and I will sue you for all you're worth."

And with that, they walk off, followed by Kiki, leaving the rest of us with nothing but the shambles of our farce.

Fauzi arrives, out of breath, with two security guards at his heels.

"Took you long enough," Eighth Aunt barks. She cocks her head at Rina and her camera guy. "Get this trash out of here."

As the security guards escort Rina and the cameraman away,

Eighth Aunt halts them and says, "My dear, if you want to continue having a career in journalism, might I suggest moving very far away from Jakarta? Because you will never find work in the city again, I hope you realize that."

Rina's chin wobbles, but her eyes remain defiant. "I won't be fired for doing my job well. This is going to be the story of the year."

Eighth Aunt throws her head back and gives a mirthless laugh. "Oh, you ambitious, stupid child." Even though I'm not the subject of Eighth Aunt's wrath, my skin breaks out into gooseflesh as she takes a step toward Rina. I notice that even the guards shrink back a little. "Nobody comes after my family and gets away unscathed, my dear. Now off you go. I expect you'll be hearing from your boss in about—"

As if on cue, Rina must have detected her phone buzzing, because her eyes widen and she reaches into her back pocket and pulls it out. Her face visibly pales when she looks at the screen.

"Ah, that's probably her." Eighth Aunt nods at the guards and they nudge Rina toward the exit once more. This time, her head's hung low as she walks, no longer a proud warrior but a defeated one. I don't know why, but I take no pleasure in seeing her leave. All I feel is exhausted and empty. I don't even know how Sharlot must be feeling right now. I don't know how to make it okay for her, how to make anything okay for anyone.

"Papa," I say, or try to, anyway. My voice breaks on the first syllable, and I feel so tiny and stupid and helpless and so utterly awful in every way possible. Papa comes toward me and engulfs me in a fierce hug—none of the awkward Asian hugs he usually gives—and Eleanor throws her arms around the two of us, holding us together like she always does.

"It's okay, son, we'll make it okay. It'll be okay," Papa murmurs.

I don't see how it could ever be okay, but just for the moment, I close my eyes and let myself believe in his lies. Just for a little while. Just until everything stops falling apart.

CHAPTER 27

Sharlot

A crowd has already gathered at the exit from the wings. Rina must have live-streamed her explosive reveal to the whole country, and now it feels like everyone is here, calling out my name and shouting all sorts of shit.

"Sharlot, is it true that you're pregnant?" someone cries.

"You whore!" someone else shouts.

"Shut up!" Mama shouts back, only for them to get louder.

"Did you know your daughter was sleeping around?"

"You're a bad mother!"

"Shut the fuck up, you trolls!" Kiki screams.

It's suffocating. I feel as though the air has been sucked out of the atmosphere. I think I'm gasping, or maybe I'm crying, or I don't know what. Something's happening with my lungs, anyway. Like they've forgotten how to lung. Kiki strides ahead of us, clearing a path until we break free from the growing crowd. We half walk, half jog all the way back to the villa as best as we can in our high heels and floor-length gowns.

It's only after we go inside and lock the front door that I'm able to take a proper breath. I sag against the wall and close my eyes, but once I do, I see flashes of awful images. George looking at me with shock and disappointment. Rina's horribly triumphant face. Everyone else's expressions, a mixture of gleeful, scandalized looks. I can't. I can't do this. I open my eyes again and see Mama approaching me with a glass of water.

"Drink," she says. I take it from her and drink gratefully.

"I need to talk to Bradley. I need to—Rina got ahold of those pictures, and I need to know how."

Mama sighs. "Are you sure?"

I nod.

"Are you okay?" Mama says.

No, of course not, I want to say. But I have a feeling if I said that, I'd end up bursting into tears and crying forever. So I just give a shrug before taking out my phone and saying, "I'll be a minute."

Mama and Kiki nod, and for once, neither one has anything to say. No smart-ass remarks from Kiki, no strict advice from Mama. I'm so unbelievably grateful to them for this small kindness, for everything they've done. But first, Bradley.

After they've left, I take a deep breath and call Bradley on WhatsApp. The dial tone rings and rings for what seems like ages, though in reality it's only like four rings. When he finally picks up, my throat closes up and my eyes fill at the sound of his familiar voice.

"Shar? Hey, what's up? I've been texting and calling and—"

"I know, I'm sorry. I just—stop talking, Bradley!" I blurt out.

He stops. I take a big gulp of air. "Uh. Did you . . . did a reporter from Indonesia contact you asking about me?"

"What? No. Wait, what?"

The confusion in his voice is palpable. Then the realization hits me. Of course he hadn't talked to Rina about me. Rina didn't have to reach out to him. All she had to do was look at his Insta profile. "Did you ever take down the photos of you and me from your Instagram?" I say.

"No, I didn't. I didn't think I had to? I mean, I knew you'd broken up with me, but they were good memories." There's a pause, then Bradley says, "Wait, please tell me what's going on, Shar. Are you in trouble?"

"I'm . . ." I sigh. "It's hard to explain." I close my eyes. God, how could I have been so stupid? I thought that deleting the photos from my account would've been enough. Of course it wasn't. Of course Rina, being an actual professional journalist, would've found out the truth. "I've fucked everything up," I whisper brokenly.

"Hey, come on, it'll be okay, whatever it is. You'll figure it out, Shar. You've always been the smart one."

I wince at the kindness in his voice. "I'm really not. Bradley, I'm so sorry. I fucked up." And once the words are out, the tears start rolling down my face. I've been such an asshole. I'd been so smug the whole time we went out, acting like I was a lot smarter than he is, treating him like a himbo. "The truth is, you're way smarter than I ever was," I finally tell him. "You've always been so kind and so real. You never bothered with all that fake bullshit. And I am so sorry for breaking up with you so abruptly. That was such a shit move, and I don't even know why—I just—I guess I was so ashamed about what happened—"

"I get it. It's fine." He pauses. "Um, to be honest, I've kind of moved on."

"What?" I gasp. "I mean, I'm glad to hear that, but wow. Okay."

"Yeah, I was really down at first, but after days of messaging you without any response, I had to learn to get over you. No offense, Shar."

"No, of course, that's—I mean, I'm happy for you." And I mean it too. "Um, is there someone else in the picture?"

He gives a bashful laugh. "Kind of? You know Bryan?"

"Bryan Johnson? From AP physics?"

"Yeah?"

"Wow." I hadn't known Bradley was bi. I think of Bryan—a tall Black guy two years my senior; annoyingly good at physics; moderately good at piano; kind smile. "That's a . . . you guys make a great couple." They really, really do. They're both two of the kindest people at school.

Bradley laughs in that shy way again, and I wish I were there so I could give him a big hug. "So tell me about Indonesia," he says. "Sounds intense." He says this with such sincerity that I can't help but laugh.

And somehow for that short second, everything isn't quite as catastrophic as before. I take a deep inhale and release it. How does Bradley do it? How does he make every awful situation a bit less shitty? "I had no idea what to expect before I came here. Everything I knew about Indonesia has gone through a white lens. The BBC is always showing it like it's this hell pit filled with rubble."

"Let me guess: It's not."

"It's definitely not," I agree. "I've got so many pictures and videos to show you." Then I realize that most people probably wouldn't want to look through photos and videos with their exes. "Um, but I know you're probably really busy, so—"

"What are you talking about? I'm dying to see them! We'll hang out when you come back and you can show me in person."

"Okay, and you can tell me all about Bryan."

"Deal."

I smile at this, but as soon as we end the call, I feel the smile slip off my face. I'm glad that I've finally resolved things with Bradley, but that doesn't cancel out the public humiliation I've just gone through. The weight of it bears down on my shoulders, and I don't know how I'll ever be able to lift my head high again.

The rest of the night passes by in a blur. Mama takes away my phone again because it was blowing up with all sorts of messages and notifications of news stories about me. This time, I surrender it without a fight; I'm actually grateful that she's taking it away. I find its proximity suffocating, its presence radiating poison. Mama and Kiki push the queen beds to become one giant bed and the three of us sleep in it. Even though I know there's a hurricane of badness whirling and throwing shit everywhere, I spend the rest of the night wrapped up like a burrito under the fluffy duvet, with Kiki on my left and Mama on my right, and I feel okay-ish. We trade stories about everything and nothing. At some point, way past midnight, I doze off.

In the middle of the night, I wake up with a thunderstorm raging in my chest. Too many thoughts swirling and crashing through my head. I need to do something, but I don't know what. I slip out of bed as quietly as I can, careful not to wake Mama and Kiki, and pad out into the living room. I make myself a cup of chamomile tea and settle down on the couch. I gaze out the window at the night sky, sipping at my hot drink. I think of everything that's just happened, about how I've been "disgraced" and what that means to me. It hits me that Mama must have gone through something similar. And suddenly, I know what I want to do.

I pick up my tablet from my bag and open up a new page. Then I start drawing. I draw until I'm so exhausted that I can't keep my eyes from closing and I put my tablet back in my bag and slip back into bed.

I awake to the sound of shoes clattering across the floor, which is somewhat startling given we're not in the habit of wearing shoes inside the villa. I blink against the bright sunlight streaming through the open curtains and see Kiki coming in, carrying a steaming cup of coffee.

"Here you go," she chirps, handing me the cup. She's all dressed and ready to go. Go where?

I scratch my hair and yawn. Mama is no longer in bed, but I can hear her voice through the half-closed door. "What's going on?"

"My parents managed to get us on the earliest flight out of here. Plane leaves in two hours. I've packed all your stuff up. You just need to take a shower and get dressed and we can leave here before anybody knows."

It all comes back to me in a rush. Rina's betrayal. My relationship with Bradley on the big screen. The mess that followed. My breath wheezes out in an asthmatic whistle. "Oh god."

Kiki's suddenly by my side, her arms tight around me. "It'll be fine, Shar. You're okay. You're fine. Breathe. Take a deep breath and release."

I do as she says and slowly the room stops spinning. "Thank you." Another thought strikes me. "George—"

"Um, yeah. He's been calling a lot, but we weren't sure if you were up for it."

My heart twists like a towel that's being wrung to dry at the thought of George calling endlessly, only to be ignored. "Is he okay? I should talk to him, I should explain—"

"There's no 'should' here," Kiki says fiercely. "Screw George. The only person I care about right now is you. Also, there's nothing to explain. He literally did the same thing to you that you did to him."

My mouth opens and closes. I start to speak. Stop. Start again. "But—I—but he—"

"You both messed up."

And there it is. She's right. We both messed up. I'd been so consumed with guilt and the WTF-ness of last night that I haven't had a chance to really process George's revelation. And now, in the harsh daylight, I realize that I feel . . . upset. I know how hypocritical that sounds and I am the last person who has the right to feel anything about this, but I do. The thought of someone else being behind those messages is violating. Even though I was doing the exact same thing back to him. How's that for irony? The familiar feeling of annoyance, of the easy, lazy anger toward him nudges at my senses, but I bat them away. I don't feel angry at him in the same way that I used to. It's a hell of a thing, to feel betrayed when I too was betraying him. I don't really know how I feel, I just know I'm not ready to face it yet. But I can also do better than what I did to Bradley.

"Could you send him a message from my phone?" I say to Kiki. "I don't want to look at anything on my phone yet, so you'll have to do this for me."

She nods. "Of course." Wow, no caustic remark. My phone must be blowing up with hate mail.

"Tell him I'm really sorry, but I need some time to think, and that I'll message him when I'm ready."

One corner of Kiki's mouth quirks up in a small smile. "That's very mature of you, Sharlot."

I roll my eyes and scowl at her, but I can't help throwing my arm around her shoulders and tapping my head against hers. "Thanks." I can't believe that despite everything, I have at least made a true friend in Indonesia.

The flight back to Jakarta is markedly different from our flight to Bali. No private jets, for one. I keep my sunglasses and hat on the entire flight and in the Soekarno-Hatta airport, only taking them off for the customs check before shoving them back on.

Lucky that I did, because at the arrivals, there's a knot of reporters looking around with cameras and mics at the ready. Holy shit. My heart rate doubles, triples, in the space of one second. Kiki and Mama flank me on either side, Mama talking rapidly into her cell with instructions to Li Jiujiu on where exactly to pick us up. We keep our heads down and walk quickly past the reporters—I guess we must look innocuous enough, because they barely glance up at us. Then it hits me that they're probably not here for me, but for George. Of course. My chest squeezes, as if my rib cage were turning into a vise around my heart. The poor guy.

"They'll have a better plan in place to avoid them," Kiki says, reading my mind.

Just then, one of the reporters spots us, and I guess I was wrong after all. They're also here for me, because the reporter shouts, "Sharlot? Sharlot Citra!" and a couple of them break off from the group to approach us, and when we walk faster, more and more peel off from the group toward us. Now the entire group is approaching, and Kiki, Mama, and I abandon all hope for subtlety and start running. Outside, Li Jiujiu is waiting next to his Alphard and we rush toward him and throw ourselves in. He doesn't even wait for us to sit down and buckle up before he tells the chauffeur to start driving. I fall into my seat and catch a glimpse of cameras flashing as we speed away from the airport. I close my eyes and take a deep inhale. God, please let this be over now.

I feel a bit better after we reach Kiki's house and I'm able to take a long, cold, ultra-refreshing shower. Just as there's nothing better than a hot shower in the winter, there's nothing better than a cold one after the sticky, humid heat of a tropical country. When I step outside, wrapped in one of Kiki's bathrobes and toweling my hair dry, Mama is waiting in my room. Something about the way she's sitting, straight-backed with her hands in her lap, makes me wary.

"We can leave here tomorrow," she says, and it's so far from what I had been expecting that I stop dead in my tracks, frozen while my hands are buried in a towel on top of my head.

It takes a few seconds before I am able to find my voice. "What?"

"Tomorrow. We go back to LA."

"Wait, Ma! No."

She stares at me, her eyebrows knotting in obvious confusion. "I thought you would be glad that we are leaving this place. You tell me plenty of times you hate it here, you want nothing to do with Indonesia."

"Well—I mean—but—" I flap my hands uselessly, trying to sort my thoughts out into some semblance of order. And it hits me then, the thing that feels truly wrong about all this. And it has nothing to do with me. "You're running away again."

Her mouth thins into a pinched line. "No, I do this because I don't want you to be facing all that—all those reporters."

"Well, okay. That's a good point." I soften my voice and sit next to her, trying to remember the last time we sat like this, just the two of us and no battles raging between us, no barbs or walls or moats filled with resentful silence. "But, Mama, I think . . . you've also got some unresolved stuff going on here." I've clawed and prodded her my whole life for the truth about Indonesia and all it did was turn her scars into a web of hard, healed skin around her that I couldn't penetrate. Maybe it's time that I stop attacking her and start with offering her some of my truth instead. "I haven't been honest with you, Ma. Back in LA, I . . ." I gird my insides. This is it. "I was going to sleep with Bradley."

Mama takes in a sharp breath, her eyes narrowing with displeasure.

"I had thought very logically about it and I was being careful about it too. I'd prepared condoms, and Bradley and I had talked about it beforehand. I did everything right—"

"You are too young!" Mama snaps before she manages to stop herself. She turns away from me and takes a shuddering breath, her hands squeezed together on her lap. "You can't understand the—the—what it means to have sex."

"Of course I don't fully understand, Ma, I haven't done it yet. Just like I didn't fully understand what it's like here in Indonesia because you never tell me anything about it and I've never been here before."

Mama flinches like I've struck a blow, and I guess in a way I have. She looks down on her lap and clears her throat. "It changes you. After you do it. It changed me. And I regret it so much, after I do it. I wish—I keep thinking—"

"Because you got pregnant with me?" I can't quite keep the bitterness out of my voice. It's hard not to feel defensive when your mom is telling you that you're the biggest regret of her life.

"No," she barks, and looks straight into my eyes. "I don't regret having you. I don't regret choosing to have you instead of . . . not."

Whoa. I was not prepared for the revelation that there was an option of not having me.

"But I regret how it happened."

"Oh, Mama." Horror creeps up on me. "Were you—was it nonconsensual?"

"Nothing like that," she says quickly. "I wanted it too—or I thought at the time I did—I don't know, it's very complicated!" Her voice rises and breaks, and she sits there, looking defeated.

And I know then what I need to do. "Mama, I have something to show you." I get up. Mama watches me in confusion, frowning when I pick up my tablet. "I drew something last night."

Mama sighs. "This is not the time to talk about art—" The words die halfway out of her mouth when I show her the picture I drew last night, when I had woken up, cuddled safe between her and Kiki and couldn't for the life of me figure out why I was awake. I had only figured it out when I started drawing, and now I finally get to show it to my mother.

It's a picture of her and Eighth Aunt standing on the beach, just as George and I had seen them. Eighth Aunt is tucking a stray lock of hair behind Mama's ear and they're smiling at each other with the tenderness of two people who have loved and lost and only just found the other again. There is history written on their faces, rich and complex and painful and sweet. I glance at Mama's face nervously, gnawing on my bottom lip.

Mama is staring at the picture with such a shocked expression that I half wonder if she's going to collapse.

"I saw you in Bali with her," I say softly. Gently. "And, um, I'm happy for you."

Mama gapes at me, then back at the tablet. Then back at me again. She reaches out for the tablet and I give it to her as gingerly as though it were a newborn baby. She studies the picture for a long time, her breathing going from ragged to a steadier pace. Tears shimmer in her eyes, and when she finally looks up at me, she's smiling, her face radiant.

"This is—" She pauses to catch her breath. "This is beautiful, Sharlot."

"Oh, Mama." I can't stand it anymore. I catch her in a tight hug and squeeze my eyes shut. She puts her arms around me and hugs me back and just for the moment, I feel as though everything really is okay.

By now, we're both crying happy, relieved tears. We laugh, hug each other again, and cry some more. At some point, we start talking. Really talking this time—Mama telling me the stuff that actually matters.

"When I was your age, that kind of thing is considered very bad," she says with a sigh. "Very taboo. I tried not to be like this, because it'll bring so much trouble to my family."

I put my hand over hers, my heart cracking at my mother talking about her teenage self like this. I can't even imagine the weight of it. It would've been before the Internet was around, before LGBTQ activists were able to spread their message of love and acceptance more widely. She must've felt so alone and so, so frightened. "Can you tell me more about Eighth Aunt? Like, how did you two meet, when did you realize that you liked each other more than friends? I want to know everything, especially when you were my age."

"Ah, girl talk," Mama says. "I always wanted to have girl talk with you. I never expect our first girl talk to be about me!"

We both laugh. "Well, you gotta start somewhere," I say. I make myself comfortable, settling in to listen to the greatest romance of my mother's life.

A small smile touches the edges of her mouth and her eyes get this faraway look. "I was very beautiful when I was your age. What? You don't believe me?"

"I believe you!"

"Oh yes, so many boys liked me. Your grandparents, they were so worried. But I wasn't interested in any boy, of course not. When I met Eighth Aunt, it was like wah! Suddenly everything became so clear. It was like meeting my best friend and my soul mate and just—my everything. We were inseparable. At first it was okay, people just think we were best friends, like sisters, you know? My parents were so relieved, because I wasn't going around bu san bu si with boys. Wah, Eighth Aunt and me, we spent all our time together." She laughs softly at the memories of her and Eighth Aunt, and the joy on her face makes me smile. "But then people started to talk, started getting suspicious. My parents were so worried. So were hers. They talk about moving her to Singapore, away from me."

"Oh god," I mutter, squeezing her hand.

"So I tried, Sharlot. I tried to be 'normal.' I had boyfriends. When this handsome exchange student came from America, I thought, 'Ah! This is a very good chance for me to prove that I'm normal.' So I go out with him, even though I don't like him like that. And I decided that best way to prove to everyone, and also myself, that I am normal is to go all the way with him. Who knows, maybe it turns out I will like it? Maybe I will start liking boys."

"That's terrible," I say.

But Mama just touches my face and gives me a sad smile. "It's not all bad. I didn't like it, but it could have been worse. Then I ended up pregnant—aiya! Suddenly I don't have to worry about people finding out that I don't like boys. Suddenly I have to worry about them thinking I am a slut. Somehow, even though they think I am straight, I still manage to make my family lose face. Oh, it was so awful. Nobody wanted to talk to me. People left very bad messages in my school desk. Parents called the school, asked them to expel me because I am a bad influence. They think I will seduce their sons and encourage their daughters to be like me."

"Holy shit, that's terrible."

She shrugs. "I don't want the same thing to happen to you. I know you say times are better, times change, people are more open-minded. But it's not that different. You see what happened in Bali, when they found out you had boyfriend back in LA?"

I'm about to argue that it's different back in LA, that people are way more open-minded. It's true, to a certain extent, but she's right that even though it's more progressive, every time there's gossip or a scandal, the one that comes out worse for wear is the girl. The guy gets away unscathed or with a reputation of being a player, which elevates his status instead of destroying it, while the girl is demeaned and shunned.

"I wanted to protect you, but I ended up making things worse for you," she says.

"I'll be fine. I've got you and Kiki, and that's already more than what you had when you were my age."

She smiles.

"And I'm so sorry that you had to go through that on your own, Mama. I um." I don't know why this is awkward to say aside from that talking about your parent's love interest is always 100 percent awkward. "I just want you to know that, like, I . . . um. I like Eighth Aunt. I think you two make a cute couple."

A whole bunch of emotions cross Mama's face, so many and so varied that I swear she's about to implode. If I had to guess, I think she's feeling: 1. Embarrassment. 2. More Embarrassment. 3. Denial. 4. SO MUCH EMBARRASSMENT. 5. A not-so-tiny spark of joy.

Finally, she clears her throat and turns away, mumbling, "Aiya, we'll see."

I'm not letting this one go so easily. I know my mother well enough to know that she's the best cockblocker—er, blocker—of her own happiness. "No, Ma. I don't want to leave it at 'we'll see.' I haven't seen you this happy in . . ." My voice trails off as I try to remember the last time I've seen Mama this joyous, this alive. "I can't remember," I whisper, the words coming out hoarse with emotion. She's given up so much for me. "You've got plans with Eighth Aunt, right? Like, you guys are adults, you've worked out how to make it work, yes?"

"Aduh, don't be ridiculous. She lives all the way here, I live in LA . . ."

"Those are just bullshit excuses and you know it."

Mama's eyes narrow, and I reach out for her hand.

"Please, promise me you won't give up again just because you think it's not proper or normal or whatever? Please try to make it work with Eighth Aunt? It's different now. You can FaceTime each other whenever, and she's filthy rich, so she can fly to see you whenever, and we can visit Indonesia often too, and of course, you have the rest of this summer with her!"

A single tear slips down Mama's cheek, followed by another, and another. She nods wordlessly. "But we need to go back to LA because—"

"No, actually." It's not until I say it that I realize it's true. I don't want to go back to LA. Not yet, anyway. Even though I've crashed and burned so spectacularly here, even though I've managed to turn this trip into a hellfire scandal of Miley Cyrus proportions, even though a huge part of me is scrambling to escape and get the hell out of here. Despite all those things, there is still a small kernel of defiance inside me. A voice, tiny but impossible to ignore, that tells me I should stay. That I'm strong enough to stay. For all of my life, I've run away whenever things get too real. But this is my chance to get to know my roots, and I'm done running.

I look at Mama and smile my first real smile since we left Bali. "I want to stay, at least until the end of the summer. And this time, I want to get to know everything about Jakarta and our family."

CHAPTER 28

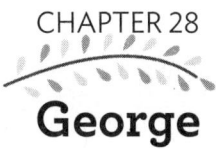

George

"You want the truth? The truth is I'm the liar. I was the one who misled Sharlot into dating me."

"George!"

I hit the Pause button. Rewind a few beats.

"The truth is I'm the liar. I was the one who misled Sharlot into dating me."

"George!"

"George!"

I frown. It takes a second for me to realize that someone outside of the video has actually called my name. I look up to see Eighth Aunt, Papa, Nainai, and Eleanor bunched up at the doorway. I sigh, letting my head drop back onto the bed so my face is buried in my fluffy duvet. I understand why I have to stay locked up in my own house—and honestly, there are worse places to have to be locked up in—but seeing my family is a very painful reminder of how I've hurt them and everyone else around me, especially Sharlot.

"Son, why don't you come out of your room, ya? It's been three days now," Papa says.

"When we asked you to lie low and not leave the house," Eighth Aunt says, striding in, "we didn't mean for you to literally stay in your room."

"Yeah, gege. We do have an actual mansion for you to prowl in," Eleanor says, plopping onto the foot of my bed.

"I'm fine," I say, or start to say anyway, but get derailed when Nainai yanks my ear. "Ow!"

"You are obviously not fine," she warbles. "Not ever since that no-good girl tricked you. Took advantage of my grandson!"

We all stare at Nainai guiltily, and then look back and forth at one another, like who's going to be the one who reminds her that I wasn't exactly innocent in the whole debacle? I sigh and say, "Nainai, I was doing the exact same thing to her as she was to me."

"Yes, but you didn't have any malicious intent!" she snaps.

"Well, I mean, she probably didn't either."

Nainai makes a "pfft" noise. "I know these no-good girls, always trying to worm their way into our family. When your mother died, I had to fight off many of these no-good women who tried to claw their way into your papa's heart."

I've been brought up not to argue back with my elders, but Nainai's misogyny is unbearable, and exactly the kind of crap that all the gossip sites have been spouting. Somehow, in the eye of the media, my transgressions matter less than Sharlot's. She's the witch harpy, the gold digger, the snake who schemed her way to my side, and I'm just the clueless, sweet-natured boy who was taken along for the ride. I only know this from TV, of course, because all of my electronics were quickly confiscated just in case I got the urge to ruin everything for the family company. Because of course, everything is about keeping the family company intact, keeping our image clean and our stocks up.

"Nainai, I love you, but you're wrong."

Nainai's eyebrows shoots up into her hairline. "What did you say, Ming Fa?"

"You're wrong," I say this as gently as I can, because she is, after all, my grandmother. "Sharlot isn't like that at all. She's a good person. I was the one who tricked her. If anything, I'm the scumbag around here. A hypocrite, especially considering my app."

"That's not true—"

"It kind of is, Nainai," Eleanor says. "I mean, not that gege is a scumbag. But that we messed up too. It's not just on Cici Sharlot."

"It was all me," Papa says. "Don't blame the kids. I should've known better."

"Yes, you should have!" Nainai snaps. But then she sighs and says, "But I know you were just trying to help your son. That's what parents do, we sacrifice our happiness for that of our children's."

"Just like Sharlot's mom was doing for her," I point out.

Nainai frowns. Then, miraculously, she mutters, "I suppose."

Holy shit. I exchange amazed glances with Eleanor, Papa, and Eighth Aunt. We rarely ever see Nainai change her mind like this.

"Anyway, are you all here to tell me that house arrest is over?"

"Oh, son, I wouldn't call it house arrest," Papa says, wringing his hands.

"Am I allowed to leave the house?"

"Of course you are!" Eighth Aunt says with an overly bright smile. "We advise you not to, of course—"

I slump back onto the foot of the bed. Of course. "Advised." That's my whole life. I'm never forced to do anything. I'm "advised" to, for the greater good, and you don't want to be the black sheep of the family, do you, George? You don't want to be the one who brings shame to the family. We must all sacrifice for the family.

I look at Eighth Aunt and notice for the first time how she looks—well, not that she looks bad in any way—but she looks slightly less polished somehow. And then I see all the little details—the eye bags, the nails that are just a little bit chipped, like she's started picking at them before she stopped herself with her usual iron will. The makeup that is ever so slightly less perfect than usual.

"How are you doing, Eighth Aunt?" I say.

She shrugs. "I'm all right, thank you. A bit tired. So many board meetings, you know. And our investors needed a lot of reassuring because of—well, you know."

Yeah, I know. I nod, contrite. OneLiner has tanked, obviously, and tanked hard. Our stock was down three whole points the day after the launch. A disaster that has sent flocks of investors clamoring to pull their money out.

"It's not your fault, George," Papa says. "It was mostly me."

I shrug. No use pointing fingers now, and anyway, it definitely is mostly my fault. I was the one who led Sharlot on in Bali. I was the one who fell for her.

"But we'll be okay," Papa continues. "We've weathered worse. Join us for dinner downstairs tonight, okay? Please."

"I don't have much of an appetite." I've left most of the food that was delivered up to the door of my room untouched.

They sigh, looking uneasily at one another. Then, thankfully, they shuffle out of my room.

Something comes over me and I call out, "Eighth Aunt? Um, can I . . . can we talk for a second?"

Papa turns to look at us, confused, but Eighth Aunt gives him a nod and as usual, he listens to her. As soon as they're all gone, I feel my palms get clammy. I've just asked Eight Aunt to talk. Alone. A not-so-tiny part of me is squeaking in fear.

"Um, I just wanted to apologize for everything," I begin, but Eighth Aunt shakes her head and holds up her palm.

"No, George, you've done enough apologizing." She sighs and sits down on the chaise longue. "You did well, you know. In Bali, during the presentation? You hit it out of the park."

My mouth parts, but nothing comes out. I wasn't expecting this at all.

"And I've thought about your ideas for OneLiner . . . ," she continues. "They were good. The one about having a share function so users can post their stories? I love that. Building a strong community is important for the success of so many apps. You did well, George. Well, until the whole Rina thing. But it's a good lesson to learn: In business, you can do everything right, and the product can still fail because of external forces. Things you can't possibly foresee. Did you know that before Toagong built the family corporation, one of the things he invested in was a budget hotel? It was doing okay, but then one night, there was an electrical fire and the whole thing burned down. It bankrupted him."

Oh my god. I had no idea what Toagong—my great-grandfather—had to endure on his path to success.

"So, let this be a lesson. You'll be all right. We've got you."

Hearing that feels like a weight's been lifted from my shoulders. "Thanks, Eighth Aunt." I hesitate, my insides kicking because the next thing isn't for me to bring up, but I really, really need her to know that just like how she's got my back, I've got hers too. "Um, and . . . um. I, um . . ." Wow, this is painfully awkward.

Eighth Aunt's eyes narrow. "Is this about Sharlot's mom?"

"How'd you know?"

"Mostly by being older and wiser," she says, laughing. "And also because she told me you and Sharlot saw us together." Her laughter dries up and worry flashes across her face. Just for a moment, but it's enough to make her look vulnerable. "I'm sorry you had to, uh, see that."

"No!" I cry. "No, don't be sorry, please. I mean, it's awkward because you're my aunt, but, um. I just wanted you to know that I—uh—I'm proud of you?" Wow, it feels so weird telling someone twice your age that you're proud of them. "And I'm here for you too."

It takes a moment for me to figure out the expression on

Eighth Aunt's face, because I've never seen her look like that before. She's . . . surprised. Even when Rina did her takedown, Eighth Aunt hadn't looked surprised, just furious. But now, her eyes are round and her mouth is slightly open, and it's like I'm finally seeing the person behind the formidable mask. Then she smiles, and years are shaved off her face and I see her as a teen, laughing and giddy and in love.

"That's so sweet of you," she says, her eyes dancing. She reaches out and squeezes my arm. "You're a good kid, George."

After Eighth Aunt leaves, I let my breath out in one long, tired *whoosh* before flopping on my bed. I love that I had that chat with Eighth Aunt, and I'm glad she seems to be okay, but it still doesn't cancel out the fact that I've made a huge mess of things. The worst of my nightmares have come true—I've not only messed up everything with Sharlot but I've also let my entire family down. I've tanked my first-ever company-related event. I bury my face in my hands and squeeze my eyes shut, wishing I could blank out everything. I roll over to my side, and that's when I feel it. Something hard in my bed.

I open my eyes and reach down for the object. It's Eleanor's new phone, one Papa gave her just two days ago. My heart rate doubles, triples, quadruples. I jump up to my feet and pace around the room. Did Eleanor forget her phone here? Or was it on purpose? I'm about to head for her room when I pause. I look down at the phone and hit the Home button. A number pad shows up, asking for the unlock code. My thumb moves as though of its own accord and hits several numbers. It unlocks, and tears rush into my eyes because Eleanor's unlock code is Mama's birthdate, and this means that she's left the phone here for me. She knew that's the first thing I would've tried.

Now that I'm in Eleanor's phone, I have no idea what to do. I should call Sharlot. Yeah, okay. I look through Eleanor's contact list until I find Sharlot's name, and I hit Dial. My heart thrums sickeningly, a guitar string strung too tight. It immediately goes to voicemail. Her phone's off. My heart plummets all the way down my body into my feet and onto the floor. Okay, maybe that was melodramatic, but, god. I feel sick. I try again. Voicemail again. I hang up without leaving a message and I close the call window and frown down at Eleanor's phone. Huh. There's only one app on her home screen, and it's ShareIt. Okay . . . my little sister's not known for subtlety, and her clues aren't so much bread crumbs as they are entire loaves of bread. I have to laugh at that.

Sure enough, on her ShareIt app, Eleanor's following only one person. But it's not Sharlot, because Sharlot has taken down her ShareIt profile. I shudder to think of all the hate messages she must've received. Eleanor is following Kiki. Of course she is. I shake my head. The world is not ready for an Eleanor-Kiki partnership. I open up Kiki's profile and my breath stops short in my chest, because there she is. Sharlot, I mean, not Kiki.

I'd assumed that Sharlot would've flown back to America as soon as she could, but here she is still in the city, only a few miles away from me. So close.

And they're doing everything. Everything that Jakarta has to offer—all the chic, rooftop bars, the hipster cafés, the roadside food stalls, and the swanky restaurants. They hit all the tourist destinations—Taman Mini, where they have a huge display of all the different traditional Indonesian huts and wooden stilt houses. They went to Monas, the national monument commemorating the independence of Indonesia from the Dutch colony, and took pictures of themselves having kue apeh—coconut-flavored pancakes—in front of the monument. They went to all the museums, even the Wayang Museum, which houses one of Indonesia's most celebrated art forms—the shadow puppet.

I smile at the photos of Sharlot discovering her heritage, but my heart cracks at the realization that she's doing it all without me. Stop being so melodramatic, I scold myself. It's not my place to show her around Jakarta. It makes sense that she'd do these things with her cousins. Yep, not singular "cousin," but plenty of them. I guess Sharlot has reconnected with the rest of her family. They look so happy and vibrant. In one photo, they're all caught mid-jump. In another, they've coordinated their poses to spell out the word *cousins*.

Her mom has come along on some of their excursions too. In one photo, it seems they went to Sharlot's mom's old school. There's a picture of Sharlot and her mom, sweaty and smiling while eating ice pops outside of the school, and Sharlot is gazing fondly at her mom, who's looking at the school with a thoughtful expression. There's so much love in Sharlot's face that I feel guilty for trespassing on their privacy and swipe down to close the app. Instead, my thumb slips and taps the picture twice, liking it.

ARGH. Oh no. I double-tap again to cancel out the like, but now that I've done it, I realize that's worse, because Kiki will get the notification about me liking it, and then she'll see that I didn't in fact like it and she'll totally figure out that I canceled out my like, which is passive-aggressive to the max. Plus, I should've just let it be because this is Eleanor's phone, and it's totally fine for Eleanor to like Kiki's pictures because of course she would, why wouldn't she? So now it's going to look really weird that "Eleanor" had liked it and then disliked it. Dammit, technology! I shut down ShareIt and shove the phone under my duvet as though that would solve anything.

It rings.

OH GOD. IT'S RINGING. An actual ringtone that means that someone's calling and not texting. Who even calls in this day and age? That's so intrusive.

I last about two seconds before I pounce on the duvet and paw through it. My hand closes around the phone and I see the name on the screen and IT'S KIKI. A half moan, half whine squeaks out of me. I am terrified of this girl. But. I take a deep breath. It's time I grow a spine. I hit Accept.

"Ellie, my girl!" Kiki shouts. Why can't anyone in Indonesia learn to speak in a normal voice? "I was just about to call you. Did you give your phone to your idiot brother yet?"

"Yeah, she did."

Kiki doesn't miss a beat. "Hey, idiot brother!"

"Hey." Despite myself, I'm kind of smiling at "idiot brother."

"How're you doing, Kiki?"

"Pretty good. Tired. Been traversing the city with your girlfriend."

She's not my girlfriend, I want to say, but my heart twists at the word *girlfriend* in a painfully hopeless way and I can't bring myself to correct her. "Yeah, I saw. It looks like you are having a great time." I clear my throat because my mouth has suddenly turned into a desert. "Um. Is Shar, um. Is she—"

"She's good and bad. You know how it is. I hear you've been the same. Well, I hear you've mostly been moping around in your room like the count of Monte Carlo."

"I think you mean Monte Cristo?"

"Don't mansplain to me, George Clooney."

"I'm not—never mind." I take a deep breath. "So Shar's good and bad?" What does that mean, exactly? "I tried to call her using Eleanor's phone—"

"Oh, she gave me her phone for safekeeping. She was getting really bogged down by all the hate mail, you know how it is."

"Ah." The thought of Shar receiving hate mail crushes me. She doesn't deserve them. As far as I know, I haven't received any hate mail, aside from, you know, the whole scaring-investors-away thing. But that's a very different issue from public opinion. In the public eye, I'm just a "normal teenage boy" who pulled some normal-teenage-boy bullshit. All in good fun. "Boys will be boys!" But not so for Shar. I grip the phone tighter. I've had enough of staying here and lying low and letting the wolves prowl and lunge and bite at Sharlot. "Hey, Kiki? Do you think you could pass the phone to Shar?"

There's a pause and I hear whispers in the background—low and frantic like she's arguing with someone. Just as I'm about to lose hope, someone picks up the phone again and says, "Hey, George." And it's her, and her voice sounds exactly as I remember it, soft and low and a little bit scratchy and the smile spreads across my face because I can't not smile at the sound of her voice.

"Hey, Shar. Can we talk? I have an idea."

CHAPTER 29

Sharlot

My heart is crashing like cymbals, and honest to God, Kiki has had to stuff wads of tissue in my bra underneath my boobs to soak up the *boob sweat*, because despite the AC that's being blasted in the room, I can't stop sweating. She's even put special little sweat pads in the armpits of my blouse, thank the lord for Kiki's forethought. My mouth is dry and my throat is sore and I'm pretty sure I'm coming down with a cold. Or maybe this is what nerves feel like?

"Ready?" Kiki says.

No.

I nod. She taps a button. Her phone screen switches to the selfie camera and there's a big red button that flashes for two seconds, and then we're live. Live on ShareIt.

Join us for THE BIG CONFESSION! Tonight on ShareIt, a LIVE EVENT with George Clooney Tanuwijaya and Sharlot Citra. We will answer ALL your questions! #GeorgeAndSharlot #OneLiner

George came up with all the social media stuff. To be fair, he didn't have to do much—all he did was post on Twitter and

ShareIt and Instagram twenty minutes ago and suddenly we were trending. We couldn't leave it too long because he didn't want to give his family's publicity team time to find out what we were up to and stop it. So here we are, live in front of the entirety of Indonesia.

The phone screen splits in half and George's face appears next to mine. He waves and smiles. "Hey, Shar."

I gulp, because I've just noticed that on the upper left hand side of the screen is an eye symbol with a number next to it, and the number says 51,032. Holy shit. Over fifty thousand people are currently watching, and that number keeps rising even as I watch. Behind the phone camera, Kiki gestures to me and waves her hands in front of her face. *Smile.* I do so. Or try to, at least. I've never done a live anything online and it is a lot more unnerving than I'd thought it would be. "Um. Hi," I squeak.

On the lower right-hand side of the screen is a comment box that doesn't stop scrolling as people send all their hate.

Ew, she's not even that pretty.

What do you see in her, George?

Sharlot the Harlot, lol.

"Yeah, I'm nervous too," George says with an awkward laugh, and the realness of it is an anchor. I take a deep breath. I can do this. I can speak my truth here, right now, on ShareIt. I can share it. Ha.

"Same." I tear my eyes away from the comment box. "Um. So?"

"So, I asked you to do this event with me today because I thought, you know, maybe we could offer our version of what went down the past few weeks leading up to the launch of One-Liner. Our truth."

"Yeah," I say softly. I've rehearsed this with Kiki, but now the words won't come.

"Can I start with mine?" George says.

I nod.

"Okay, so the truth is, my dad caught me jacking off—"

HOLY SHIT. WHAT? I choke on my own spit. In front of me, Kiki's jaw is mopping the floor and I can't blame her because WHAT?

The comment box is exploding, shocked emojis everywhere, people screaming, WHAT? LOL. HUH???

"Yeah, my dad caught me masturbating to porn—it was vanilla porn, in case anyone's wondering—and I closed the tab and the screen went to a game I'd had running in the background, and of course my dad thought I was, uh, masturbating to a gnome and a badger."

Oh.

My.

God.

I burst out laughing. I can't help it. I clap my hands over my mouth to try and stop the laughter, but it just comes and comes and all the emojis spilling out of the comment box are cry-laughing. George laughs too. He's still talking. How's he still talking?

"It was the craziest, most humiliating time ever!" he cries, half laughing. "But come on, you are saying nothing like that has ever happened to you?"

And now the comments are full of people agreeing.

My mom walked in on me one night—

My sister found my porn on my laptop when she was trying to print out her algebra homework—

"Yeah, you know what I'm talking about," George says. "Anyway, so of course my dad freaked *out* and was like, George, you are a loser and I need to find you a real human girlfriend so you'll stop jerking off to gnomes."

I'm literally shrieking with laughter by now.

"So he confiscated my phone, and then my little sister, who was also very horrified by my gnome fetish, went and helped my dad find me a girlfriend. And that was how they found Sharlot." His face softens and the laughter subsides. "They found her profile on ShareIt and . . ." He sighs. "Look at her, it's impossible not to fall for her."

Never mind my cheeks, my entire body is blushing. I steal a glance at the comments, expecting more hate, but there are actually people agreeing with him. And now I see what he's done. He's made them see me through his eyes.

"I never would've had the guts to talk to Sharlot myself. In a way, I'm grateful that my little sister and my dad did what they did. I know it was wrong, and I know I fucked up in the worst possible way. I'm so sorry, Sharlot."

"I understand." And I do. I really do. I no longer feel such conflicting emotions about him. I smile at George and he smiles back and we're almost okay. Almost.

There's a moment of quiet, and I realize this is it. My cue. My turn to share my side of the story. "Well, George," I say, my voice sounding extra loud in the silent room, "funny you should say that you got caught masturbating, because I got caught almost having sex."

George goes bug-eyed. Kiki, who was already gaping from George's reveal, looks like she's about to have an aneurysm. This is *not* what we practiced earlier on. But I've had enough of practicing. It's time for the truth. No more bullshit. No more neat publicity packaging.

"Yeah, back in California, I had a boyfriend. He's really sweet and we liked each other very much and we decided we were ready to have sex. As it turned out, I wasn't actually ready, and he respected that and stopped when I asked him to stop, which—you know—I think that's so decent of him. He's a great person and a wonderful human and I'm glad that he was my almost-first."

George nods like he gets it, and I think he does. He really does.

"And I think it's important to be honest about these things. I hate that there's such a double standard when it comes to sex. It's a healthy part of growing up for many people, and I don't think there's any shame in that. But girls carry so much societal expectation when it comes to sex."

George nods again. "Yeah, I can't even imagine."

"It's very confusing. We're supposed to be alluring but like, also modest?" I start listing out all the crap that has been thrown on our shoulders from even before puberty starts, and George listens without interrupting me, frowning at some parts and laughing at the lighter ones. And the comment box is full of girls sharing their own experiences too. "Anyway, as I was saying, I'd discussed this stuff with Bradley and we were going to do it, but then when we were about to, I decided I needed to wait, but my mom walked in on us and freaked out."

The comment box scrolls superfast. *OH NOOOO!*
Aahgfshafsfahsjsksksksk
My worst nightmare!

I laugh. "Yep. She basically put me on the next flight out to Jakarta, and that was how I ended up here for the summer. I guess she thought that my ex was a bad influence on me or whatever, because she was determined to find me a new boyfriend—one who was brought up well enough to not try to get into my pants. She confiscated my phone and put her version of my profile on ShareIt. That was right around the time you messaged me. Or rather, your dad and your sister messaged me."

"So our parents catfished each other?"

There's a pause, and then we both burst out laughing. I bury my face in my hands and cackle so hard that tears roll down my cheeks. "They really, really did!"

Oh my god, that is BONKERS.
LMAO!

"Come on, you folks saying your overbearing Chinese Indo parents haven't ever done anything like this?" he says into the camera.

The comment box fills with anecdotes of the weird shit that parents have pulled.

My dad literally followed me when I went out on a date . . .
My mom created a fake FB profile to internet-stalk my boyfriend . . .

"That's what I thought," George says. "I'm glad you all can

relate. But, Shar, you know what the worst part of this entire thing was?"

"What?"

"That your mom thought I was the kind of boy who wouldn't want to have sex with you," George says, grinning.

Oh my god. I am dead. There's just something about the way he said that which is so full of nudge/wink. I swear there are literal flames licking at my face.

"I am totally the kind of guy who would try to have sex with you!" he says with faux indignation. "I mean, after discussing it with you very respectfully, of course."

If I'd been drinking coffee, this is where I would've laugh-spit it everywhere. But I'm not so I just cackle out loud, blushing so hard I swear my cheeks are melting off. When I finally manage to catch my breath, I say, half cringing and half giggling, "I would be open to having that discussion."

Now it's George's turn to go red. His face shines like a tomato under the sun, and the comment box has exploded and is just a continuous scroll going almost too fast for me to read.

LMAOOO—

These two—

I STAN!

"After we go out on a few more dates, though!" I add belatedly.

"As many as you want. And if you change your mind about it, that's also legit. I mean, I—"

The door bursts open and we both glance up to see George's dad and grandmother rushing into the room, out of breath. I look at George, who's been sitting next to me the entire time. We wave at our phone cameras, turn them so that everyone watching can see that we're actually sitting next to each other, and lean into each other.

"No—" Nainai says.

We kiss.

The internet explodes.

EPILOGUE

George

My hands are sweaty, my throat has forgotten how to swallow, and my heart thinks it's a bass set being used at a rock concert. All the hallmark signs of nervousness. Despite everything we've been through, I am nervous as hell. I guess because this will be the first time that I'm seeing Shar minus everything else.

The last week or so has been a whirlwind of interviews and appearances. We foolishly tried grabbing a coffee at a small café in Kemang, a hipster area in Jakarta that's frequented by celebs, and it took no time for someone to spot us and for a crowd to form around us.

At least it's not crowds with pitchforks chasing us down now, but crowds who adore us and want us to take selfies with them. Our ShareIt live video has gone viral, and although there are still some haters, the bulk of viewers who watched them *loved* us, especially Sharlot. My approval rating is the highest within my family among the eighteen-to-twenty-five-year-olds, our target audience for OneLiner. Speaking of OneLiner, it hit the #2 position on the Most Downloaded App yesterday, so Eighth Aunt is (grudgingly) happy and Papa is (literally) teary with joy and pride.

They had a talk with me, and it was the funniest thing. It was so obvious that they couldn't decide whether to praise me or scold me.

That was so brash, what you did, you could have—

Yes, you could have! But also it was great instincts. You knew your audience well, and you knew exactly what to say, and—

Yes, very good instincts. Really good social skills, which is so important in business.

So important! You're not as clueless as everyone in the family thinks.

No, not as clueless, but still young. So brash.

So brash. But promising.

In the end, Papa patted me on the shoulder and told me, with tears in his eyes, that he was proud of me, which also made me teary-eyed. And now that I know I'm not—as Papa said—as clueless as I thought I was about business, I'm actually looking forward to learning more about the family company and how I can contribute to it.

My phone rings, and when I hit Accept, Eleanor's face appears on my screen. "Are you there yet, gege?"

"Almost. Jakarta traffic, you know how it is." I glance up at our driver, who's expertly navigating the stop-and-go traffic.

Kiki's face squeezes onto the screen and they both sit there just grinning at me.

"What?" I say. I can't be too pissy; after all, Eleanor was the one who helped me get back in touch with Shar, and she was the one who helped distract Papa long enough for me to let Sharlot sneak into the house to do our ShareIt event.

"Bow-chicka-wow-wow," Kiki sings.

"Okay, gonna hang up now."

"Wait, gege!" Eleanor shoves Kiki aside and puts her face all the way up against the phone so all I can see is one eye and half of her nose.

"Yeah?"

When she next speaks, she says in her most serious voice, "Wear a condom."

"Oh god. Be a *normal thirteen-year-old*," I say, and hang up on the peals of laughter coming from her end. I can't help but smile as I shove the phone back in my pocket, though. I love that Kiki and Eleanor hang out with each other, even though they are unbearable together. I love that Eleanor has a big-sister figure to help guide her—okay, maybe not guide her since the only place Kiki is likely to guide anyone is straight to trouble. When they grow up, they'll probably form a multibillion-dollar corporation that will take over the world.

The sun is still not up when the car pulls up in front of Sharlot's house, but Shar comes running out looking very awake and cheerful. Her mom walks out behind her and gives me a reserved smile.

"Hi, Auntie. You're up early."

She shrugs. "Gotta send my daughter off. You take good care of her, okay? Otherwise your aunt will hear of it."

Shar rolls her eyes and kisses her mom on the cheek. "Go have fun with Eighth Aunt. I love you."

Her mom sighs, still smiling, and waves us off as the car trundles out of the driveway. "Your mom seems a little bit tired."

Sharlot snorts. "She stayed up until two last night, chatting with Eighth Aunt. It was kind of cute, actually. They're making plans to 'bump into each other' over the holidays."

I hand her a cup of coffee I'd bought on the way over. Thank god Indonesia is so coffee-mad that there are cafés that open before dawn. Sharlot thanks me by kissing me on the cheek, and though it's a simple act that I should be used to by now, my skin still tingles and my heart still skips a beat.

"It sucks that they have to keep everything under the radar," Shar's saying, "but I think they've got it figured out for now."

I nod. Change doesn't happen overnight, but it's happening slowly, a huge machine shifting its course, wheels and cogs turning in the right direction. Eighth Aunt and Shar's mom at the helm. The thought of it makes me smile.

The whole drive out of the city, we chat about nothing and everything. We play Scrabble on my phone and Sharlot punches my arm when I try to make the word *squaffle*—"a squabble over waffles!" And then we're out of the city, away from the concrete jungle and hurtling past green fields, and Sharlot looks out the window with eyes wide and mouth slightly open, slightly smiling. It's so obvious how much she loves Indonesia, and I can't help but love this about her too.

We reach the hills of Cikampek just as the sun is about to make its appearance, and we climb out of the car and stretch a bit before we start walking. I take Shar's hand and we walk up a trail, breathing in the damp morning air, our breaths coming in and out at the same time as each other's. It's different out here, without the lights and the noise of the city. Without the cameras and the crowds following us. For the first time, it's just us.

"I'm starting to realize why this is your favorite part of Indo," Shar says.

"Look at you calling it Indo like a proper local."

She rolls her eyes at me and we continue chatting as we walk up the hill. It's a short walk, and before long, we reach the summit and Shar stops still and looks out silently at the sight before us. It's an amazing sight to take in, I know.

We're above terraced rice fields, a vast collection of hills whose slopes have been painstakingly shaped into steps to plant rice. This land is among the richest in Indonesia, its soil fertilized by volcanic ash to produce the most fragrant rice, rice that smells of vanilla and tastes like sweet milk. From where we stand, we can see the terraced ponds of water reflecting the sky and the hills, and men and women wearing traditional batik are working the fields. A lot of the agricultural land in Indonesia is still owned by independent farmers—farmers whose sons and daughters work their own fields instead of corporations who employ hundreds of people to work them. In recent years, various tech companies have invested in small, independently owned farms, delivering their produce from the farms straight to customers in the city. I love this spot because it's a reminder of how tech can do good, that it's not always about being the biggest techbro, that it can be about spreading the wealth.

We sit down and Shar takes out her drawing tablet and begins sketching, her hand moving as swift and light as a butterfly as she captures the scenery around us. It's a place untouched by time, and I can't believe I get to share it with Shar.

She glances at me and I know that she gets it. She gets how much it all means to me and I see that it means just as much, if not more, to her.

"I love this place," she says, smiling as she adds another stroke to her sketch. I'm pretty sure she's talking about more than the rice fields.

"Yeah, same."

She takes a deep breath. "You know, times like these, I feel like I could live in Indo forever."

I cock an eyebrow at her. "Really?"

"Well, just times like these. Once we get back into the city, I'll go back to craving LA again."

"Okay, that sounds more like the Sharlot I know."

Her smile is short-lived.

"What's wrong?" I say, squeezing her hand.

"I'll be leaving in a week's time."

"I know." Each morning, I wake up with a sick feeling in my stomach because that's one more day gone, one less day I can see her. Again, my heart rate quickens and my palms start to get slick. This is it. I'll tell her now. I can do this. "But, um—so. I wasn't sure, um."

"Oh my gosh, what is it? Just say it."

"Well, um. I was wondering how you'd feel about me, um, maybe applying to some of the same schools as you?"

She stares at me. Oh god, she's going to freak out. It's too much. College is a time when we should be free or whatever, and of course she's not going to want to go to college shackled to a boyfriend, of course—

"Oh my god, yes!" she screams, and before I know it, her arms are around me and I barely react fast enough to catch her as she flings herself into my arms.

I close my eyes tight. "Really?" Please don't let this be a dream.

"I mean, I don't know if your grades are good enough to get into the schools I'm aiming for—"

"Whoa, okay, sorry I didn't realize I was talking to the next Rhodes scholar."

She laughs and leans in, and we're kissing and laughing and our eyes are tearing up a little. I'm torn between relief and excitement and every other emotion that's possible to feel, because thank the universe, the end of the summer doesn't mean the end of Sharlot and me, and wow, I really was not expecting any of this to happen, and isn't that just the best goddamn feeling in the world.

ACKNOWLEDGMENTS

I wrote *Well, That Was Unexpected* while still riding the amazing *Dial A for Aunties* wave, and I knew I wanted to write something joyous to celebrate my heritage and my beautiful country. First, thanks to my agent, Katelyn Detweiler of Jill Grinberg Literary Management, for encouraging me to write what is essentially a love letter to Indonesia. Thank you for being the best everything: cheerleader, advocate, strategist, and accomplice! To world domination, mua-ha-ha!

Katelyn found this book the absolute perfect home with Wendy Loggia at Delacorte. Wendy is an actual legend, so when the book landed with her, I was starstruck and really very, very intimidated. I sweated through my shirt the first time I spoke to her. (I completely empathize with Sharlot's need for boob deodorant!) Fortunately, Wendy is not only humble and kind, she is also a freaking genius. Thank you so much for elevating the book, for coaxing it into the lively, colorful story it is now. Truly, I still can't believe that I'm lucky enough to call you my editor!

Thank you to the rest of the team at JGLM: the superstar foreign rights agent Sam Farkas, Sophia Seidner, and Denise Page, without whom so much of my life would be a complete mess.

I can never write an acknowledgments page without thanking my amazing, long-suffering writing friends. To Laurie Elizabeth

Flynn, who is my inspiration and my soul twin! Thank you for basically holding my hand while I wrote this, and for cheering me on literally every day. Thank you to my menagerie family: Toria Hegedus (kind, pure-hearted hedgehog!), Elaine Aliment (wise puppy!), Tilly Latimer (superbat!), Lani Frank (best beef!), Rob Livermore (wild Muppet!), SL Huang (brilliant pencil!), Maddox Hahn (funniest monster thing!), Mel Melcer (wait, we haven't come up with an animal for you!), and Emma Maree (cozy tea dragon!). A huge thank-you to Kate Dylan for reading and giving me such insightful feedback, Nicole Lesperance, whose wisdom has never led me wrong, and Grace Shim for being such a great critique partner.

I don't know why my husband, Mike, sticks with me, but he does, and I'm so grateful for it. Thank you for believing in me all these years and supporting me in every way possible. My husband, a gifted Oxford-educated physicist, uprooted himself and left his career and family behind to ensure my happiness, and still has it in himself to push me when I wanted to give up writing. Without him, none of my books would have gotten published. Thank you for being so invested in every single part of the writing journey. It's so priceless to have someone to share this wild ride with.

Thank you to my family, especially my mama and papa, for celebrating my publishing journey. My parents have been so wonderful, rallying their friends to do photo shoots and to share in the joy of publication. They've made the dream so much more lively and real.

One day, my baby girls will be old enough to read this book, and I hope that you, Emmeline and Rosalie, will be proud of it. I hope that like Sharlot, you have all the support you need to weather any storms that may come your way, and that you will fall in love with Indonesia the way that Sharlot, and I, and your dad, did.

Last but not least, thank you so much to my readers! I am so happy to be able to share a slice of Indonesia with you. It has been a dream of mine for the longest time to write a book set in Indonesia, and the fact that this is the book—a love story with meddlesome aunties and uncles and lots of coffee!—is so perfect. I'm so grateful that you took the time to read it, and I hope you've enjoyed this glimpse into Jakarta and Bali. I hope that one day you have the chance to visit and have a cup of strong, sweet Indonesian coffee next to the beach.

ABOUT THE AUTHOR

JESSE Q. SUTANTO grew up shuttling back and forth between Indonesia, Singapore, and Oxford and considers all three places her home. She has a master's from Oxford University, but she has yet to figure out how to say that without sounding obnoxious. Jesse has forty-two first cousins and thirty aunties and uncles, many of whom live just down the road. She used to game, but with two little ones and a husband, she no longer has time for hobbies. She aspires to one day find one (1) hobby.

jesseqsutanto.com

JESSE Q. SUTANTO

"There's a kind of magic to Sutanto's writing... She tackles complicated issues of culture and family ties while also creating convoluted plotlines that'll make you squeal with laughter."
—*The Wellesley News*

For a complete list of titles, please visit prh.com/sutanto